A SAWBONES WESTERN

NEVER SEEN DEADER

WILLIAM W. JOHNSTONE
WITH J. A. JOHNSTONE

WHEELER PUBLISHING
A part of Gale, a Cengage Company

GALE
A Cengage Company

Wheeler Publishing Large Print Western.
The text of this Large Print edition is unabridged.
Other aspects of the book may vary from the original edition.
Set in 16 pt. Plantin.

LIBRARY OF CONGRESS CIP DATA ON FILE.
CATALOGUING IN PUBLICATION FOR THIS BOOK
IS AVAILABLE FROM THE LIBRARY OF CONGRESS.

ISBN-13: 978-1-4328-8695-0 (softcover alk. paper)

Published in 2021 by arrangement with Pinnacle Books, an imprint of Kensington Publishing Corp.

Printed in Mexico
Print Number: 01   Print Year: 2021

NEVER SEEN DEADER

NEVER SEEN DEADER

CHAPTER 1

Dr. Samuel Knight flopped on his belly and stared at the dusty, bleak New Mexico Territory back trail, hunting for any sign his pursuers were sneaking up on him. He lifted the spyglass he had found alongside the road a few days earlier and started to peer through the cracked lens, then stopped and lowered it again. He used a thumbnail to scrape dried blood off the eyepiece to get a clearer view. Who had dropped the spyglass remained a mystery since he hadn't overtaken any rider on the lonely trail and none had passed him riding east.

He blinked twice, pressed his right eye into the lens, and slowly scanned the heat-distorted horizon. The burning desert sun caused his eye to water as he tried to penetrate the shimmering, silvery curtain of mirage. He pulled away, drew out the tube to its full length, and anxiously focused on a green spot south of the road. His study was so intense that he suddenly gasped, having held his breath without realizing it.

There were riders in the stand of cottonwoods.

Several riders.

Knight swallowed hard, rolled onto his back, and stared up at the cloudless sky so he could draw his revolver, hold it at arm's length, and check the load in the Colt Navy's cylinder. Every chamber was full.

Riding with the hammer resting on an empty chamber kept accidents from happening. Otherwise, the constant bouncing of a horse sometimes caused a round to discharge. But Knight preferred to take the risk so he had an extra bullet in a shootout.

Just in case.

That caution summed up his life ever since he'd been released from the Yankee prisoner of war camp at Elmira, New York. He had been captured after the Battle of the Wilderness and sent to a hellhole where one in five prisoners died from disease, abuse, and all too often, their own hand when life became unbearable. His skills as a doctor had been pushed to the limits of his endurance, but he had saved the lives of dozens of his fellow Johnny Rebs using nothing more than stolen spoons sharpened into crude surgical instruments and water boiled over fires better used for staying warm during the fierce northern winter.

His life had been a living hell — he was not the only one calling the Yankee prison camp Hellmira — but all that should have changed when General Lee surrendered and he and the others were released. On his own, on foot, with nothing but the clothes on his back, he had nearly frozen and starved to death as he made his way home to Pine Knob, Texas, and his loving wife Victoria.

If his life as a prisoner had been horrific, what he'd found in the town where he was born and raised proved worse. A lot worse. His wife had remarried without first divorcing him. Adding insult to injury, she hadn't even picked one of the local boys. She had married a carpetbagger from Boston who had come to Pine Knob to rob the citizens and steal as much as he could, all in the name of Reconstruction. Why she had given Gerald Donnelly the time of day, much less her hand in marriage, still puzzled Knight, but she had. She had married the Yankee and had rejected Knight when he returned.

Knight smiled grimly. Gerald Donnelly had plenty of reason to send his hired gunmen after the rebel doctor after getting his

Achilles tendon severed and his trigger finger shot off, both done with Knight's surgical precision.

The Federal cavalry officer in command of the garrison in Pine Knob had reason to come after him, too. Stolen horses, dead soldiers, shouted insults — it was as personal with Captain Norwood as it was with Donnelly.

And it wasn't just the trouble in Pine Knob that Knight fled.

He didn't even want to think about all the folks in Buffalo Springs who might want his scalp after the saloon got burned down to the ground, the town shot up, and bodies left all over. Then there was Amelia Parker . . .

Knight's guilt about abandoning the lovely woman the way he had tore at him like ants chewing away his very soul. But there hadn't been a choice, not after he had killed half an outlaw gang comprised of his old friends, some former inmates at Elmira who once upon a time had saved his life, and then shot up a band of Texas State Police Donnelly had sent to kill him.

His life swirled with death and double dealing, and it made him sick to his stomach.

He tried to push that feeling away as he

10

pouched the iron and rolled over to study his back trail again. Nervous fingers slid back and forth along the slick brass tube of the spyglass as he tried to make sense of the blurred image from the stand of trees. Two miles behind him? Maybe less.

They had to be after him. When he thought he would go blind staring at the treetops swaying in the sluggish desert wind, not seeing another hint of movement, he realized he was fleeing ghosts. There hadn't been anyone behind him for more than a week. He had left Buffalo Springs in the middle of the night and ridden until his horse threatened to collapse from exhaustion.

That forced him to rest, but he pressed on when he could, heading westward into New Mexico Territory. So many of the men from Buffalo Springs had come this way to find their fortunes in gold and silver strikes that he expected the road to be crowded. Instead, the vast desert had afforded lonely traveling for him and his tired horse. He'd appreciated that solitude more and more as he rode.

After he'd passed a range of mountains to the north of Paso del Norte, he had slowed his pace. Watering holes were scarce. From what he had heard in the past, the Apaches roaming these barren lands were the only ones who knew where to find water that was fit to drink. Even the river he had crossed had been mostly dry.

"The Rio Grande," he had scoffed aloud. It had been misnamed, though the banks were wide, hinting that vast amounts of water sometimes raged between them. Not this year. Not so he could do more than find small holes in the sandy bottom filled with enough water for his horse and him.

He considered following the dry bed south until he reached Paso del Norte and then riding into Mexico. The only drawback he saw to that was the army detachment at Franklin on the Texas side of the border. They must have a telegraph. He didn't doubt that Captain Norwood had sent warnings to every army post in the south and west warning about the horse-thieving criminal Rebel doctor.

"West." He pushed to his feet, collapsed the spyglass, and squinted once more along the road he had traveled earlier that day. A small dust devil swirled around and danced across the trail. Nothing else moved out there, not even circling buzzards.

Knight trudged to where he had left his horse nibbling at a patch of grass. He stashed the spyglass in his saddlebags and put his foot into the stirrup to mount.

Distant gunfire made him freeze. Trailing the gunshots came the swift pounding of horses' hooves. He pulled himself up and settled into the saddle before tugging down the broad, floppy brim of his hat to keep the sun out of his eyes. The stand of cottonwoods still looked like it had a few seconds earlier, but the commotion steadily grew louder. Slowly turning, Knight searched for the origin of those sounds of battle.

Directly south of him, loud whoops suddenly rang out. He edged his horse in that direction, alert for a trap. When he caught sight of the drama playing out across the desert, he almost wheeled around and rode off.

Two Indians rode with their heads down, firing arrows at a cowboy not twenty yards ahead of them. The cowboy swung from side to side, thrusting his revolver out and getting off wild shots that did nothing to slow the pursuit.

Knight knew that hitting anything while firing from horseback was difficult. Shooting over a shoulder as he galloped from two Apaches trying to turn him into a pincushion presented the cowboy an impossible task. He might get lucky and score with one of those wild shots . . . but from where

Knight sat, the man being pursued so aggressively had chased off Lady Luck a lot earlier.

Knight drew his rifle from the saddle sheath, levered a round into the chamber, and snugged the weapon to his shoulder. He held his horse steady with his knees as he swung smoothly from behind the Indians and then past them in a slow arc. When he came even with the lead Indian, he squeezed the trigger but kept swinging to be sure he didn't pull the shot.

His round missed the lead rider but hit the second, jolting him halfway around even though he didn't fall from the racing pony. Knight shook his head. The cowboy was out of luck, but Knight's was damned good at the moment. He had only winged the Apache, but that was enough to cause the warrior to veer away from the chase.

Although he'd evened the odds, leaving the cowboy only one adversary, Knight realized the luck still rested with him. The fleeing cowboy's gun clicked on empty cylinders. The Apache still had a quiver filled with arrows. Judging by the smooth pluck, draw, and fire, the warrior had a good chance to skewer his quarry.

Knight reacted without thinking. He spurred his horse down the sandy slope and across the sunbaked desert in pursuit. Trying to fire his rifle while riding would only waste ammunition. Head down, riding like the wind, he closed the gap between him and the Indian. At some point the Apache realized he had a decision to make. He either kept chasing the defenseless cowboy and got shot in the back — or he whirled around and confronted his new attacker.

As he galloped closer, Knight saw this was no young buck on his first raid. He was facing a grizzled veteran of too many ambushes and battles. The Indian brought his horse to a dead halt, drew back on his bow, and let fly an arrow. It spun a little as it flew toward Knight.

That saved him. The fletching on one side was torn off and the unstable flight sent the arrow angling to the right, away from him.

Knight hauled back on the reins, his horse kicking up a cloud of dust as he duplicated the Indian's ploy. On a stationary mount he had a better chance of making a killing shot. As he fired, the dust blew off to one side, giving him a distorted glimpse of the Apache.

For an instant he thought he had made a clean miss. Then he saw fortune still favored him. The rifle slug tore through the Apache's head and knocked him clean off his horse.

Knight levered in another round as he heard a horse galloping for him. He lowered the rifle when he saw the frantic cowboy waving at him.

"Behind you! Damn, there's the other one behind you!"

Knight jerked forward, bending at the waist as an arrow sailed past. His horse began crow-hopping, forcing him to fight to keep his seat. If he got thrown, the horse would race off and leave him stranded — and at the mercy of the Indian he had already wounded.

By the time he got his horse under control, the cowboy had flashed past, screaming like a madman at the top of his lungs and waving his empty pistol over his head. Knight brought up his rifle but couldn't fire without hitting the cowboy.

The young man launched himself from his horse and crashed into the charging Apache. He brought his revolver down hard on the warrior's shoulder. The crack sounded loud enough to convince Knight that the collarbone had broken under the blow. Cowboy and Indian crashed to the ground. Knight had trouble maneuvering his horse around to get a clear shot as the two men wrestled desperately with each other.

In spite of the broken bone and what had to be intense pain, the Apache fought like ten men. He kicked out and forced the cowboy away. A silver-bladed knife flashed in the sunlight. His grip weak in his right hand, the Apache dropped the knife, bent, and picked it up with his left just as the cowboy surged forward. He swung his gun again, aiming for the warrior's skull.

He missed and lost his balance as the Indian twisted out of the way. The cowboy sprawled facedown to the ground. The Apache reared above him, the knife clumsy in his hand but still potentially lethal. In spite of the pain and weak grip, the man prepared to deliver a death blow.

Knight's bullet reached him first. The Apache took a half step back, stunned by the impact. His right arm twitched. He tried to touch the red flower blossoming on his chest with his left hand. Unexpectedly, he threw back his head and unleashed an ululation that chilled Knight.

Then he toppled backwards like a felled tree, dead when he hit the ground. Stretched out on his back, he didn't even give a small twitch or tremor.

The cowboy got shakily to his feet, still holding his revolver. He stared at the fallen warrior and shook his head. Then he looked up at Knight. "I got a lot to thank you for, mister. You saved my life."

"You probably saved mine, too, from that one." Knight pointed with the muzzle of his rifle to the sprawled Apache. "I never heard him coming up behind me."

"You winged him when he was chasing me. See?" The cowboy nudged the body with the toe of his boot, lifting slightly to show where Knight's first bullet had cut through the man's rib cage. "Went in and bored clean through, came out the back. Didn't even hardly slow this red bastard none."

The cowboy began reloading his revolver.

"How'd you get them on your trail?" Knight slid his rifle back into the scabbard and then swung down from the saddle. He cared less about the cowboy's story than getting on his way, but he felt he owed the young man something for coming to his aid the way he had. Hearing his story would take care of that obligation.

The cowboy was barely twenty, if that. He had a short, dark stubble on his lean jaw that might have taken a week or two for him to grow. He wore a green vest with two buttons popped off, a shirt that had been white at one time, and blue denim pants worn white in patches. A gun belt was strapped

18

around his hips, but Knight doubted the boy was a gunslinger. He held his weapon with authority but not the arrogance of a killer. Though Knight couldn't be sure, he thought the cowboy's hands shook just a mite.

He was sure of that tremor when the cowboy pulled his battered hat up from behind where it hung by a chin strap around his neck. Likely, the youngster was no more than a down-on-his-luck wrangler caught on the range by a pair of Apaches who mistook him for easy prey.

"Just more bad luck," he said in answer to Knight's question as he reloaded his pistol. "I lost a spare horse and gear coming up from Big Bend, following the river. Down south there's plenty of water. Not so much up here." The cowboy looked around and snorted in disgust. "The Journey of Death they call this stretch all the way up to Socorro or maybe Albuquerque. *El Jornado del Muerto.* Not hardly anybody calls it the King's Highway, not even the Mexicans that named it."

"El Camino Real," Knight said, exhausting his Spanish and knowledge of the region. If he knew so little about this territory, that meant Gerald Donnelly knew nothing at all.

"That's what they called it, too. The Span-

19

ish came through, naming everything that didn't move and some of the things that did. The Organ Mountains back there look like organ pipes. I doubt they named that, not having an organ to play on. But to the west of us are the Peloncillo Mountains." He pointed.

Knight shrugged. He had no idea about the terrain ahead. All he knew was that he could never go back to the piney woods of east Texas.

"That means *little baldy* since them mountains are as naked as a jaybird. Nothing grows on them that doesn't have thorns or is poisonous. I reckon the Spaniards that explored the region weren't so far wrong. Journey of Death. Bald Mountains." The cowboy slid his revolver back into its holster, made a point of fastening the leather thong around the hammer, and came over to thrust out his hand. "I apologize for my bad manners. The name's Dave Wilcox."

Knight shook. He had developed a set of calluses from riding, but his surgeon's hands were soft compared to the rough hands of the young man. If there had been any doubt about whether or not Wilcox was a gunman, that grip dispelled it. No gunslick had calluses from roping and wrangling like the ones Wilcox had.

20

Knight caught himself before he introduced himself as Dr. Samuel Knight. He had no call to claim that profession anymore, not after all the dead bodies he had left in his wake. Worst of all, he had felt good about slapping leather, drawing and killing when his victim was a gunman bought and paid for to kill him . . . or even a man who had been a friend before turning to a life of bank robbery and murder.

"Sam Knight," he said simply.

"Well, Mr. Knight, we make a pretty durn good pair, I'd say." Wilcox looked to the west. "I was heading toward Ralston City. That's a mining town just north of the Peloncillos. A silver strike there's got everyone all worked up and champing at the bit to get rich."

"You're going to try your hand at prospecting?"

"Not me, sir. Nope, not me. I know better 'n that. I've heard the stories of prospectors all my life. Better to work in a mine already discovered."

"Mining's a backbreaking job."

"But in a successful mine, it pays real good. I've never been afraid of a bit of work. The only thing that I'm not sure about is being underground like that."

21

"Are you afraid of the dark?" Knight asked.

"Not that as much as being all squeezed into a tight space. It must be a little like getting buried alive, the rock walls all around. But I can find out if that's for me by trying it."

"And if it's not?"

"Then I'll look for something else. I'm what you call versatile. You know what that means?"

"I do."

Wilcox studied him for a moment, then said, "You talk like an educated man. Me, I finished the sixth grade. I can read and cipher. My writing's not great, but folks can make it out if they try, especially if I don't rush at it. Hell, I might even get a job with a newspaper. Most of the men in a mining camp can't even write their own name." Wilcox grinned. "In comparison to them, I reckon I'm an educated fellow."

Knight had to smile at the young man's optimism and determination. He had listened to Wilcox's story and was ready to move on. He put a foot in the stirrup and swung onto the back of his horse.

Instantly, Knight had to struggle to control the suddenly skittish mount. "There, there, settle down," he said as he patted the horse's neck, but as the gelding turned and danced, Knight caught sight of something in the distance that sent a shiver up his spine. He asked Wilcox, "How many Apaches were on your trail?"

"Well, now, sir, I ran afoul of them two days back, a lot farther south. I'm no expert, but they might be Chiricahua Apaches."

"I don't care about the tribe. How many chased you?"

"Those two were all I saw. Why do you ask?"

"It behooves us to get on the road and ride like we mean it." Knight stared at the horizon to the southeast and the dust cloud building there. It could have been another dust devil; the spinning tornados of dirt reaching hundreds of feet into the air were common in the desert. It *could* have been . . . but Knight believed it was a third Apache making tracks.

The Apache might have been running away, but Knight felt his luck evaporating.

More than likely, the third Apache was riding hell-for-leather to bring back a full war party.

CHAPTER 2

"They might be Mescalero," Dave Wilcox said as they rode past the second of the fallen Apaches. "I ought to study up on identifying them. Know your enemy." The cowboy rubbed his left arm vigorously, making Knight wonder if he had been injured.

"You catch one of those arrows?" He indicated the way Wilcox acted by mimicking the movement.

"What, this? No, they didn't put a scratch on me. I fell off my horse earlier on and banged up my arm. Wrenched it some more when I grabbed the reins to climb back up. The horse reared and damned near kicked me."

Knight shot a quick look behind as he had been doing since he had left Texas. If he spotted riders coming after him, they would really be there and not just figments of a guilty imagination. "Does it matter if the Indians are Mescalero or Chiricahua?"

"Might be Warm Sands, too, but I doubt it," Wilcox said. "One of these days, they'll all be tucked away on reservations where they can't hurt anybody. General Carleton tried that with the Navajo, but that didn't work so well since he put 'em with the Mescaleros over at Bosque Redondo. The Mescaleros stole all the Navajos' horses and snuck out to go raiding. That made life hell for the cavalry because they'd sneak back onto their reservation and claim it was the Navajos doing the thieving. To the army, one Injun looks like another. That caused a passel of trouble for everybody."

"You know just about everything about the Indians in these parts. How's that?"

"My pa was an Indian agent for a while. He would spin yarns constantly at the supper table, though he dealt with the Lipan and none of the New Mexico Territory Apaches."

Knight nodded. "I've had some dealings with the Lipan over in East Texas. They and the Comanche never got along too well."

"All the tribes spent their time fighting each other until the white man came. Then it was easier for them to fight us." Wilcox slapped his holstered gun to emphasize what he meant. "Comancheros sold guns and firewater to any tribe that stole enough money or cattle to satisfy their greed. We got to keep an eye out not only for armed Indians but double-dealing white men, too. They're all our enemies."

Knight glanced back and caught sight of a larger dust cloud. He hadn't wanted to mention it to Wilcox, but now he had to. "There was a third Apache. We got rid of two while the third rode away. I hoped he was going to hightail it and make himself scarce. It looks like he found some friends to avenge what we did to his partners."

Wilcox turned in the saddle and half stood, then twisted back. ""Damn me, you're right. I don't have much ammunition. Enough to reload three or four times. How about you?"

"I'd rather not fight anyone who can fire an arrow, then come pick it up and fire it at me again." Knight had left Buffalo Springs with scant supplies. Along the way into New Mexico Territory he had lived off the land, having become a crack shot. One rabbit, one shot. He had started his escape with a box of cartridges for the Winchester and enough caps, slugs, and powder for fifty shots from the Colt Navy. Facing one or two more Apaches was possible. If an entire hunting party — or a war party — came after them, he needed five times that much ammunition.

"I'd rather not fight them at all. They carry a grudge something fierce. If they've slipped off a reservation, they won't want us reporting to the cavalry. That would give them a one-way ticket back."

The way Wilcox winced as he gestured wildly worried Knight. He almost offered to check the cowboy's arm to be sure the injury was as minor as he claimed, but Knight wanted to distance himself from his prior life as much as possible. Not practicing medicine went a ways toward cleaning the slate and letting him start over.

He touched the gun at his side. He was more than passably good with it, but turning into a gunfighter, no matter how fast he was, didn't appeal to him. Sitting at a table covered with green felt and gambling suited him better. Most cowboys lacked even passing acquaintance with odds and how to bet and when to fold. Back in Buffalo Springs he had found gambling more lucrative than tending to sick and injured patients.

Mining towns were lush pickings for a determined, knowledgeable gambler.

"Is there anywhere we can lay low so they'll pass us by?"

"This is new country for me. I glanced at a map back in El Paso, but I didn't do

27

anything like memorize it. There wasn't much need. Just head west and eventually a road would take me to Ralston City, or so I thought."

"What are the odds of us outrunning them?" Even as he asked, Knight knew the answer. His horse was fresh enough, though he had been pushing hard to get away from any unseen pursuers. Wilcox's horse, though, was close to dead. Its lathered flanks gave mute testimony to how hard he had ridden to get away from the two dead warriors.

"About zero now." Wilcox lifted his injured arm, winced as he pointed, then dropped it back to his side.

Knight caught sight of three Apaches not a half mile distant, riding along a ridge parallel to the trail. He looked around for a place to hide, if the Indians hadn't spotted them. He knew at least one Apache was behind them. "We need to find a place to hole up."

"You want to hold them off? You have enough ammunition for that?" Wilcox heaved a deep sigh when he read the answer on Knight's face. "We're getting into foot-hills, but the three to our left cut us off from reaching them."

Knight's thoughts flashed over a dozen

possibilities, none of them good, and settled on the least bad. It meant not only luck, but outright courage had to triumph. "We take on the three Apaches. If we get past them, are you sure we can hide in the mountains? What did you call the range? The Peloncillos?"

"That's the name, but I'm not sure about anything, Mr. Knight."

"Call me Sam."

"Dave."

Knight drew his rifle and slipped a few rounds into the magazine to replace the ones he had fired earlier. They would need all the firepower they could get.

"Well, Dave, it comes down to this. We get lucky, get into the mountains, and find a place to hide . . . or we get killed right away."

"That surely does take away the uncertainty, don't it?" Wilcox laughed. "Been good knowing you, Sam. Yeehaw!" He raked his heels against his worn out horse's flanks, drew his revolver, and led the attack.

Knight trailed him, but not to let the young cowboy get killed first. He wanted the Apaches to focus their attention on the wrong point of attack. And it worked. Kicking up rocks and sand, the three braves sent their horses straight down a steep incline from the ridge toward Wilcox. Their descent was more an avalanche than controlled riding.

Knight's quick eye picked out the spot where the Indians had to end up at the bottom of the hill. He began firing with measured accuracy. Every few seconds he sent a leaden message to let the Indians know that they had made a mistake.

His first slug took one from horseback. His second hit a horse, spilling the Apache to the rocky ground, where he moaned and struggled to sit upright. From the trouble he had, the warrior had either broken his back or strained it so badly that even standing would be excruciating. Knight tried to get the third rider in his sights, but Wilcox blocked his shot.

Knight trotted forward, waiting for a clear field to fire. A quick exchange of gunfire ended that need. Wilcox used the last seconds to empty his gun before the remaining Apache reached level ground. How many times he actually hit the warrior didn't matter. One of the slugs caught the Indian in the gut and knocked him off his pony.

"Grab his horse!" Knight shouted. "We can use a spare." He veered away from the battlefield to capture another of the Apaches' horses as Wilcox obeyed his command. By the time Knight snared the hacka-more and tugged to slow the animal, Wilcox trotted up beside him.

"That went better 'n it had any right to. You're my good luck charm, Sam. And you're one hell of a marksman."

"No time to slap each other on the back. Where are the mountains we can hide in?" Knight glanced over his shoulder, worried about the other Apaches. With so many of their number dead or seriously wounded, it had become a matter of pride to bring the white eyes to Apache justice. Knight had heard stories. Better to save a round for himself if capture looked like it would become a reality.

"Up and over the ridge. There's an easy way to get to the top." Wilcox tried to point and again he flinched. In spite of his obvious discomfort, he led the way.

Knight was content to fall behind to guard their backs. They reached the ridgeline, giv-ing him a chance to study the countryside they had just crossed. "At least four more braves are coming for us."

"And our luck is holding, Sam. See? Toward the southwest is the mouth of a canyon. The Peloncillos got a reputation for being all twisty and turny. That can be bad if you're on your way into Mexico because it doubles the time to get across the border, but for us it's salvation. There has to be a spot for us to hole up."

Knight wanted more than that. He wanted a spot where they could disappear. The chance of finding that increased when he saw how rocky the canyon floor became. Their horses left only sporadic tracks. Keeping to the side of a rocky game trail hid the hoofprints entirely, but slowed them down. The decision between speed and caution was settled fast.

"Get a move on, Dave. Change horses if yours is too tired to get us as far from the Apaches as possible."

"There's not a saddle on either of the captured horses," Wilcox said. "I'm not so good riding bareback."

"Try. I'll hang back to guard our trail."

Wilcox kicked free of his stirrups, then jumped to the captured horse. The animal tried to rear, but contrary to what he'd said, Wilcox proved too good a rider to lose control. He gentled the horse, then set a faster pace.

Seeing his new partner making better progress, Knight watched the trail for any sign of pursuit. If he had seen any, he knew this would be where he made his stand. Likely his last stand.

After a full minute, no Indian popped into view. Canting his head to one side, he listened hard for sounds of pursuit. Nothing. The clop of the horses ahead of him echoed down the canyon, making him even less sure they would get away.

Caught in the canyon, they had nowhere to go but ahead. A quick study of both canyon walls showed no trail to the rim. Every time Knight found what looked like a promising path, it turned too steep or petered out halfway up the sheer rock walls. Unless he changed his mind and returned to fight his way past the Indians, he had only one direction to flee — straight ahead.

He heaved a sigh of relief as he rounded a bend. Wilcox had stopped and looked left and right. The canyon forked off due south and at an angle to the southeast. The cowboy turned and shook his head. "Can't say which way to go."

"Does it matter?" Knight looked at the canyon floor. A game trail went down each canyon. No hint there. He considered the choices, then headed into the southeast branch.

"Why this way?" Wilcox drew up beside him. "What did you see that I didn't?"

"Nothing. It heads away at an angle to the border. That's all."

"The only reason? If the canyon stretches long enough, and there are plenty in these mountains that must, we'll still cross into Mexico."

"If we avoid the Apaches, I don't care where we are. It won't be that hard riding back into New Mexico."

"The Federales might have something to say about that. They're all up in arms about U.S. troops chasing outlaws into their country. Hanging us might be a good lesson for eager cavalry troopers. Plenty around here, from what I've heard."

"They're doing a terrible job of keeping the Apaches from attacking travelers."

Knight felt a little easier as the walls stretched out wider in either direction, relieving his feeling of being in a rocky coffin. One thing remained the same, though. His sharp-eyed study failed to reveal any trail to the rim on either side.

Wilcox looked around. "One of these canyons is called Skeleton Canyon. They call it that because so many people have died in it."

"I can see why. Not only are you right about the lack of vegetation, there's not a drop of water to be seen along the canyon floor." Knight drew rein and stared ahead. He felt as if he had stepped into a mile-

34

deep well and only waited for the impact of landing.

It came when Wilcox saw what he already feared. "Box canyon. We got to hightail it back and try to get down the other fork before the Apaches overtake us." Wilcox wheeled his pony around and started back without waiting for Knight to join him.

Knight thought his luck had finally run out. He had taken a trail that was a dead end. Then he thought his luck had come back as they neared the fork. The split in the trail lay only a dozen yards ahead.

Then he knew his luck had disappeared entirely. The Apaches were there, dropping from their horses and fanning out to take cover. They had effectively bottled up Knight and Wilcox in the box canyon.

"Been nice knowing you, Sam," Wilcox said again, "even if it was only for a couple hours."

"Do you always give up so easily? I'm disappointed in you, Dave. We can get out of this." With that bit of bravado, Knight dismounted and led the horses into a tumble of rocks at the base of a steep cliff. Making his way through ever tighter crevices, he reached a point where the horses no longer fit. He fastened their reins down with rocks, took his saddlebags and rifle, and climbed

35

higher still. Flopping on a large boulder gave him a view of the fork in the trail.

"They're hidden pretty good," Wilcox said from beside him. The cowboy gripped his revolver with both hands as he stretched out on the rock slab.

"That arm bothering you? The left one?"

"I'm just shaky at the notion of getting my scalp lifted." He looked sideways at Knight, then nodded. "Yeah, the arm's all swole up. That doesn't mean I'm not shaking in my boots from the prospect of getting killed dead."

Wilcox jumped when Knight pulled the trigger on his rifle. The answer came immediately. His marksmanship hadn't suffered any from the afternoon of running from the Indians. He nailed one in the leg, bringing him down amid a torrent of Apache cursing — if Apaches cursed. He thought he recalled hearing somewhere that Indians didn't.

"You're a good shot. Wish I could handle a gun like that."

"I'll teach you," Knight said, levering in a new round. "When we get out of here."

Wilcox laughed without humor. "You always see the bright side. What else do you see, Sam? Out there. How many Injuns are ready to rush us?"

Knight pulled his hat down a little lower to shield his eyes. The sun dipped low, making it difficult to see well. With such high walls, twilight would settle down over the canyon in less than a half hour, he estimated. Darkness favored an Apache attack, unless what he had heard about them not fighting after dark was true.

As if reading Knight's mind, Wilcox said, "They don't like to fight when it gets dark because the rattlers come out then. They're feared of rattlesnakes more 'n anything else in the whole danged world, but that doesn't mean they'll pack up their bows and arrows and go home. We left too many of them dead already for them not to want us killed or captured."

"So they'll fight all night long?"

"Won't much matter. If they just keep us bottled up here, they can wait us out. How much water you got? I have about a canteen's worth, maybe less. Two days from now, we'll be dried out deader 'n lizards. You've never seen deader than what we'll be."

"They have to have water, too," Knight pointed out.

"Yeah, and they likely know where to find it in these hills. One of 'em can ride out and fetch more for them. We're in a bad

37

spot, Sam, a really bad spot."

Knight wanted to argue, but his mouth already felt as if it was filled with cotton wool. Talking about how little water they had made him think of the last time he had taken a swig. Even worse, he couldn't remember. Sometime before he had spied that cowboy running from the two Apaches was when he had swallowed a pull of tepid water from his canteen. "Will they come for us in the dark?"

"What are you thinking about? Taking the fight to them? I don't see too good in the dark, Sam."

"You can cover me while I go after them. The best count I have is six of them, and one's carrying a bullet in his leg. They've posted him as lookout."

"He's got a grudge, that's for sure. He won't go to sleep if there's any chance he can spot one of us for himself. And if he's really mad, he'll rouse the whole band to take turns torturing us."

Wilcox had said something Knight hadn't considered. The Indians could take turns on lookout and rest up for a real battle. All they needed to do was pull back a few hundred feet, start a fire, cook food, sleep, and dream of lifting the scalps of two white men who had humiliated them.

38

He fired again when a brave poked his head above a rock. The Apache was already ducking back before the bullet got there. Another popped up and another and another. Wilcox shot at both of them. His aim wasn't any better than Knight's.

"They're getting us to waste our bullets." Knight chewed his lower lip for a moment. "That means they aren't going to wait us out. They're going to attack when it gets a little darker."

He checked the sun dipping lower over the western canyon rim. If he had been in the place of the Apaches, he would launch his assault in less than fifteen minutes. Shadows would hide the advance, but enough light remained to make the attack possible without getting lost in the rocks.

"I never expected going to Ralston would end up like this. Damn me, I never laid eyes on that mining town. Maybe I would've got rich, but all I really wanted was to make a few dollars before moving on. I've heard that Tucson is a place where an ambitious young man can make a decent living. Don't reckon I'll find out now."

Knight didn't try to boost his companion's spirits this time. He checked his Colt Navy and made sure the Winchester carried a full magazine. "Here they come! We keep them back, and we might see sunrise." He began firing.

Two rounds from his rifle found targets. The Apaches' screams were as much pain as they were anger. Knight finally came up empty, drew his revolver, and rested the butt on the rock. Using it to steady his hand, he emptied the cylinder as the Indians darted through the gathering shadows and tried to rush the rocks. With practiced ease, Knight knocked out the spent cylinder and put in a loaded one. The first two shots proved to be duds. The next four drove the Apaches back to cover.

"I'm out of bullets," Wilcox said.

Knight replaced his spent cylinder with another spare. "Unless I miss my guess, we spooked them enough to hold off any new attack until dawn." He sounded more confident than he felt.

He and Wilcox were dead men if he was wrong.

CHAPTER 3

A gray tinge was creeping upward in the eastern sky. The night had been an eternity long. The Apaches had retreated after a second failed advance. Not attacking during the night had proven nerve-wracking for the trapped men. The slightest sound — a falling pebble, the soft whistle of wind through the rocks, small animals scurrying about — all had caused them to jerk awake. Neither had more than a few minutes' sleep the entire night, waiting for the attack that had never come.

Knight shook his head, trying to dislodge some of the cobwebs from his brain, and checked his gun even though he knew it had three rounds remaining in it after the last skirmish the night before.

One shot for the Apaches when they attacked, one for Wilcox . . . and then a final round for his own brain.

"It's almost dawn. Another half hour at

the outside, even with the canyon walls cutting off the light."

Wilcox fumbled about, drew a pocket watch from his vest and peered at it. "Hard to read."

Even in the dark, Knight saw shadows begin moving closer. "You might want to throw rocks or see if you can lever a big rock down in an avalanche. This is going to be over quick, no matter what we do, but I want to go down fighting."

"Hasn't been long," Wilcox said, "but damn me, it's been good knowing you, Sam." He thrust out his hand.

Knight hesitated an instant, then shook. "I can't say you're the one I thought I would die with, but I could have done a lot worse." Memories of Milo Hannigan's treachery back in Buffalo Springs flashed through Knight's head, but his one big regret was losing his wife to a carpetbagger.

The Apaches creeping forward stopped that morbid chain of memories from lengthening. Knight rose, took careful aim, and fired. Whether nerves got the better of him or he just wanted the fight to end, he squeezed off all three rounds. The Colt's hammer slammed down with a haunting metallic emptiness on a spent chamber. He was out of ammunition, too.

"Let's see how good your arm is, Sam." Wilcox jumped to his feet and heaved a fist-sized rock. He failed to reach the first Apache making his way through the maze leading to the boulders. That didn't stop him from hefting another rock and lofting it with no better result.

Knight slid his knife from a sheath and stood alongside the cowboy. Pale morning light shone behind them. That put the sun in the Indians' eyes. It also showed the inexorable tide of death flowing toward them.

An arrow sailed past his ear. Knight stood his ground and took a deep breath to settle his nerves. Panic would only speed his death. He intended to use his knife and take at least one Apache with him to the happy hunting ground since he had missed with all three of his last rounds.

"Sam. Sam!"

"What?" A flash of irritation made Knight grip his knife even tighter. Distracting him meant an easier victory for the Indians.

"Do you hear that? Music. Heavenly music!"

Knight thought the young cowboy must have gone loco from fear, only Wilcox didn't sound like he had lost his mind. Before Knight could say a word, he heard the trumpet's wavering notes echoing from the canyon leading south. "That's not Gabriel. That's a cavalry bugler sounding *Charge.*" He had heard plenty of those commands during the war. Mistaking the sound was impossible.

Wilcox heaved a rock and hit a brave in the head. The impact only staggered the Apache but caused him to spin and face the first of the soldiers pouring from the southern canyon mouth. At the head of the column rode an officer, his saber swinging. In spite of the officer being a Yankee, Knight cheered when he saw the flashing blade cut deeply into an Apache's neck. Blood spurted.

The officer raced past, his horse's hooves thunderclaps against the rocky canyon floor. "Forward! Take no prisoners!" he bellowed hoarsely.

His troopers understood and fought with a fury Knight hadn't seen since the war. What he had never seen were black soldiers.

"Damn me," whispered Wilcox. "A white officer and colored soldiers. I'd heard of them buffalo soldiers but thought it was only a tall tale."

"Buffalo soldiers?"

Wilcox shrugged. "These must be troops

from Fort Bayard, a day or two north of here."

Knight watched the tide of bluecoats drive the Apaches from the field. He tried to count the bodies. Lingering shadows kept him from getting a good count, but he saw at least two Apaches sprawled on the ground. There had been no more than a half dozen pinning them down.

Now what was he to do?

His trouble back in Pine Knob with the army commander there probably hadn't reached the distant outpost, but he couldn't take that chance. Captain Norwood's fury might have forced him to send out wanted posters to every U.S. Army post connected to a telegraph.

Knight didn't know if Fort Bayard had a telegraph. If it had been built just after the war to keep the Indians in line, the so-called singing wires might not have reached it yet. Could he take that chance?

"Come on, Sam. Let's go congratulate them. I don't care if they're black as night. They saved us from hours of torture if the Apaches captured us." Dave Wilcox slid down the rock, landed hard, then twisted his way agilely through the rocks.

Their horses whinnied as Wilcox took the reins and led them downhill. Knight almost called out to his unexpected partner and told him to leave one horse behind. If he tarried and let the squad of soldiers move on, he might avoid talking with the officer. Sneaking off after they rode back to their post presented an even better solution, but he had to have a horse.

He hesitated and Wilcox led all four of their mounts down to where the officer waved his saber around, the dawn sending shards of reflected light in all directions.

"Hey, Sam, come on down. It's all right. The lieutenant's got it under control. We're safe!"

"There's someone else in the rocks?" The lieutenant stood in his stirrups and peered into the sunrise, trying to find Knight.

The dilemma resolved itself in Knight's head. If he tried to run, he would create too many questions for the officer to ignore. He had ridden far and fast from Pine Knob. Captain Norwood was a thousand miles to the east, although Knight still worried that he couldn't run far enough, fast enough to get away from all he had done.

He made his way down, stepping over the body of a fallen Apache on the way. He wondered how the man had died, but he wasn't curious enough to examine the body. A random shot or an accurate one, none of that mattered. The Indian had died in the assault on Knight's secure rock fortress and Knight was still alive. That was all that counted.

"You sho' 'nuff look like you's been through a fight."

He turned to a gray-haired sergeant who studied him closely. Too closely for comfort. The man stood almost as tall as Knight's own six feet but outweighed him by fifty pounds. While Knight had regained most of the weight lost during his incarceration at Elmira, he hadn't built up the muscle he once had.

The sergeant's extra weight was nothing *but* muscle. He had the look of a man who could hoist a horse above his head, then brag about it being light because it hadn't eaten that day. Hands like quart Mason jars clenched and unclenched. A single blow from either of those ham hocks to the chin meant instant death. Knight was glad the noncom wasn't his enemy.

At least, he wasn't if Captain Norwood hadn't contacted Fort Bayard about the murderous Rebel outlaw fleeing from Pine Knob.

"I have, Sergeant," Knight replied. "We ran out of ammunition just before dawn. Holding them off meant fighting with this."

47

He showed his knife, then slipped it back into its sheath.

"We kin give yo' some rounds. Leastways, if the lieutenant says so." The sergeant spat.

Whether it showed his disrespect for the officer or just came from too much chaw made Knight wonder about the unit. Being a Confederate captain, he had never seen one comprised of black soldiers before. Certainly no one in his medical unit had.

"Sergeant Lawrence! Get that man over here, now!"

"A pleasant fellow," Knight muttered. He could tell that the sergeant overheard from the way the man's lips pulled back into a feral smile. With more confidence than he felt, Knight went to greet the officer. Wilcox already had made his acquaintance. If Knight read his newfound partner's expression correctly, there wasn't any love lost between the two. And that had taken less than a minute to accomplish.

"Sam, this here's Lieutenant Billings. He done rescued us from them red devils."

"Much obliged, Lieutenant." Knight shook hands with as much distaste as the lieutenant showed, which was plenty.

"This is a filthy place filled with sneaking redskins and more Johnny Rebs than you can shake a stick at." Billings squinted as he studied Knight like a bug under a magnifying glass. "You fight for the South?"

"No, sir, I did not," Knight said, glad he didn't have to lie. He hadn't killed Yankees himself during his enlistment. As it was, he kept Confederate soldiers from dying so they could do that chore. Saving as many as he had, his efforts undoubtedly had resulted in the deaths of hundreds, if not thousands, of Federals.

"From your accent, you're from Texas."

"And from yours, I'd say New York."

"I am, sir, and proud of it. I graduated from West Point only this year."

"First assignment," Wilcox said in a neutral voice. From the slight curl to his lips, he mocked the officer.

Knight had never found out where the cowboy's sympathies lay, North or South, and since the Yankees had won the war, it hardly mattered. Reading anything other than scorn for the greenhorn officer personally was wrong. He suspected that to know Lieutenant Billings was to hate him, in or out of uniform.

Pulling himself up to his full five-foot-nine height, Billings said in response to Wilcox's comment, "That hardly matters. Whether I rescued you or Colonel Patterson with his twenty years of service had done so should

49

not affect your gratitude."

"Thank you, Lieutenant," Knight said. "You surely did pull our fat out of the fire. Are there other Apache war parties in the area?" He felt itchy and ready to ride away, It was as if he played with fire by staying close to the lieutenant.

"I led my patrol to the Mexican border chasing a dozen of the bastards. My standing orders are not to engage if they escape into that godforsaken country, and I obeyed."

"Always obey your orders. Yes, sir, that's the kind of soldier you are." Sarcasm dripped from the cowboy's words.

Knight almost poked him in the ribs with his elbow, but the lieutenant took no heed and regaled them with stories of his daring pursuit of the hostiles.

In his time, Knight had heard many a story spun around a campfire. What he heard from the lieutenant was likely true, just a little. The embellishment that added flair — and the hint of an officer's outrageous bravery — did not ring true. If Billings intended lying about his exploits, he needed more practice. If he lived long enough, he would learn. He wasn't the sort of officer to take kindly to advice from anyone else, though.

50

"Suh, patrol's ready to move on." Sergeant Lawrence threw a sloppy salute as he came up. "We got them redskins all buried. I found this on the one what's they leader." The sergeant passed over a deerskin pouch.

Billings recoiled from it as if it would bite. "Why give that filthy thing to me?"

"Suh, it's a *hoddentin* bag off their medicine man. You want to see this here map." The sergeant pulled out a tattered scrap of paper and blew off yellow pollen.

Knight almost laughed as Billings backed away as if he might catch the plague from the dust.

"It don't hurt you none, suh. It's what a medicine man uses to cast spells and such. But this here map?" Lawrence shook it off again and handed it to the officer.

Billings took it gingerly, then turned so he could study it in the bright rising sun. His finger traced over lines and his lips moved. Standing on tiptoe allowed Knight to catch a look at the map. From the quick flight down the canyon and the Apache pursuit, he got the lay of the land quickly. The spots smeared with animal grease marked watering holes.

"What do you make of this, Sergeant?"

"Looks like places where they intend to lay ambushes. Them's waterin' holes, but I

51

know two of 'em ain't got good water. Al-kali."

"Why mark them, then?"

" 'Cause they can lure unsuspectin' sol-diers there and spring traps."

"Or let the soldiers drink bad water and get them and their mounts so sick they can't fight worth a hill of beans," piped up Dave Wilcox. "I've heard of them doing such a thing before, down in the Big Bend area where I'm from. They —"

"Thank you for your astute analysis, sir," Billings said sharply, folding the map. He hesitated, then shoved the filthy paper into the front of his uniform. "This is important enough for the captain to see. Sergeant, mount the troop. We're returning to the fort immediately."

"But, suh, we got another week of patrol."

"You heard my order. This is vital intel-ligence that requires me to report back im-mediately."

"You could send it by a courier while —" Wilcox snapped his mouth shut at the look of pure hatred Billings shot at him.

"You and your partner will return to Fort Bayard with us. Your story will add credence to this discovery." Billings patted the front of his jacket where he had stashed the map.

"Wait, Lieutenant," Knight objected.

"There's no need for us to go with you. We can follow you out of the canyon and then we can go our separate ways." He kept the panic out of his voice only through sheer effort. Being taken to a Yankee stronghold was the last thing he wanted.

"Both of you. Mount. That's an order. *My* order." Billings spun and stalked to his horse. He waited a moment until a private came and helped boost him into the saddle. With a grandiose arm gesture he motioned for the troopers to follow. He kicked at his horse and got it moving back toward the mouth of the winding canyons.

"We gonna keep them two Injun ponies," the sergeant said. "Spoils of war. That and we be a dozen head short back at the post. No matter how the colonel begs, we don't get no supplies worth a bucket of warm spit, much less fine horses like these."

"We risked our lives to get those horses," protested Wilcox.

Knight put his hand on the cowboy's shoulder to quiet him. Arguing got them nowhere.

"Don't," Wilcox said, pulling away. His entire left arm sagged from just that light touch. "Don't grab hold of me like that."

"Sorry." Knight fought down the urge to examine his new partner's injury, but that was what a doctor did. He had to leave all the medical knowledge behind. It hadn't gotten him anywhere and only left him aching and hollow — and his friends dead.

Sergeant Lawrence watched them like a hawk, his brown eyes missing nothing as they stepped up on their original mounts.

Knight settled down, working over how to separate himself from the squad and get on his way. If he had to abandon Wilcox, so be it. He liked the young cowboy and admired his bravery in the face of what had seemed unavoidable death. Wilcox had some knowledge of this part of New Mexico Territory that could come in handy, but if he had to leave him behind, he would.

"I didn't expect to see blacks serving in the army," Knight said, riding alongside Lawrence.

"You bein' a Southern man from the way you talk, I don't doubt that none. I signed up early on and saw more fightin' than I care to think on. After the war, the War Department decided on sendin' all us Negro units to fight them Indians."

"The unit's not all black, though. You have to put up with him." Knight stared at Billings's back, as if he could drill holes through the officer's body.

"He's a caution, that one. Wet behind the

ears, sho 'nuff, but he's not as bad as some of the others at the fort."

"The captain?"

"Now, how'd you know that? You been to Fort Bayard?" Lawrence fixed him with those brown eyes that should have been soft but took on a hardness matching Apache arrowheads.

"I figured it out from the way he talked about the man. Billings wants to curry favor. He thinks the captain's approval will get him promoted or moved to a better command. More than that, he thinks this is a punishment detail for him."

"For most all of 'em, it is."

"You don't mind?" Knight saw that they were approaching the mouth of the canyon. The hilly land beyond could provide cover when he chose to make his bid to escape. A half dozen different ways of accomplishing that stirred in his mind. He felt a little regret that none of them included Wilcox riding off with him, but so be it.

" 'Course I mind. Be a damn fool if I didn't. But buffalo soldierin's a hell of a sight better 'n workin' in some plantation owner's cotton fields."

"I can't argue with that." Knight fell silent, letting Lawrence sway along with his horse's uneven gait.

The sergeant's eyes became hooded, then the eyelids sagged shut.

Knight had guessed right that the lieutenant had kept the squad on patrol all night long. Taking the Apaches by surprise hadn't drained much more energy, but the rush of fear and anticipation before any battle had to be slipping away from the soldiers. All of them were drifting off in the saddle as they made their way north toward Fort Bayard.

Knight considered warning Wilcox of what he intended, but at the moment the cowboy was riding alongside Billings and keeping the officer occupied. Their pace slowed as they trudged up a steep hill. It took little effort for Knight to slow his horse and fall back even more. When the soldier riding in front of him disappeared over the crest of the hill, Knight turned abruptly and followed the elevation away.

He had ridden for almost fifteen minutes before he felt he had succeeded in getting away. He slowed his horse to let the animal take a breather.

"You sho' do take the long way 'round, mistah. Why doan we ride on back to the rest of the patrol?"

Knight jumped at the sound of the familiar voice. He looked back to where Sergeant

Lawrence sat astride his horse, a carbine resting across the saddle in front of him.

CHAPTER 4

Gerald Donnelly hobbled along, leaning heavily on his cane to take away some of the pain radiating upward from his severed Achilles tendon. With every step a monumental agony, how could he ever forget the man who had done this to him?

Dr. Samuel Knight.

The name rolled through Donnelly's head like thunder. They had fought and the damned surgeon had gotten the better of him, just for a second. He had used his scalpel and surgical skills to cut the tendon and forever force his bitter adversary to limp about like some damned cripple.

Donnelly tried to get a better grip on the gold-knobbed cane and lost his hold, sending him crashing to the parlor floor.

"Damn it. Matty!" He bellowed for the maid but his wife came running instead. He glared at her with unbridled fury. She had been married to that son of a bitch who had done this to him. Somehow, it was all her fault.

"Are you all right, Gerald?" she asked as she leaned over him.

"Do I look all right? Help me stand, Victoria. And don't take your sweet time, either, like you always do. You enjoy seeing me like this, don't you?" He got to his knees, but the cane slid from his grip again and thwarted him. "Help me, woman!"

"Your right hand," she said in a low voice. "Without an index finger, you lost your grip on the cane."

"Damn it, yes. Is that what you want to hear from me? Your husband shot my trigger finger off. He murdered Alton and shot me in the hand. Your *former* husband turned me into a cripple!"

"The cane does have a rifle mechanism," Victoria said, getting her hands under his armpits. She heaved. Too heavy for her, he slipped away and crashed back to the floor, cursing. "And Hector Alton was a gunfighter you hired to kill Samuel. He got the better of a professional gunman, too."

"He ambushed Alton. Gunned him down from ambush. Then he shot me after he had cut my feet." Donnelly shoved her away. He crawled to a settee and pulled himself up. "You shouldn't take his part. You're *my*

59

wife. You owe me for marrying you when no one else would."

"It wasn't like that, and you know it. I thought Samuel was dead. You came along and were so sweet then. So nice to a woman grieving over a lost husband." She stepped away and stared at him with soft brown eyes flooding with tears. "You've changed so much, Gerald. You've turned bitter."

"Bitter? Bitter? Of course I'm bitter after what Knight did to me! He left me an invalid."

"It's more than that, Gerald. You've become an ogre. All you do is plot and scheme how to steal more land. You're foreclosing here and running men off their homesteads there. It's all you do."

"It's what I have been entrusted to do by no less authority than Secretary of War Edwin Stanton himself. Government policy demands that I humble you Rebels in any way I can."

"Do you count me among 'you Rebels,' Gerald? I never supported slavery. My family never owned slaves, and Papa spoke out against those who did. You have no call lumping me in with the others in such a callous fashion." Tears flowed freely down her cheeks. She made no effort to wipe them off. "And it doesn't matter to you if it's an old woman's house you foreclose on with that horrid Mr. Fitzsimmons at the bank. Or someone unable to properly tend their house."

"Another cripple? Are you saying I have no mercy for *other cripples*? Well, madam, I do not. I have no pity, no mercy, not a speck of sympathy for those who fought against the Stars and Stripes. That includes you, it seems."

"Oh, Gerald." Victoria fled from the room, openly sobbing.

He started to call her back, to *order* her to return, but a knock at the front door stilled his desire to make her apologize. Pressing business demanded his full attention, and dealing with an ungrateful woman could be postponed until later.

"Come in, damn you. Come in!"

Donnelly sagged farther into the cushions when he saw the commander of the local cavalry detachment in the doorway. Captain Norwood tucked his hat under his left arm in perfect military manner. Everything about the tin soldier was perfect. The creases on his trousers were sharp enough to cut a man's hand. The sheen on his boots had required hours of work by his aide to achieve such perfection, and the brass buttons blazed like the very sun. Donnelly hated slovenly dressers. He should have liked Norwood, but he loathed the man for no reason he could pin down. Something in his gut churned whenever he faced the military man.

"Sir," Norwood greeted him.

"Get in here. You took your time responding." With his cane, Donnelly imperiously tapped the spot on the floor directly in front of him.

To spite him, Norwood marched in, cadence parade-ground-perfect, and stood off to one side, forcing Donnelly to turn slightly and put pressure on his bad leg. The officer did this on purpose. He had to. Donnelly refused to show any discomfort. Weakness now would be used against him later.

"What do you want, Donnelly?"

"Civility," he snapped. "You will address me by my title."

"You are a civilian and are not my superior." Norwood spoke louder to drown out Donnelly's protest. "You might have pull with my superiors. If so, there is nothing I can do to keep you from complaining to General Sheridan. Until he or another in my immediate chain of command so orders, I am not your personal servant nor am I obligated to jump whenever you call out *frog.*"

"Your insolence is exceeded only by your incompetence. What do you have to report about him?"

"Him?"

"Damn you! Dr. Samuel Knight! Have you found him?"

"I tracked the Hannigan gang to Buffalo Springs," Norwood said. "They were also pursuing Knight. What happened there is confusing. They tried to rob the bank and, from some accounts, Knight killed them all. Others claim he took part in the robbery. Whichever it was does not matter. From there, he simply disappeared. The townspeople know nothing of his whereabouts and some show intense dislike for him, one woman in particular."

"Who? What's her name? If she has reason to despise him, she can be made to talk."

Norwood shook his head. "She doesn't know anything, Donnelly. Nothing at all. I am confident of that. Because Buffalo Springs lies so far away, I cannot afford to patrol there or pursue the matter more."

"You've failed!"

"I want to bring him to justice as much as you." Norwood pointedly stared at Donnelly's leg, then his mutilated hand. A tiny smile curled the officer's lips. "Perhaps not quite as much, but I know my duty. He stole government property and must pay for it. However, it is beyond my command's ability to track him down. I follow orders about keeping the peace in Pine Knob and the surrounding area. That mission takes precedence. Now, I must return to my *assigned* deputation." Captain Norwood executed a half left-facing movement and strode from the parlor.

"Get back here. I haven't finished with you, Norwood! Get back here!" Donnelly half rose but lost his balance. By the time he got to his feet and hobbled after the retreating officer, Norwood had mounted and was halfway to the road leading into Pine Knob. All Donnelly could do was shake his walking stick in the officer's direction as he stood in the open doorway, gripping the jamb. His anger had passed beyond words.

He looked over his shoulder. His black maid Matty stood in the doorway leading to the kitchen.

"Prepare my buggy. I have to go into town." He reached for his hat on a rack beside the door. "What's wrong? Have you gone deaf? My buggy! Now!"

Matty turned away without a word.

Fuming at the incompetence all around him, Donnelly shuffled onto the porch to wait. His mind raced wildly, producing no decent plan of action to bring down Captain Norwood. The man's intractable nature was not to be tolerated. There had to be some way to get him transferred to a dead-end command. That would fix him. After the war, a surplus of experienced officers threatened to bloat the army. Many accepted demotions, some from general to as low as captain to remain in the service of their country. Others, like Norwood, stayed in the army because they could find no other employment.

"Sheridan," Donnelly mused aloud. "He might be the one to contact, but Edwin Stanton is a better way. Yes, he's a good friend. He's commander-in-chief of Reconstruction policy. Civilian, yes, but he *is* Secretary of War. How can he be pleased that an officer in his army performs so poorly?"

Matty drove the buggy around and passed the reins to him. Donnelly climbed awkwardly and painfully into the vehicle, then flapped the reins and started the horse moving. He muttered to himself as he drove, composing a letter to Stanton damning Captain Norwood. The wording had to be precise, not too vitriolic or Stanton might want to send someone to investigate. Failing to arrest Knight hardly constituted major malfeasance on Norwood's part, but there had to be more at which to hint. Innuendo worked better in Washington circles than outright accusation.

By the time Donnelly drew to a halt in front of the city hall, he had the letter perfectly formed in his mind. His mood lightened, and he had an unusual spring to his step that got him up the steps more easily than at any time in the past week. In the town hall foyer, he bellowed for his assistant.

Leonard popped out of his small coffin-sized office like a prairie dog coming to attention above his burrow. His rheumy eyes shone big and fearful through the lenses of his eyeglasses. Even in his debilitated condition, Donnelly thought he could outrun the clerk, outfight him, and best him in just about any physical contest. The man was so scrawny, he ought to be fearful of a high wind blowing him away.

"Sir? They aren't here yet. I can look for them."

"What are you prattling on about?" Donnelly demanded.

"Your appointment with the men recommended by Mr. Seward."

Donnelly had forgotten, but the reminder

made him feel even better. If Norwood had failed, the men so highly recommended by William Henry Seward would not. Seward and he had become more than casual acquaintances, drawn by their anti-Masonic feelings. In charge of the Secret Service, Seward had contacts even Stanton lacked.

"Later. They will be here, I am sure. They are dependable men. So says Mr. Seward. Bring me paper, pen and ink, and an envelope. I have an important letter to write. When I am finished, you must post it immediately."

"Yes, sir, of course. I —"

"The stationery, Leonard. Now."

As the clerk scurried off like a small rodent, Donnelly made his way into his office. He paused in the doorway and looked around. Two windows looked out onto a forested area. The furnishings befitted the man whose word was law in this town. The office had belonged to the mayor until Reconstruction.

The mayor had complained, but there wasn't anything he could do about getting evicted from his own office.

Donnelly went to the lushly padded chair behind the desk and sank into it. Being called a carpetbagger had taken on an air of prestige. He had been sent to wipe out any trace of rebellion from any Southerners and Southern sympathizers — basically all townspeople — and bring a stronger moral character to the town.

He was well on his way to doing that and would have accomplished his task if he'd brought Samuel Knight to heel.

"There. Put it on my desk, Leonard."

The clerk placed the paper, pen, and inkwell in front of Donnelly and bobbed his head up and down as if it were mounted on a spring. He clutched his hands together in front of him like a squirrel with an acorn, but Leonard's thin, sandy hair had nothing in common with even the meanest of squirrels.

"What is it you want?" Donnelly slid the paper into place to begin the letter that would terminate Norwood's military career.

"Those men. The two you wanted to see. They're here."

"Tell them to wait." Donnelly looked up when Leonard didn't budge. "Did you hear me?"

"They said they'd leave if they had to wait. They have important business elsewhere." Leonard bent forward and whispered confidentially, "I think they might be government agents."

"Of course they are," Donnelly snapped.

"They're Pinkerton men. Very well. Send them in." He pushed aside the paper, not liking how the two unknown, unseen men manipulated his staff — and him. Seward would hear about them if they proved less than he had boasted.

Donnelly involuntarily reached for his cane with the rifle mechanism and forced himself to take a breath. This was his office. He was in charge. But seldom had he seen men as hard looking as the pair who entered the room.

"Gentlemen, be seated." He motioned to the two straight-backed chairs in front of his desk. "Would you like a drink? Whiskey, perhaps?"

"We don't have time to lollygag," said the taller one. He had the look of a sailor cured into a piece of light brown leather from the sun and wind. Donnelly expected the face to crack as the man's lips moved.

Nothing of the sort happened. The grid of scars held the skin in place. Eyes so black they might have been endless pits fixed on him. The man's jacket and vest were plain, nondescript, but clean and durable. His trousers were a tad on the tight side, as if he had put on weight. Donnelly didn't see how that was possible since there didn't seem to be an ounce of fat on his body.

Most obvious, there was no mistaking that the Walker Colt slung in a cross-draw rig had seen frequent and hard use.

Donnelly blinked and looked at the man's partner. If there had been a complete opposite in the world, he stood there: short, corpulent, dressed like a gambler or riverboat dandy. The man's round, pudgy face radiated nothing but friendliness. He didn't wear a gunbelt but Donnelly saw flashes of a shoulder holster and a small-caliber gun hung under the man's right arm.

"Don't let my good friend's brusque manner put you off, sir. I am Henry Hesseltine, of the Baltimore Hesseltines. Have you heard of my family? They own, oh, most of the city and a shipping line carrying half the freight between the United States and Rotterdam." Hesseltine smiled ingratiatingly. "My friend here — Rance Spurgeon — used to work on the docks for my uncle. Rance is quite civilized in spite of his roughhewn demeanor."

"You and, uh, Mr. Spurgeon *are* Pinkerton agents?"

"We are, sir. Mr. Seward recruited us to aid in breaking a strike in Baltimore that affected the shipping of supplies vital to our nation's economy. I found myself serving double duty." Hesseltine chuckled. "The strike was against the family shipping company, so I got paid to do what I would have done for nothing. Mr. Seward approved of our efficiency and commended us to Pinkerton. It turned out there was no need. Allan had donned one of his clever disguises and was in Baltimore watching us the whole while."

"Some disguise," grumbled Spurgeon. "I saw he had a fake beard."

"Yes, yes, you did, my friend. But it was foolish letting him know the way you did. Allan thinks he is a master of disguise. Remember when he uncovered the assassination plot against —" Hesseltine abruptly stopped speaking.

Donnelly felt a chill up and down his spine at the sudden change in the man's demeanor.

"Rance is right, sir. We have no time for reminiscing. Allan Pinkerton ordered us from our headquarters in Chicago to this nothing of a town as a favor to Mr. Seward. What do you require of us?"

"Sit down," Donnelly said again. Having the pair hovering at either corner of his desk, towering over him, made him feel small and insecure.

Spurgeon glanced at a chair and shook his head.

Hesseltine never bothered to even look. "We prefer to stand. We won't be here long enough to get comfortable."

Spurgeon snorted at the very idea those chairs were comfortable.

Donnelly had ordered them to be adequate for holding a visitor's weight but nothing more than that. He preferred anyone in his office to be at as much a disadvantage as possible. Like Norwood earlier, Hesseltine and Spurgeon refused to take the bait and give him even a small edge over them.

"Very well. Mr. Seward was kind enough to send you. There's no reason to waste your time. In a nutshell, I want a man brought to justice. Whether you return him alive to stand trial or dead is of no consequence."

"The pay's the same?" Spurgeon rested his left hand on the butt of his revolver.

"Rance, my friend, we are paid by the Pinkerton Agency. We draw a salary, so of course the result is the same." Hesseltine made it sound as if they worked for a set fee, but Donnelly heard the edge in the man's voice and knew what to do.

"Your salary is sufficient for two such accomplished agents, I am sure, but you should receive a per diem — a fee for any extraordinary expenses — to be determined when you return with Dr. Samuel Knight."

"That's who we're after?" Spurgeon rummaged in a coat pocket and pulled out a wanted poster with Knight's likeness on it.

Donnelly started to speak, but words failed him for a moment. He had not expected the agents — especially Spurgeon — to be aware of their mission.

"We always know what we're getting ourselves into." Spurgeon thrust the reward dodger toward Donnelly. "This is the owlhoot?"

"It is. Any reward is, of course, yours. Captain Norwood failed to capture Knight when he was in town, riding with the Milo Hannigan gang. Norwood is —"

"We know who he is," Hesseltine said. "We'll speak with him to find out anything you can't tell us." He pulled out an ornate pocket watch and studied the face as if reading a book. He snapped it shut and tucked it away. "We have five more minutes. Be concise, sir, as you tell us everything we need to know to capture this Samuel Knight."

"Yeah, capture him." Rance Spurgeon ran his fingers over the butt of his gun, leaving no question how they intended to bring Knight to justice.

That suited Gerald Donnelly just fine. He

spoke quickly, telling them all he knew.

The pair left exactly five minutes after he began, although he hadn't finished. He stared at their backs as they left his office. He sighed, then pulled the paper into place and began the letter that would get rid of another problem vexing him in Pine Knob.

CHAPTER 5

Sam Knight sat straighter in the saddle when he spotted the flag flying high on a flagpole. The last time he had seen a flag that large, it had been flying over his prison camp. The commandant had assembled the prisoners every morning, no matter how bitter the cold, and forced them to pledge allegiance to the red, white, and blue. Those who refused ended up in pits dug for the purpose of solitary confinement.

Knight had been thrown into those holes in the ground secured with metal grating across the mouth more than once, but for other offenses. He tried to pick his battles, and those he had lost all had to do with trying to save the miserable lives of injured and sick prisoners.

"You doan want to go to the post," Sergeant Lawrence said as they rode closer. "Any reason for that, suh?"

"It's a waste of everybody's time. What

75

can I tell your captain that the lieutenant hasn't heard already? Wilcox and I were ambushed by Apaches. We tried to escape and went down a box canyon by mistake. Before we got out, the Indians trapped us. Your squad saved us. That's the whole story."

"From what Ah know, that ain't the whole story. Ain't never the whole story, no suh. You got some real fear about comin' to the fort."

"I never fought against the Union. I can swear on a Bible and do it with clear conscience."

"Ah believe you, Ah do, but like Ah said, there's more you're not tellin'." Lawrence shrugged his broad shoulders, brushed off trail dust in huge clouds from his uniform, and stared straight ahead. "None of that's my concern. Them officers, now, thass what they's paid to do . . . to find the truth, the whole truth, and nuthin' but the truth." He turned to Knight and flashed a toothy smile. With that, he kicked his horse into a canter to enter the fort.

The fort lacked the tall palisade often found at posts back east. A knee-high adobe wall kept in chickens and other small animals. Two watchtowers at opposite sides of the compound provided the only defense. If the sentries failed to call out, the post could be overrun in a few minutes, even with soldiers flopping on their bellies and using the low adobe walls for protection.

Knight found himself wishing the Indians would launch such an attack right now. Being interrogated by the lieutenant had been annoying. The brash young snot showed the arrogance of class and upbringing that made him feel superior to anyone not wearing a Union uniform. Feeding him answers that satisfied him was easy enough. Knight had tried to find out more about the captain immediately in command over Billings but hadn't reached any conclusion other than he was a son of a bitch, too.

Knight swallowed hard. That was how he considered all Federal officers. They had won the war, and his side had lost. He needed to get over the prejudice of being a loser and find a way to get on with his life, if that was even possible after all that had happened to him after his release from the Yankee prison camp.

A squad of buffalo soldiers marched out and escorted him and Wilcox to an adobe building with two-foot-thick walls and a thatched roof. Knight held in check the impulse to light a lucifer and toss it onto the roof. He sagged when he remembered he didn't have a lucifer. For that matter, he didn't have the makings for a cigarette. A few puffs might help settle his nerves. A stiff drink would go down even better.

Wilcox moved closer, his arm brushing Knight's. In a low voice he asked, "You in trouble with the Army?"

"Why do you ask?" Knight wondered if the cowboy would turn him in in exchange for his own freedom. Then he realized how ridiculous that was. Wilcox knew nothing of him or his past. They had been together for a couple days and mostly they had talked about how soon they would die at Apache hands. They had not talked about their pasts, though Wilcox had been far more talkative.

"You get real tense around them. Especially the officers."

"Inside." Billings motioned for them to enter then turned, preceded them into the small office, and took a seat behind a small desk covered with a thin layer of dust.

The lieutenant sneezed as he used his sleeve to swipe away the dust. He succeeded only in getting his uniform jacket dirty. Very little of the dust vanished from the desktop. He sneezed again, then took off his hat and laid it in the clean spot before looking up.

"I want a full report from you two." He

opened a drawer, took out a sheet of paper, pen and ink, and poised to take notes.

Knight exchanged looks with Wilcox. The cowboy took the hint, stepped up and put both hands on the desk to lean forward. "You know most all of what happened, Lieutenant. Why don't you —"

"Hands off my desk." Billings stabbed at Wilcox's hand with his pen. The steel nib missed his fingers and dug into the wood top. "You first." He prepared to take notes again.

"Well, sir, it's like this." Wilcox launched into a long, windy tale of how they had been run ragged by the Indians and barely avoided getting their scalps lifted.

Knight appreciated how Wilcox embellished the truth without ever actually lying about what happened. The cowboy made them into heroes holding off half the Chiricahua nation and the cavalry arriving had been a boon to beating the Apaches. Otherwise, they would have suffered a devastating defeat at the hands of two men rather than an entire troop of soldiers.

Billings stopped writing, leaned back and glared. "You want me to put that into an official report?"

"Might be you and them black soldiers kept us from losing our hair," Wilcox allowed. "That'd make for real good reading, wouldn't it — how you rescued two grateful cowboys who had made damn fools of themselves by tangling with an entire Apache war party."

"Yes, well, that is closer to what happened."

Knight appreciated the way Wilcox maneuvered the lieutenant into composing a self-congratulatory report. By the time Billings finished, it sounded more like the white officer had led a solitary charge and his black troopers had done little more than tootle on the bugle and lend support when he needed it — and he'd needed very little.

Billings used a blotter on the ink, blew away some dust, and stood. He tucked his hat under his arm and marched to the door where he stopped and pointed at them. "Don't leave the post. The captain might have more questions for you."

"Aw, Lieutenant, that report you just penned is the gospel truth. Damn me if it isn't. What more could he want from us?" Wilcox hinted that they should be released.

Billings wasn't having any of it. "Stay on the post. You don't want to make me angry." With that, the young lieutenant marched across the parade ground to a larger adobe building.

Knight looked around, trying to figure out how soon he would be run down if he ignored the orders and fled. From the number of troopers practicing close order drills and the men in either of the watchtowers, he figured the lieutenant could field fifty men in a matter of minutes to catch anyone escaping.

Knight stepped out and squinted in the sun. He stared at the huge American flag snapping in the wind. It had been raised on a peculiar pole with support wires fastened to a disk halfway up the shaft.

"I've seen poles like that before, down in Corpus Christi," Wilcox said. "That's a sailing ship's mast. They must've used it instead of a standard flagpole because the wind's so strong here."

"They wouldn't need it if the flag was smaller," Knight said.

Wilcox laughed. "You are an unrequited Johnny Reb, aren't you? Don't get so het up. I won't say a word to any of them. I wasn't in the army but I suspect you were."

"I wasn't lying when I told the sergeant I never killed a single Union soldier."

"There's other ways to serve. I knew a gent who never heard a single shot fired, much less saw fighting, and he worked as a shipping clerk. Did a whole lot to keep the soldiers fed and in ammunition shipped from Europe and snuck past the embargoing warships. He'd have been a complete waste in the front line since he was blind as a bat without his spectacles, but behind a desk, keeping tally of cargoes and making sure supplies got to where they were needed most, he was as good as any general."

Knight stepped back when a squad of soldiers marched past, their sergeant chewing them out for lack of coordination. He had to smile. They were raw recruits and some had no idea how to perform close-order drill without bumping into each other. Before the sergeant finished with them, they would know their right foot from their left.

He and Wilcox began circling the parade ground. Billings had ordered them not to leave the fort. Knight wanted a better idea of the layout, the number of troops, and what he would be up against if any of the officers recognized him from a wanted poster.

They came to a well with a wooden awning built over it. "You fellas want a dipper o' water? The trail was dry." Sergeant Lawrence held up a tin dipper sloshing water over the rim. He took a long drink, refilled the dipper from a bucket that sat on a rock wall around the well, and held it out.

Wilcox took it gratefully, then followed it with a second. Knight hesitated when it came to his turn, then lost all inhibition when the warm water touched his lips. He was about as parched as a man could get without cotton growing in his mouth.

"How long has the post been up and running?" Knight doubted it had been commissioned for too long.

"We're the first soldiers posted heah," Lawrence said. "Gettin' used to this heat's been hard."

"Where were you stationed before?"

"Ovah in East Texas."

Knight almost bolted and ran. "Do tell. I hear that's good country. What part of the piney woods?"

"Danged near in Louisiana. I ain't pleased with none of that land. I was born 'n raised in Indiana, near White City. You know the area? 'Course not. You both Southern boys."

"How long were you stationed in Texas?" Knight feared the answer wouldn't please him.

"You askin' fer a reason?"

"Captain Norwood. I knew an officer there named Norwood." Knight blurted the explanation out before he realized it. Then he relaxed as he read the answer on Lawrence's dark face.

83

"Don't reckon I've heard of him. You and him, you were friends?"

"Something like that." Knight wanted to say *Nothing like that,* but he had better control of his emotions. Fear of discovery still burned in his breast, but nothing so far hinted that he had anything to worry about. After all, his luck had held and the blue-coats had saved him from getting turned into a pincushion by a half dozen Apaches all firing arrows at him.

Out of the clear blue, Lawrence said, "Pine Knob. Thass where —"

"What?" Knight's mouth turned dry again . . . from fright. He wanted to make a living as a gambler. To do that, he had to keep a poker face. He fought not to show his shock that the sergeant had crossed paths with his nemesis.

"I never served under him, but I heard tell of him in a place called Pine Knob. That where you knowed him?"

Knight bobbed his head, not trusting himself to answer. The reply gave him a chance to get his rampaging emotions under control. Lawrence had never served under him, so the chance that he had ever heard of Dr. Samuel Knight was small.

"If he's a friend o' yours, don't tell him, but nobody I know had a good word to say 'bout him. Him and Lieutenant Billings would git along jist fine, all spit and polish."

"Yup, that's Captain Norwood." Knight had himself under better control. The sound of hammering made him look around. "What's going on?"

"They's buildin' a gallows to string up white folks."

Any relaxing Knight had done vanished in a flash. Panic seized him. Wilcox grabbed his arm to steady him.

"You're joshing us, aren't you, Sergeant?" Wilcox spoke loud enough to drown out the carpentry.

"Shore am." Lawrence chuckled. "Ain't much to keep a man amused at Fort Bayard. The look on yo' partner's face was worth it."

"Funny," Knight said weakly. He pulled free of Wilcox. "What is being built?"

"A gallows. Weren't funnin' you 'bout that, but it's for a Mexican bandit we caught rustlin' beeves. Claims it was to keep him and his family fed, but he done other things worse, and thass why he's gettin' his neck stretched tomorrow morning."

"So you mostly keep the peace from here to the border?" Wilcox edged around to insinuate himself between Lawrence and Knight. "Catching *bandidos* must be high

85

on your list of things to do before breakfast."

"An' after, too. All the livelong day. That and tryin' to corner the Apaches and put 'em back where they belong." Lawrence shook his graying head sadly. "Most all the men what gets killed from this fort are victims of the Indians. Never seen fiercer fighters, and they know this country better 'n anybody. I guarded a survey team a while back. Even them mapmakers don't know the land like the Apaches. Don't matter what tribe they're from, they know it all."

"You have chosen a profession sure to keep you busy for the rest of your life," said Wilcox, then hastily added, "Not that I mean you'll ride out any time soon and get yourself killed."

"I'm in the army for the duration, as they say. Don't know nuthin' else but shootin' a carbine and bossin' them lazy-ass privates around." Lawrence heaved a sigh and looked toward the post headquarters building. "And then there's gettin' bossed around by the likes of them."

Knight almost bolted and ran again when he saw Lieutenant Billings storm from his captain's office and make a beeline for them. His scowl told of bad things to come, and he fixed his eyes squarely on Knight.

A quick glance toward the gallows showed

room for a second noose. Knight moved his hand to the butt of his Colt. Whatever happened, he wasn't going to be strung up alongside a Mexican outlaw. If necessary, he'd go down shooting.

"You, Knight. Come here!" Billings motioned and pointed to a spot directly in front of where he had stopped on the parade grounds.

Knight slid the leather loop off the Colt's hammer and walked toward the lieutenant.

CHAPTER 6

"You, Knight. Were you telling the truth?" The lieutenant clenched his hands into tight fists at his sides. His arms shook with the strain of his barely suppressed anger.

It wasn't the accusation Knight expected. Billings's question took him off guard. "About what?"

"What happened out there! Damn it, man, we rescued you. *I* rescued you."

Knight didn't trust himself. He nodded slowly but kept his hand on his gun. Something was powerfully wrong, and he wondered what it was. From the way Billings acted, his commanding officer hadn't chewed him out for not arresting a fugitive from East Texas.

"Wilcox and I held off the Indians until dawn. That's when we heard your bugle. You attacked the Apaches and killed them."

"I led the attack. I did it."

Knight started to point out that the soldiers had been there, too. The lieutenant had charged into the middle of the war party and taken out at least one warrior with his saber. But his troopers had dispatched the rest.

With Knight's initial shock subsiding, he knew better than to throw fuel on the fire. He nodded. "You did, Lieutenant. You were about the bravest soldier I ever did see."

"With me. Both of you. Now." Billings spun on his heel and marched back to the captain's office.

The few yards gave Knight a chance to compose himself. He guessed what had happened, and it had nothing to do with him running from Captain Norwood. It had everything to do with the report Billings had filed.

Standing stiffly before his commanding officer's desk, Billings said, "Captain, these are the men brought in after the Apache attack. Knight and Wilcox, as I stated in my report."

The captain looked to be a hundred years old. Knight took him for one of the senior officers accepting demotion rather than being mustered out of the army.

He never took his eyes off the stack of papers in front of him on the desk. "Lieutenant, leave us. Now."

89

Billings clearly didn't want to go, but he wasn't going to refuse a direct order. He grimaced slightly, turned on a heel, and stalked out of the office.

The captain rocked back in his chair and hoisted a boot to the desk. It wasn't so he could get a better look at the two civilians. He closed his eyes and massaged his knee. An old battle injury, Knight supposed.

"You tell me what happened out there," the captain said. "I have to be on the parade ground for review in five minutes. Don't waste my time, gentlemen."

Knight motioned Wilcox to silence and gave a quick summary of what happened. He played up the lieutenant's role because he knew that was what had caused this meeting. The captain doubted Billings had played such a prominent part in the rescue.

"You're saying the lieutenant, by his lonesome, killed five of those Apache warriors?"

"I wasn't in any condition to count," Knight said, realizing Billings had embellished his role more than expected. "We were pinned down all night. I swear, it was as if the entire Apache nation was out there. It could have been fifty of them, for all I know."

"It wasn't. This was a war party making its way up from Texas. If there were as many

90

as ten fighters in the group, it would surprise me." The captain lowered his leg and leaned forward. His eyelids rose to half mast. "You swear to the veracity of Lieutenant Billings's official report?"

Knight heard the verbal trap snapping shut around him and chose his words carefully. "We were pinned down. After dawn, the Indians were dead and we were brought back to the fort. That's really all I know."

"Look, Mr. Knight, Mr. Wilcox, this is a touchy matter and that young fool isn't making it any better. The 25th US Colored Infantry Regiment just settled in at Fort Bayard, and we're working to keep Company B, 9th Cavalry Regiment properly outfitted. The War Department isn't happy with having Negro soldiers, but the president is. Any heroics on the part of my soldiers goes a long way toward keeping President Johnson happy because that shows his judgment was correct."

"You want the president to be happy," Knight repeated.

"Hell, yes, since he decides on supplying us. I am sick and tired of buying worm-infested beef and grain lousy with bugs that afford more nutrition than the grain itself. He has powerful enemies that hold the War Department in check. It's all a mess of politics and I have no idea why I am saying a damned word to you about this."

"You want the enlisted men's part in the fight beefed up?"

"That would be fine, Mr. Knight, but only if it is true."

Knight never looked at Wilcox when he said, "The lieutenant's report is accurate."

The captain grumbled under his breath and motioned for them to get out of his office. Knight herded the cowboy ahead of him into the cool breeze kicking up from the west.

"What the hell did you say that for?" Wilcox asked. "The sergeant and his soldiers risked their lives to save us. That's their job, but you heard what the captain said. If they get credit, it reflects well all the way to Washington and —"

"Let's get out of here." Knight stepped around Wilcox not bothering to see if he followed.

Within three steps, the cowboy caught up with him. He grabbed his arm, but Knight jerked free.

"You lied so we wouldn't get caught up in a squabble between the two officers and the buffalo soldiers?" Wilcox tried to grab him again, but Knight sidestepped, turned away, and went directly to their tethered horses, ignoring the strange look Sergeant Lawrence gave him. He mounted, jerked the horse's head around, and aimed directly for the low gate in the adobe wall surrounding the post. He didn't look back, but he heard hoofbeats behind him and knew Wilcox was coming along.

Knight wanted to rage about how unfair it all was, to apologize to Lawrence and the others who had saved his life, but he fixed his attention on riding out of the fort and whatever else it took to get away from the Federals and the chance that someone would identify him. While Sergeant Lawrence hadn't served under Norwood, one of the others in his newly transferred regiment might have. Let the Yankees work out their own problems as long as he was far, far away while they did it.

No one tried to stop them. And nothing suited Knight more than being away from the sound of the gallows being built.

Three days' hard ride through the mountains gave Knight time to settle down. He wasn't sure Dave Wilcox forgave him for not telling the truth back at Fort Bayard, but he had felt so confined that he would have done anything to get away from the soldiers. The sight of the gallows being

93

nailed together had spooked him more than he wanted to admit. He touched his neck, imagining the feel of the rough hemp rope followed by the sudden drop and —

"That sign. Did you see it back there?" Wilcox jerked his thumb over his shoulder.

"I missed it."

"You've been all wrapped up in yourself since we left the fort."

"What'd the sign say?" Knight wanted to divert Wilcox from getting into another discussion about giving the buffalo soldiers their due. He had taken a shine to the cowboy and wanted to count him as a friend rather than parting company. On the trail, having someone to watch his back, to split the chores, to just *be* there mattered more than Knight would have believed possible. Worst of all, he agreed with Wilcox on the matter of stealing away the glory and giving it to that lickspittle lieutenant.

"Ralston City. There's some mining going on nearby, but mostly it's a town where the stagecoach and freight wagons drop off supplies for the surrounding area. That's where I was headed when we run into each other, remember?"

"It sounds like my kind of town, if there's a saloon and gambling going on."

"Never saw a boomtown where there

weren't a dozen saloons and a hundred times as many drunk miners." Wilcox chuckled. "I may soon be among 'em."

"I didn't peg you as a man who drank to excess."

"That might be the only way you'll ever beat me in a card game. I'm the best what ever played, slipping those pasteboards across the table and betting like I've got all the money in the world."

"That means you bluff?"

"Every chance I get."

"It's not a bluff if you tell people ahead of time," Knight pointed out.

That drew a laugh from Wilcox. "Hell, I trust you, Sam. Just don't tell nobody else."

A short time later, Knight drew rein and peered through the twilight haze at a town set out in the middle of the arid plains. The hills seemed to run away from Ralston, leaving the town to shine like a glowing jewel as pale yellow lights winked on in windows.

As they rode down the main street, he spotted low slopes a half mile ahead on the far side of Ralston with the dark mouths of mine shafts cut into them. From the lack of activity around the mines, he wondered if they had played out. Even if there wasn't any gold or silver left, the activity told of other strikes not too distant. The streets were crowded with men in canvas pants and denim shirts, marking them as hard-rock miners. They shoved and called to one another, preparing for a night of debauchery.

"Must be Saturday night," Wilcox said. "I lost track of the days."

"So did I. I'll stand you to a shot of whiskey."

"You want to scout the saloons to see where the pickings are easiest. I know you gamblers too well."

Knight and Wilcox went into the nearest saloon, the Last Nugget, and were almost forced back outside. The small room was packed with men sloshing beer on each other and angling to get to the half dozen gaming tables set around the room.

"Now there's the game for me," Wilcox said, his attention fixed across the crowded room. "Faro."

"You just want to ogle the pretty dealer." Knight watched the short, dark-haired woman bend over the table to rake in the lost bets. She hadn't worn the low-cut dress with the fancy white lace trim for nothing, and the practiced way she stood on tiptoe revealed just a hint of ankle. None of the men at the table paid any attention to how she also raked in winning bids. She gave

96

them a show for their money, and that was why they'd come to Ralston.

"Not saying you're wrong, Sam, not at all. Let me go place a bet." Wilcox took a step, then turned. "Can I borrow a dollar?"

Knight laughed in spite of himself. He fished out a many-times-folded greenback and gave it to the cowboy.

"I'll repay you. After I win."

Knight made his way to the bar, elbowed his way in, and dropped a nickel to ring a few times before it stopped spinning. Somehow, in spite of the din, the barkeep heard and came over with a mug. The foam made a thin crown around the top. Knight knew what the beer tasted like before he sampled it — bitter — and he didn't care. It cut the trail dust and took the edge off all the aches and pains he felt from being so long in the saddle. More than that, it relaxed him. Ever since the ordeal with the war party and being taken to Fort Bayard, he had jumped at every shadow and sound behind him.

He wanted to forget all that. Ralston was a thriving town. A boomtown feeding smaller strikes all around. Making a new life here not only seemed possible, it became inviting when a gambler left a nearby table and signaled to Knight to take his place.

Without looking too eager, he took his

beer with him, dropped into the vacated chair, and put down a stack of two-bit coins on the table as his stake. From the look of the miners around him, it was about the right poke. He fell into easy play, getting the sense of how good the others were before upping his bets and taking ever larger pots until he was almost ten dollars ahead.

"There room for one more?" Dave Wilcox stood beside Knight and held out his hand. If Knight had won steadily, Wilcox had won big-time. He held fifty dollars.

"Pull up a chair," Knight invited. "How'd you get so lucky?"

"I found me a partner. Let's say we split the take." He tipped his hat in the direction of the faro dealer. She smiled prettily and curtsied.

"You looking to get even luckier?" Knight dealt the cards.

"When the Last Nugget closes, I might just find almost getting scalped by Indians and traveling all the way up from Texas was worth it."

Knight had to grin. Wilcox reminded him so much of Seth Lunsford, left back in Buffalo Springs. Seth had ridden with the Milo Hannigan gang because his older brother had urged him to, but in his heart he had always sought the straight and nar-

98

row. Knight hated leaving the young man behind, but Seth had a good job apprenticed to a gunsmith. That job carried more benefits than oiling trigger mechanisms, too. The gunsmith's daughter had taken a liking to Seth. Before he had ridden out in the middle of the night, Knight had figured out Seth and Marianne Yarrow were destined for the altar. Of all those in Hannigan's gang, Seth had not only survived but had come out a winner with a job and a fine woman.

"What's her name?" Knight looked at his cards, saw no way to play the hand, and folded.

"We never got that far, but that's going to change any second. Here she comes." Wilcox stood and held out the chair for the woman if she wanted to sit in at the game.

Knight had no objection to having a professional gambler join them. The miners around the table certainly wanted her presence. More than one of them lost concentration and let his cards show. After seeing those cards, Knight was sorry he'd folded.

"No thanks," she said. "I . . . . I don't know how to ask this, uh . . . ."

"Dave. Dave Wilcox."

"Justine Delmarre." She looked upset and kept glancing toward the bartender.

99

That put Knight on his guard. If her name was really Justine Delmarre he was Jefferson Davis. "What's wrong?"

"A friend of mine's been hurt something bad, and *what passes for a doctor* is working on him. He's drunker than a skunk again — still. I don't reckon I've ever seen him sober."

Wilcox asked, "How'd your friend get hurt?"

Justine smiled weakly. "He got himself stabbed in a fight over at the Friendly Cuss Saloon." She looked at Knight. "I thought maybe you could do something for him."

"Where is he?" Knight rose from the chair, damning himself for so easily being pulled back into performing as a surgeon. That had given him nothing but heartache since leaving the Yankee prison camp, and it gave those hunting him a chance to track him down. But he had taken an oath to preserve life.

"He's in the back room. Doc Murtagh is with him." Justine shivered all over. Under different circumstances it would have been a delight to view, but her expression showed only panic, and she folded into herself, arms hugging her body to hold off some unseen horror. "Can you help Red?"

"If he's already got a doctor . . . ." Then

Knight remembered what else Justine had said. Doc Murtagh was drunk. That wasn't any condition to be in with a man's life hanging in the balance.

Knight should have returned to the card game. He knew that, but instead he went with Justine and Wilcox to the back room. The door stood ajar. Just beyond he saw a man wobbling above a man stretched out on a table. The doctor held a bottle of whiskey in his hand as he bent over his patient and probed with fingers into a gaping wound. Knight thought Murtagh intended to use the whiskey as disinfectant. Instead, he reared back and took a long pull on the bottle, draining a full inch of the amber liquor.

Justine and Wilcox hurried past him to the prone man's side. It was easy to see how he had gained the moniker of Red. He had long unkempt red hair that flowed off the end of the table to hang down a foot or more. His face showed considerable sunburn, but the exposed chest where he had been stabbed was pasty white.

"What's it look like?" Knight sidled up to the table and peered over Justine's shoulder at the patient.

"Got it unner control. You the one to pay me fer my ser-services?" Murtagh belched loudly and took another drink from the bottle. At the rate he was going through it, a full quart wouldn't last him a half hour.

"Pour some of that into the wound to clean it out and disinfect." Knight grabbed for the bottle, but before he could take it, the shaky doctor sloshed some where it did the most good.

Red moaned and turned slightly.

"He's bleeding profusely. You have to stop the bleeding or he will die."

"St-stop it? I kin do that. Outta my way." Doc Murtagh poured more whiskey over the wound and dug around inside with his filthy fingers. He smiled crookedly. "Got the bugger. The bleeder. The artery what's spurting out the blood. I got it pinched off. Tie it. Need to tie it off or he'll for certain sure die."

"Do it quick. He's turning pale." The woman clutched Red's hand. Tears welled in her eyes but did not spill. "That's not good, is it, Doc?"

"It's not good," Knight answered automatically.

Justine's eyes widened and she mouthed *Please!* He understood what she wanted. She needed someone other than the drunkard to work on the man who was probably her boyfriend.

"Here's the thread. Got it all r-ready." Doc Murtagh tugged at his lapel and a thread came free. He released his grip on the severed artery and tried to make a slipknot in the thread. Such fine work was too difficult for a man with liquor-addled fingers.

"Here." Knight took the thread and expertly formed the knot. "Can you close off the bleeder?"

"Nuther shot and ready to save this son of a bitch." Murtagh dived back into the wound, poked about, wiped his blood-soaked fingers on his coat, and returned to the injury. He chewed on his tongue and then lifted one end of the thread. "That did it. All's good now."

"Is it?" Justine asked Knight, but Wilcox answered.

With one arm around her waist, he said, "The blood's not gushing out the way it was." He poked Murtagh in the chest with his free hand. "You sew up the wound. You can't leave it gaping like that."

Knight watched Murtagh stitch up the cut with surprisingly adroit needlework.

When he finished, his shaking hands again grabbed the bottle. "Time to celebrate. And somebody owes me fer my work. Ain't him gonna pay up. I went through his pockets and he's got nuthin'."

"He was robbed. Stabbed and robbed." Justine's voice sounded small and distant. She clung to Red's limp hand.

The man's breathing was shallow and ragged.

Knight put his hand on Wilcox's shoulder and said softly, "Let's get a drink and leave her with her beau."

"I . . . you don't know that. He might be somebody she works with." Wilcox's tone implied that he knew Knight had hit the nail on the head. The pretty faro dealer was staying with her boyfriend.

The pair left the back room and found a spot at the end of the bar. Knight used some of his winnings to buy them both shots of whiskey — the good stuff, not the trade whiskey peddled to most of the customers. He appreciated the smooth warmth all the way to his belly, but it did little to quiet his anger at the doctor.

Wilcox took a swig, "He's a quack, isn't he? You should have worked on Red."

"It's not my place."

"He was drunk and you're not."

"Murtagh's a doctor." Knight let the rest of the sentence hang, implying that he wasn't a doctor. He knew Wilcox was too upset to mentally follow that false path in his thinking. Any need to outright lie about his training was avoided when Murtagh stumbled from the room, bottle empty and clutched in his hand.

"Done good work tonight. I have. Time to cel-celebrate." Doc Murtagh staggered past them and out of the Last Nugget.

Knight ran his finger around the rim of the shot glass, licked away the solitary drop he captured, and heaved a sigh. "With him out of the way, let's check to see if Red's doing all right. Red and Justine."

Wilcox didn't have to be asked a second time. He swung around and went into the back room where Justine still clung to Red's hand. The instant Knight entered he went cold inside as he saw the stark look on Justine's face.

"How is he?" Wilcox asked the woman.

"All right," she said in a hollow voice. "Red's just fine now. He's not in pain anymore."

Knight balled his hands into tight fists and wanted to lash out at the drunken doctor. Justine knew as well as he did that Doc Murtagh had killed Red with his inept treatment.

CHAPTER 7

"Sierra Rojo is gonna make us rich, Sam. I feel it in my bones." Dave Wilcox kept looking back over his shoulder as they followed the increasingly steep trail toward the mountain mining camp due north of Ralston. "We're gonna need pack mules to carry all our money."

"Don't take it in greenbacks. Union money's not worth the paper it's printed on." Knight knew that Wilcox wanted to stay in Ralston City since that was where Justine Delmarre worked as a faro dealer. The woman's loss when her boyfriend died had left a void in her life that Wilcox obviously intended to fill.

The memory of how the quack, Doc Murtagh, had let the man die in the saloon's back room turned Knight cold inside. He had wanted to help, to do what he could to save the injured man's life. But keeping his background hidden gave him a better chance of avoiding any pursuit. Gerald Donnelly had shown he was willing to recruit the vilest, most lowdown men to come after him. He had even paid off Milo Hannigan and his entire gang to find Knight.

That hadn't worked out well for Donnelly since Seth Lunsford's friendship had been enough to make him face down even his own brother to defend Knight. But doctoring in Buffalo Springs had shown him that such a high profile worked against him. It made him too prominent and more easily tracked down.

Still, letting the man die because of the drunk doctor's ineptness rankled. Dave Wilcox suspected Knight knew more about medicine than he let on, and clearly Justine had sensed the same thing or she wouldn't have approached him for help to start with. But his new partner had the good sense not to press him on the issue.

Wilcox's own background was no secret and he willingly spun tales of even the most trivial details of his life. In spite of that, he didn't press Knight for equally revealing details of his journey to reach the gold and silver mines of New Mexico Territory.

"A pocket filled with twenty-dollar gold coins will do me just fine," Wilcox said.

"Why, I might make enough to settle down. I hear that the grasslands over in Arizona are mighty fine for grazing. A small herd would keep a family going for years."

"Settle down? Family? Aren't you getting ahead of yourself?" Knight had to laugh. "She might not want to give up dealing faro."

"I don't know what you're talking about." Wilcox settled down and stared at the road winding around the mountainside ahead. Then he laughed, too. "Her name's not really Justine. That's only what she calls herself to snag a few more tips from the drunk miners. If the men think she's from France, that makes her more exotic."

"Where is she from?"

Wilcox shrugged. He turned to Knight and said, "I suspect she's from Kansas City, but I wouldn't swear on a Bible that's so. I don't even know her real name, but I will. One day, I will."

"It's good to know where you're headed in life." As those words left his lips, Knight turned morose again. He hadn't saved the man in the Last Nugget because he intended to forsake his entire life as a doctor. Worse, Red's killer would never be brought to justice because neither Ralston nor Sierra Rojo had a marshal. He had no idea where the nearest sheriff hung his hat or if there was a federal marshal in the region. From all he could tell, if the cavalry at Fort Bayard didn't enforce the law, it was ignored.

He forced himself to think of other things, such as what he sought in going to Sierra Rojo. Wilcox had a goal. It lit him up like a bonfire in the night. Knight wondered if Wilcox realized the man he rode with had nothing to look forward to. For all he knew, Knight was nothing more than a saloon gambler looking to find the next drunken miner who had no idea about odds in a poker game. Knight tried to decide if that was enough for him since there wasn't a Justine in his life — and never would be.

Finally he saw the crudely painted sign announcing they were entering Sierra Rojo. The mining camp had become a boomtown almost overnight because of silver strikes in the surrounding hills. Knight had asked around Ralston and quickly came to the conclusion that the Sierra Rojo strike was the real thing. Enough silver, along with a trickle of gold, had made its way down the mountainous road to be shipped from Ralston to the big banks in California that he knew a fortune awaited an ambitious man.

His own intention to give the miners a decent poker game hardly matched Wilcox's vaulting desire to get rich. Swinging a pick or using a shovel for a mine owner was hardly the way to achieve that, but Wilcox had hinted that his plans would make him rich without the need to spend long, lonely hours prospecting on his own. Too many of those men died in the hills, victims of claim jumpers or outlaws or disease or accident. Not only was it a lonely pursuit, it was a dangerous one that Knight couldn't see his partner doing.

"Did you ever see a lovelier sight?" Wilcox took a deep breath and coughed. "Even the air's full of silver dust. Might be gold dust."

"I certainly smell sulfur from the smelting going on."

"Ore feeds the smelters and silver comes out. And gold. We're gonna be rich, Sam. Wait and see. This is the place where it all starts."

Ralston had a population of almost five hundred because it was on the stage route. Ben Holladay's stagecoach line freighted as many passengers into that town as could be packed into every coach. Knight tried to estimate Sierra Rojo's population and decided it might equal Ralston. Wagons laden with supplies rattled along the broad main street. Carpenters hammered furiously, putting up new stores. Sierra Rojo even boasted a bank to store all the precious metal being pulled from the rock. From there it moved on to Ralston and then by stagecoach to the money centers on the Pacific Coast.

"I count three saloons, Sam. Which one are you staking out? Or will you drift from one to the next?"

"I'll figure that out after a night or two of drinking in each," he said.

"Hell of a profession, gambling. You have to rustle up your own job. Look at the signs. I've counted ten advertising for miners. I can take my pick." Wilcox laughed. "Did you get the joke? I can take my pick? I can take it into the mines and pick out lumps of silver the size of my fist!"

Knight knew better than to point out any such mammoth nugget belonged to the mine owner and not the miner. He didn't want to throw cold water on Wilcox's enthusiasm.

"Let's get down to settling in," Knight said. "I'll buy you a drink, then you can scout around for the best place to make your fortune."

He heard Wilcox mutter under his breath, "What'll it take for Justine to notice me?" Louder, he said, "That one's closest, so let's start there. Damn me if the Red Mountain doesn't look good, even if its owner didn't show much imagination."

"How's that?" Knight swung his leg over and dropped to the ground. For a moment, his legs wobbled after so many hours in the saddle, but it didn't take long to get his balance back.

"Sierra Rojo. Red Mountain. You need to learn a *poco Español* to live in this part of the country."

"A little Spanish? I reckon it'll come with the territory."

Knight and Wilcox entered the Red Mountain Superior Drinking Emporium and looked around. The place had quite a few customers. They went to the bar. Knight bought Wilcox the drink he had promised, then they shook hands, and the young cowboy left to find himself a job.

Knight had gotten used to having Wilcox at his side out on the trail and would miss him. Turning around, he rested his elbows on the bar so he could study the action at the nearby tables. A faro setup stood empty. That would become the center of attention if a young lady as comely as Justine Delmarre dealt. At the moment, only three tables filled with gamblers intent on various forms of poker showed any action.

After watching how the betting went at

112

one table, Knight rummaged about in his vest pocket and got out his poke. It was time to launch his career as a professional gambler.

Knight tried to remember when he had settled into the straight-backed, shaky chair to begin the epic poker game. Two days ago? It might have been that long. His belly rumbled from lack of food. He pretended to sip at the whiskey occasionally set beside his hand on the table. He knew better than to lose the edge he had over the other three players. Two were professional gamblers, but the third was the reason he and the other gamblers stayed in the game. He owned a gold mine and had more money than Croesus. He was rich and ready to be plucked, only he was no pushover. He knew odds and he played well.

Even with everything going for the mine owner, Knight had steadily eaten away at the man's poke. The other gamblers saw their piles of chips evaporating while Knight's and the mine owner's slowly grew. Knight kept eyeing the other man's stack. Better than a thousand dollars rested in front of him.

"Raise two hundred," Knight said, pushing a pile of chips into the center of the table.

"Now that's a mighty bold bet when you don't have anything. You're bluffing." The mine owner stared hard at Knight. "I'm looking at three of a kind. No, wait. Three of a kind and another pair."

"You have a full house?" Knight allowed himself a small smile. Whatever the man held in his pudgy fingers, it wasn't a full house. But how good was it? All Knight had was a pair of deuces. Every bet he'd made during this hand was a flat-out bluff. "What'd you say if I told you I have two pair — and both are the same card."

"What card?"

"Sevens. I've got four of a kind. Four sevens." Knight wanted to reach for the shot of whiskey at his right. He kept his hands pressed into the table to prevent them from shaking. He was bluffing for close to two thousand dollars in the pot. He would bust out one of the other gamblers and seriously cut into his stash. But the real money came from the mine owner.

"You don't have a hand stronger 'n a pair. I know it." The miner matched Knight's bet and bumped the pot five hundred.

Knight knew better than to react instantly. He ought to fold and lose the money he had in the pot. Otherwise, he stood to lose everything. Instead of tossing in his cards, he carefully counted out five hundred and pushed that much more into the pot.

"You're mighty confident for a man with a losing hand." The miner looked at his cards, then squared them up, and tossed them into the middle of the table. "I think you've got a losing hand, but I'm not paying to find out if I'm right."

Knight thought his heart would explode. He realized he had stopped breathing. He forced himself to breathe slowly and evenly as he put his cards facedown on the table and raked in the pot. Keeping track of it hadn't been possible, but he estimated at least five thousand dollars was piled up in front of him.

"I'm wiped out," said one gambler. He pushed back and left.

The other looked at his diminished pile of greenbacks and chips, raked them in, and left without another word.

Knight looked across the table at the mine owner. "Another hand?"

"I've got to get back to digging precious metal out of hard rock before I take you on again." The man stood, patted his ample belly then paused. He looked down at

Knight. "Tell me. You were bluffing, weren't you?"

"You've got good instincts. What do you think?"

"Son of a bitch." The mine owner shook his head and laughed. "Son of a bitch." With that he left the saloon.

Knight reached for the man's discarded pasteboards. He wanted to see what the mine owner had folded. Before he could flip them over, a heavy hand came down on his shoulder. He reached for his revolver before he saw Dave Wilcox looking distraught.

"Sam, I thought I'd never find you."

"I've been working. Profitable work, too, but the hours are long."

"I got a job out at the Lucky Draw mine."

"Congratulations. Does it —" Knight cut off his question when Wilcox swung around and sank into a chair. "What's wrong?"

"There's been a mine collapse. It's pretty bad, Sam. I tell you, we've found three dead men already and there are that many more in a bad way. They need a doctor. A real doctor."

Knight sat frozen, not sure what to say or do. He had trained as a doctor all his life, but he had turned his back on it. He couldn't save everyone in the world. While he had been in the Yankee prison camp, he had failed so many, although he had saved some who would have died without his medical skill.

"Why come to me? Is there a doctor I can fetch?"

"Sam, *he's* out there."

"Who?"

"The butcher from Ralston. Murtagh. And he's as drunk as ever. He has to sit down because he can't even stand without wobbling. We need you there, Sam. Please."

"Why me?"

Wilcox stared at him, his eyes boring into Knight's very soul. "You never fessed up to it, but you know more than Doc Murtagh ever did. I don't care if you were a doctor. In my book, you still are, no matter your reason for denying it. You're a hell of gambler." His eyes flashed to the pile of money on the table. "Unless I'm mistaken you're as good a doctor. Maybe better. Why you stopped practicing, I don't know, but even if I'm wrong about you knowing how to be a sawbones and you can't actually figure which side of a scalpel to use, your hands are steady and you're a mile better than that drunk Murtagh on his best day."

Knight scooped up his winnings and pushed back his chair. He turned away from the table, then stopped and reached back to flip over the mine owner's hand. Two pair. Knight had bluffed himself into a small fortune, his deuces against jacks and tens. He damned himself for being a fool as he asked, "What needs to be done? Supplies? What do we need to take from here in town?"

Samuel Knight realized he had never seen a real working mine before. The stark reality compared to what he expected shook him. The Lucky Draw bustled with miners lugging timbers to shore up the mouth of the mine while others lit miner's candles for their helmets and disappeared into the black maw. Dust still floated out, billowing from deep in the ground.

"When did the mine collapse?"

"Two days ago. It's a bad one, Sam. I had just hired on and never got a chance to even work a shift. Never in all my born days did I think I was lucky, but that proves Lady Luck is my best friend."

"Where are the wounded being tended?" Knight looked around and couldn't find a tent set aside as a hospital, then remembered this wasn't a military unit. When he had been a surgeon with the CSA, the headquarters company always made certain the hospitalers had a secure spot before

118

moving troops into battle. Expecting the same concern for civilians, for miners, was out of the question.

"It's kind of haphazard, dealing with the ones we've pulled from the mine. Everyone's thinking more about the trapped miners than the ones who got out already." Wilcox looked anxiously to the mine when two men hurried out with a stretcher bearing another injured miner. "Help me with the supplies." Knight dismounted and grunted as he pulled two large bags of medical supplies from behind his saddle. A considerable portion of his gambling earnings had bought the contents. If it saved even one life, it was money well spent.

"There's where the owner set up the tent for the wounded." Wilcox pointed toward a ravine formed by two large piles of black tailings. He helped with the bags and hurried toward the ravine. Nestled between the manmade hills a tarp had been strung from one side to the other. Beneath its flapping canvas five pallets had been laid on the ground.

The men on the pallets were in bad shape. Just a glance at them told Knight that much. He stopped and glared. Across the covered area sat Doc Murtagh, taking a long pull from a bottle. Knight doubted it was tea the doctor downed with such gusto. The drunker Murtagh got the less he cared for the five wounded men. Ironically, that increased their chance of survival.

"Can you do anything for them?" Wilcox anxiously pressed the bag of medical supplies into Knight's hand. "I don't know these men. I never got a chance, but I want to be able to. Going to their funeral isn't what I signed up for."

Knight ignored Murtagh and made a quick circuit of the five injured miners. More than once, he had worked in field hospitals not far from the front lines of battle and had learned how to make a snap decision. Some men would die no matter what he did. Others required only a pat on the shoulder and would recover on their own. Those who needed direct medical attention and would die without it held his attention. He dropped to his knees beside a man with half his skull exposed. The white bone shone in the light of a lantern hung from a post.

"Bring that light closer." Knight took off his long black coat and tossed it aside. He rolled up his shirt sleeves and splashed carbolic acid on his hands before lightly touching the protruding bone.

It didn't look promising. The man didn't

bother flinching, moaning, or showing any hint of life. Knight pressed his fingers into the man's neck and felt the thready, distant pulse. He bent closer and examined the wound. A rock had crushed part of the man's head. Tiny pieces of ore glittered in the light of the lamp that Wilcox held.

"I've found the mother lode," Knight said. "Time to do some digging." He grabbed the pliers he had bought at the hardware store, dipped the tips into the carbolic acid, and then gently probed for the bits of rock in the man's brain.

"Whatcha doin'? That man's not gonna make it. I salute you, dead man." Doc Murtagh hoisted the bottle and downed a healthy gulp. "Lemme a-anoint you 'fore the burial." He poured some of the whiskey over Knight and across the miner's exposed brain.

That brought a reaction. The miner snapped to attention, then began shaking all over.

Knight straightened and backhanded Murtagh, knocking the drunk away. "If I find you in this tent when I finish here, I'll rip your gonads out through your left ear."

"G-gonads?" Murtagh clutched his crotch. "Who're you to mess with these men? I'm the doctor."

The light vanished for a moment, then returned.

"Sorry," apologized Wilcox. "I had to take the garbage out."

"I hope you shoved him downhill. That'll keep him occupied until he sobers up." Knight dived back to his patient, pressing his hand into the miner's chest to quiet him. The shivers subsided, letting Knight carefully grip one piece of ore after another and pull them from the skull cavity.

"How's he doing, Sam?"

"I have two pieces of skull bone to pluck out before I'll know." Knight wiped sweat from his forehead in spite of the chilly wind blowing through the tent. The first piece of bone was only a sliver. He popped it free easily. The larger piece required him to use not only the pliers but a knife blade to get under the bone. It came free with a lewd sucking sound, but Knight didn't remove it.

"Damn me, aren't you taking that out, Sam?"

"It's about where it ought to be, even if it's not connected to the rest of his head bone. If I took it out, I'd have to put in a metal plate. Better to leave it this way."

"Where would you get a metal plate?"

Knight laughed without humor. "This is a mine, isn't it? Pounding a silver ingot into the right shape would do him just fine. The man with the thousand-dollar head." He dropped the pliers and knife to begin bandaging the wound. It took a few turns before the blood seeping out was stanched.

Knight wiped his hands off on a rag Wilcox handed him.

"Which one's next, Sam?"

Knight looked at the man who had received the benefit of his surgical skill. His breathing came more easily now that the debris had been removed from his brain. He might never be the same after he recovered as he was before the accident, but he would recover. Knight saw the signs of a man tough enough to live.

The former Confederate doctor pointed to one of the stretchers. "That one. The one with the compound fractured leg."

Dr. Samuel Knight worked through the night, no matter that it had been two days since he'd had even a wink of sleep. It felt good, helping people again. But he worried that his work would set dangerous men on his trail as it had before.

CHAPTER 8

"One thing's for sure," said Henry Hesseltine, looking around as he and his partner rode into Buffalo Springs. "We can save a lot of ammunition. This town's been shot up already."

He drew rein in front of what had been a saloon. Careful study told him there hadn't been a living soul in the burned-out husk for months. What few sections of wall still standing threatened to tumble from being turned into Swiss cheese by more bullets than he cared to count.

"Might have been bees. Lots of bees. Or termites." Rance Spurgeon smiled crookedly, causing the scars on his face to stretch into obscene spider webs.

Hesseltine had spent two years trying to figure out his partner's sense of humor. Why it was the least bit funny that bees and not bullets might have chopped up the wood escaped him. No matter what caused the

124

man's wooden expression to break into a hideous grin, Hesseltine had never ridden with a man who was quicker with his revolver, better in a fistfight, or more loyal to his job and whoever rode with him.

"The bees have gone back to their hive, wherever else that might be." Hesseltine saw that many other buildings had been damaged by gunfire, but repairs had patched them. More than one wall remained unpainted and displaying the results of battle, but most had covered the damage with paint or putty.

"You notice anything strange about this town, Henry?" Spurgeon asked.

"More women than men on the streets," Hesseltine said after a moment's reflection. "Did the men die fighting off whoever hurrahed the town?"

"That's something to ask about. If there aren't many men, Knight will stand out like a sore thumb."

"He *is* a sore thumb," said Hesseltine, smiling, "and we're the hammer to hit it again and again." He unconsciously touched the butt of the pistol slung under his right armpit.

Gerald Donnelly had hired the Pinkertons to bring back Dr. Samuel Knight dead or alive. Keeping such a desperado alive only

125

added to the complications of returning to Pine Knob. Hesseltine, of all people, liked things simple. If his bosses in Chicago didn't care if Knight was dead or alive, and Donnelly paid either way, a corpse would be shipped back. That simplified things, and he wanted that right now.

Interrogating the cavalry's commanding officer had been frustrating — Captain Norwood had been tight-mouthed. From all the Pinkertons had learned by asking around Pine Knob, it was with good reason.

When they returned to Pine Knob with Knight's body slung over his horse, the cavalry officer wouldn't be there. Hesseltine had seen how Reconstruction judges and administrators ran their towns, who they favored, and how they operated. Donnelly didn't have to tell him of the letters sent to Washington and the political favors being swapped to remove Norwood. Hesseltine felt the cold currents swirling around Pine Knob and read them accurately. It bothered him because of the familiar patterns. Once, just once, he wanted an assignment to run differently.

He and Spurgeon had found enough evidence to be sure that Knight had come to Buffalo Springs. What had happened after that and why the town got shot up was a mystery, but not one worth investigating unless it affected their quarry. If it took them longer than a day or two to run Knight to ground, it would surprise him.

"Is there a place serving a good steak?" Hesseltine stopped in front of the solitary hotel. Windows had been replaced. From the caulking and lack of paint on the trim, the glass had been put in not too long ago. In spite of himself, he felt a growing curiosity to find out what had happened to the town.

"Not here," said Spurgeon, sniffing the air. "They burn their meat."

Both liked their steaks so rare that they mooed when stuck with forks. Hesseltine considered himself more of a gourmet than his partner, and lack of decent food in the town and along the trail made it all the more imperative to bring down Knight so they could return to Kansas City or even the home office in Chicago. Decent restaurants serving prime steaks abounded in both cities.

"The hotel looks to be the only place to get a drink. Did you see another watering hole?"

"Only the saloon that was burned out." Spurgeon swung his leg over and dropped to the ground. He took all three of the steps up to the front door in a single stride and looked inside. He waved to Hesseltine. "They got a bar set up in the parlor. There might be a restaurant at the back."

"It's nice of them to put everything in one place for our convenience." Hesseltine dismounted with a bit more clumsiness than his partner. His bandy legs had turned stiff during the ride. He stretched and massaged his thighs before climbing the three steps to the front porch more carefully than his partner. He peered past Spurgeon into the hotel lobby.

It was everything Spurgeon had said. The bar had two customers and a tired-looking barkeep. On closer examination, he realized the bartender doubled as hotel clerk. Or was it the other way around? The clerk held down a second job as barkeep? He decided that was the way of the world, pushed past Spurgeon, and went directly to the bar, a plank laid over two sawhorses.

"Welcome to the Springs, stranger. You want a beer or a room? I can get you either. Both." The youngster behind the bar hadn't been shaving long.

"Maybe both," Spurgeon said, stepping up alongside Hesseltine. "We're looking for a gent."

The barkeep stepped back a pace and gave

them the once over. "You lawmen? Texas State Police?"

"Texas State Police? What's that? A local vigilante committee?" Hesseltine dealt with amateurs all the time who thought they could solve crimes and bring criminals to justice. Such groups always proved to be an obstacle to his work.

"Nobody we're happy with. They didn't do a thing to stop the Milo Hannigan gang when they robbed the bank."

"That's what happened to the buildings? All the bullet holes?" Spurgeon shifted his weight from foot to foot, showing he was getting antsy. They had just started and already he wanted it over.

When that point was reached, he was as likely to shoot someone or use his meaty fists. A few times that sped up their mission, but Hesseltine had found such a hair-trigger temper caused more trouble than it solved.

"They came ridin' in, shootin' and cussin'. They set fire to the saloon to keep us busy while they tried to hold up the bank."

"Do tell. So much lead flying must have caused a few injuries. How'd the town's doctor do, patching up everyone?" Hesseltine watched the reaction and wondered at the way the man's beardless face turned

129

flaccid, as if he thought it was a poker face nobody could read. Why was that important, hiding the presence of a doctor in town, he wondered.

"Why're you askin'?"

"My friend here's got a foot that might show a touch of infection. A doctor can cut off the toe and get him back as right as rain." Again Hesseltine wondered at what the barkeep hid.

"No doctor here."

"Where are the men in town? I've seen a few, but not as many as I'd expect. Not that I'm complaining," Spurgeon said. "That means more women to choose from."

"You got that right. Lots of eligible women in Buffalo Springs," the barkeep said, warming.

Hesseltine made a mental note to thank Spurgeon for the abrupt change in topic. The barkeep had started to freeze up, but this loosened his tongue.

"Were so many of the menfolk killed during the robbery?" Spurgeon made it sound as if he cared.

"Naw, most had left town before that. Hell, I'd have been gone myself, but I got a sick ma to look after. Ain't sayin' this, mind you, but when she ups and dies, I'm headin' west, too." He leaned over the plank bar and whispered loud enough for everyone to hear anyway. "Gold. Big strikes in New Mexico Territory. I heard tell one mine in Sierra Rojo takes out nuggets as big as your fist." He stared at Spurgeon's hands. "Even yours. Rumor has it some of those hunks of gold are as big as this." He held out his hands to show something the size of a steer skull.

"A lot of men getting rich, I suspect," Hesseltine said. "That might be worth thinking about, Rance. We need to become millionaires before we get too old to enjoy the money." He motioned for the barkeep to draw them beers. As the mugs were set in front of them, Hesseltine put down a ten-dollar gold piece to pay.

"Mister, I ain't got enough change for a dime out of that." The barkeep fixed his eyes on the small gold coin. He licked his lips but to his credit he never grabbed for it.

Hesseltine pushed it in the young man's direction. "I don't want change, if you can tell us where to find Dr. Samuel Knight."

Calculation flashed behind the barkeep's eyes. He pressed his finger down on the coin and moved it around, pulled away from it as if he weren't going to bite, then with a move that put a striking rattler to shame, snatched the coin and made it disappear.

131

"Folks around Buffalo Springs don't like to talk about him after what he did."

Hesseltine put his hand out to caution his impulsive friend. Spurgeon subsided and let the bartender proceed at his own pace.

"He saved plenty of folks around here, he did. He even saved Amos Palmer's life, after poor ol' Amos got himself run over by a wagon. Took off both legs, whack whack." The man illustrated with quick swipes across his thighs. "Then came the raid on the bank. Nobody knows what happened there, well, hardly anybody. Some say he gunned down all the outlaws stickin' up the bank."

"And?" Hesseltine urged more when the man slowed and threatened to balk.

"And him and Amelia Parker, they was gonna get hitched. Everyone said so. Amelia surely thought that was so. But then Knight upped and left without so much as a good-bye."

"Left? What do you mean?" Spurgeon leaned forward, his huge hands turning into balls of gristle. Anyone on the receiving end of a punch by those fists wasn't long for this world.

"He rode out. Nobody knows where he went. Amelia sure didn't. She cried her eyes out for pert near a week."

"That's not very thoughtful," said Hesseltine. "It would give me some pleasure to console Amelia. Where can I find her?"

"She works at the bank. Ain't that a coincidence? Knight keeps the bank from getting robbed or Amelia all shot up, then he turns his back on her."

"You think she knows where he went?"

"No, sir, I don't. She would have rode after him if she did. She loved him that much." He sighed. "I wish I had a chance with her. She's real purty."

"With such a drought of men in town, you just might. Don't sell yourself short." Hesseltine walked away, Spurgeon trailing him from the hotel.

Outside, Spurgeon said, "You think he knew what he was talking about?"

"He has his ear to the ground. Gossip in a town this size travels faster than a bullet. What we need to figure out is if she knows where Knight went and is waiting for him to return or if she has no idea so couldn't follow. In any case, I believe she still loves him."

"If she does, that'd be hard getting her to spill the beans."

"And if she has come to hate him for abandoning her in such a cavalier fashion, we might have a different kind of trouble."

"What's that?" Spurgeon looked curiously at his partner.

"We might never get her to shut up so we can kill him."

They walked in silence down the street. Hesseltine pointed to the bank, checked his pocket watch, and walked faster. It was almost closing time. They slipped in as the head teller closed the doors.

"We'll be out of here in a moment," Hesseltine assured him. "Where can we find Miss Amelia?"

"Amelia Parker? She's at her desk." The teller pointed.

Hesseltine clapped the man on the shoulder, thanked him, and went to the desk where the woman pored over a ledger. She looked up. Hesseltine gave her an ingratiating smile. It wasn't hard. He seldom saw a woman as comely. Her midnight black hair was pulled back from her oval face, where bright blue eyes peered up at him. High cheekbones gave her a patrician look that appealed to him. But she was only a means to an end, not a woman to woo.

Above all else, Hesseltine finished his assignments, no matter what distractions he encountered. "Miss Parker, allow me to introduce myself and my colleague. We are Pinkerton detectives."

"Detectives? Is this about bank business? I'm just the bookkeeper. You'll need to speak with the president."

"It's not about the robbery." He paused. "Well, perhaps it is. We have been on the trail of the gang responsible for the attempted robbery."

"They're all dead."

"All? Our information is that Samuel Knight escaped."

"Sam?"

"He was a member of the gang. In addition, he has charges filed against him in Pine Knob by the marshal and the commander of the cavalry unit stationed there. He is a fugitive from justice."

Hesseltine saw the emotions playing on the woman's face. When the ripples died down, he knew he was out of luck getting any information from her. She still loved Knight and would never give so much as a hint where he had fled.

"He left me without saying a word. I have no idea where he is. I wish you luck finding him."

"Thank you, Miss Parker." Hesseltine considered for a moment. "There is a reward for his arrest."

"Is that the Pinkerton Agency's interest? The reward?"

"Mr. Spurgeon and I are paid a salary and don't collect any rewards off those we find." Hesseltine lied through his teeth, but he wanted her to think he was driven by duty, not greed. If he read her right, that would work better to unlock what she knew but kept behind closed lips.

"I wish you luck finding him. Now, if you will, please let me get back to work. I have another hour's labor ahead of me and cannot leave until it is finished." She pointedly dived back into her work, the quill pen scratching furiously to transfer numbers from tiny slips into the ledger book.

Hesseltine and Spurgeon left, the teller letting them out into the increasingly chilly autumn afternoon sun.

"We can watch her," Spurgeon said. "That'd be mighty easy on the eyes."

"You certainly have an eye for the ladies, but I feel there is a quicker way to find Knight. You remember what else the hotel barkeep said?"

"Her pa was fixed up by Knight. Amos Parker."

"A few inquiries ought to find where he hangs his hat. Questioning him will more than likely give the answer we need. He cannot have any good feelings for Knight if the good doctor wronged his daughter."

"Not even if Knight saved his life?"

"No, Rance, not even that. Amos will see his life as over and his daughter's only beginning — and Knight ruined her happiness. That is enough to cause Amos to hate our fugitive enough to tell us anything we want to know."

"I hope you're right. I don't understand a lot of what you say when you get all highfalutin like that."

Hesseltine smiled. Spurgeon's talents lay elsewhere.

An hour later, they rode up to the Parker ranch. Hesseltine exchanged a quick look with his partner. A legless man sat on the front porch, a blanket tucked around him as he basked in the last rays of the setting sun. They walked their horses slowly, then halted when the man reached under the blanket. Hesseltine couldn't make out the shape, but if he had been a gambling man, he would have laid heavy odds that not only was this Amos Parker but also that he clutched a revolver under that blanket.

"Mr. Parker? Amos Parker? Can we have a word with you?"

"Who are you?"

"We heard about the trouble in Buffalo Springs a few weeks ago. We're not outlaws.

137

Quite the contrary." Hesseltine fished around in his pocket and held out a shiny gold badge. He moved it a bit so it caught the rays of the sun and reflected them toward the old man on the porch.

"Can't see what you got. Ride closer."

"We're Pinkerton detectives on the trail of a dangerous criminal."

"Who might that be? All of them what shot up the town and tried to rob the bank are dead."

"The Hannigan gang, yes, we've heard that. We also spoke to some of the citizens and learned how your marshal was brutally murdered. The one member of the Hannigan gang who escaped is likely responsible for his murder."

"One got away? That's the first I heard."

Hesseltine and Spurgeon rode closer but did not dismount. From that angle Hesseltine saw the gun more clearly. He let his horse move to the side so Parker would have to shoot across his body. If the old man moved to take a shot, he'd find himself out drawn . . . since Spurgeon had a hair-trigger response.

Hesseltine leaned forward so his left hand rested close to the pistol slung under his right armpit. "His name is Samuel Knight. He might be the worst of the lot."

138

"Do tell."

Hesseltine nodded solemnly. "A cold-blooded killer back in Pine Knob. Not only the marshal wants him, but the army does, too. The list of his crimes is a mile long."

"I don't know what became of that snake in the grass."

"So you do know him?" Spurgeon started forward, but his partner motioned for him to hold back. For the moment.

"Him and my daughter was fixin' to marry. He upped and lit out one night and never even said good-bye."

"He's a desperado, that one. He must have gotten wind of my partner and me coming for him. So you don't know where he might have headed?"

"I'd track him down myself for the grief he gave my Amelia and his friend."

Hesseltine kept from crying out in joy. "That's a terrible thing, breaking a young woman's heart like that. He must have left his friend wondering what became of him, too. That'd be Lucas, wouldn't it?"

"Don't know no Lucas. Leastways, not one who was friendly with Knight. Seth's his name. Seth Lunsford. They rode into town together."

"Did Seth ride out with him?"

Hesseltine grinned like a wolf at the answer.

CHAPTER 9

"Why are we hoofin' it around? We're horse soldiers. Old Spit and Polish must have saddle sores again to make us walk every damn place." The army private hefted his carbine to his shoulder and spun around, intending to find a place to sit down in the afternoon sun. He went pale when he saw his commanding officer glaring at him.

"You find something wrong with my command, Private?" Captain Norwood thundered his question, drawing the attention of the entire squad.

The sergeant hurried over and saluted. "Is there something wrong, sir?"

"You have a malcontent in your ranks, Sergeant. He does not understand the purpose of this exercise. Explain it to him."

"Why, uh, I don't rightly know what it is myself, sir. We ought to be ridin' horses, not trompin' around in the forest. They call us horse soldiers, not infantry."

141

"The Comanche are excellent horsemen. They count their wealth by the horses they own, the number of horses they steal. What happens when your entire squad has its mounts stolen and you must recover them on foot? What happens when you must sneak up on the savages in the dark? Astride a horse, you make too much noise. You blunder through a forested area and alert the enemy. If you haven't trained for such a contingency as this, you will die in battle. Worse, you will be taken prisoner and tortured to death by the Comanches."

"Got to say this torture's 'bout as bad," the private grumbled. He paled when he saw how he had drawn his commander's ire again.

"You will walk punishment duty for one month, Private. If you say one more word, I will court-martial you. Would you like to be put in front of a firing squad for your insolence?"

The enlisted man swallowed hard. "No, sir. I wouldn't want that."

"Please, Captain Norwood," cut in the sergeant. "Private Melloy don't mean nothing. We're all tuckered out from walkin' all day and —"

"And I'll see that you hike all night, too!"

"Yes, sir," the sergeant said, a touch of

anger in his tone. He backed down when the officer stepped forward and shoved his face within an inch of his.

"Form your squad. Get them marching — in step, in tight formation. You may rest for five minutes out of every hour. Don't let me catch you disobeying my orders or you will find those stripes are in danger. Do I make myself clear, Sergeant?"

"Yes, sir."

Norwood stepped back, waited for the sergeant to get the men into a tight formation, two men wide, eight men long. They began counting cadence. Over them Norwood called out that they could report back to the encampment for morning reveille and not an instant before.

The soldiers vanished down the road, leaving him to stew. He took out his frustration on them, but how dare they question his training methods? With a few quick movements, he brushed off leaves and seeds clinging to his uniform. His boots were coated with dust but nothing his aide couldn't clean off in a few minutes, if he used some elbow grease. They hardly needed more polishing, but he would insist. Discipline. That's what these frontier soldiers lacked, and that was precisely what he would teach them or know the reason why.

He stalked back to the camp and made a quick inspection. He handed out punishment duty freely, then abruptly went to his own tent when he realized his anger ought to be directed at Gerald Donnelly and not his own troops. Dropping to his cot, he put aside his hat, canvas gloves, and heavy cavalry saber. Stretching out for a quick nap would perk him up, but he refrained. Field reports needed to be filed. Out in the field as he was, he had scant time to tend to such duties. A clerk would have been useful, but none of the men in his command could read or write worth beans.

Moving to the small desk, he started the quarterly report, then found his attention drifting. He had pursued the elusive Indians for weeks and had never engaged them once. Always he found traces but never did they confront his superior forces. They were wily and moved fast. In a way he admired such tactics. When your enemy outnumbers you or outguns you, make yourself scarce.

He ignored the report and pulled out a map of east and central Texas, trying to guess where the Comanches holed up. If he found their main camp, he could engage them. Most of the Indians carried only bows and arrows. His superior firepower would carry the day in any outright skirmish.

Carbines, the Walker Colts, his men's horses. Those were the strong points the cavalry brought to the battle.

But the Indians were better trained. He had to be sure his men learned to obey immediately and not question his orders. If they hesitated or second-guessed him when facing a Comanche force, they were goners — dead men — unless they made use of their best advantage: discipline.

Norwood ran a finger along the course of the Sabine River, figuring where the Indians would ford its broad expanse, where their camps might be, where he might attack with greatest result. He turned the map around, putting Pine Knob at the top, and then measured distances to estimate striking ranges for his troopers. He looked up when the flap on his tent pulled back and a gust of cool air blew through. One elbow held the map in place as he glared at the youngster who interrupted him.

"You Captain Norwood?"

"What do you want?"

"Got a telegram from town for you." The boy, hardly eight, thrust out the yellow envelope. He made no move to leave, expecting a tip.

Norwood took the telegram and opened it. His mouth opened and closed like a beached fish. He looked up, shock turning into fury.

The boy backed away when he saw the captain's reaction. He wasn't going to get a tip. He was going to be lucky to escape without a thrashing.

The officer read the telegram through a second time. A third. Then he stuffed the flimsy yellow sheet into the front of his uniform jacket. Slowly getting to his feet, he belted on his saber, made sure his service pistol rested on his right hip, put on his gloves, and settled his hat. He stepped out of his tent and went directly to his horse, not bothering to return the salutes from his soldiers.

He rode slowly into Pine Knob. Rather than a jumble of thoughts, nothing in his head resonated. His mind was empty as he turned toward the town hall. When he got to the two-story building, he sat astride his horse and stared. Only then did emotions begin welling up and overwhelm him. With a quick move, he dropped to the ground, strode into the building, and marched up to Donnelly's office.

"Captain, do you have an appointment?" Leonard tried to interpose his thin body in front of the juggernaut that the officer had become. The rail-thin clerk was bowled over when Norwood never slowed.

Ignoring Leonard's bleats, Norwood stood in front of Gerald Donnelly's office door, lifted a leg, then kicked out as hard as he could. The door exploded inward to fall heavily to the floor.

Behind the desk, Donnelly jumped a foot. "Captain, what the hell?"

"You slimy toad. You're responsible."

"Oh?" The sudden, pleased smirk was evidence enough of Donnelly's guilt. "What are you talking about?"

"This!" Norwood slammed the telegram down on the desk so hard, everything on it jumped an inch. His fist smashed down again, sending a stack of papers skittering along to the floor.

Donnelly reacted, trying to grab the papers. When he failed, he settled back in the chair and folded his hands on the bulge of his stomach. The smirk grew.

The sight of it infuriated Norwood. "Who did you pay off to get me transferred?"

"Well, General Sheridan was interested in using your talents elsewhere. Where might that have been?"

"My orders are in transit for me to assume command of a post along the Canadian border."

"A promotion, perhaps?"

"*There are ten men at this post!* They keep the Crow Indians from sneaking into the U.S. from Canada."

"Ten whole soldiers." Donnelly tsk-tsked and immediately regretted it.

Norwood surged over the desk, skidding on his knees as he reached for the administrator's throat. His fingers clawed at Donnelly's skin and left bloody marks. Flailing about, Donnelly pushed back and tried to grab his cane with the rifle in it. A hard fist knocked it away, and Norwood tried to strangle his tormentor again.

Donnelly made gurgling sounds as hard fingers tightened on his windpipe. Then they vanished. Norwood thrashed around as he was pulled off the desk, kicking and screaming. A foot collided with a man's gut. The dull *whoosh!* as air blasted out gave Norwood the chance to roll onto his hands and knees, then come to his feet. With a wide flourish he drew his saber and held the two deputies still on their feet at bay. The marshal gasped and moaned, clutching his belly.

"You done attacked the marshal. We got to put you under arrest," the deputy nearest Norwood said.

"He also attacked me!" Donnelly cried. "I'm federal administrator of Pine Knob.

148

That's only a local offense kicking the marshal. It's a federal crime to try to strangle me!"

Norwood's rage built again. He raised the saber, ready to cut Donnelly in half. Strong hands grabbed his sword arm and spun him around. Somehow his feet tangled up in the still gasping marshal on the floor and Norwood fell heavily. Both deputies jumped on him and finally wrestled the sword from his grip.

By then, the marshal had pulled himself up and waved his revolver. "Outta the way, men. I'm gonna plug this son of a bitch right betwixt his squinty eyes!"

"Marshal, wait," Donnelly said. "He ought to stand trial."

"Nobody hits me like that and lives to brag on it." The marshal tried to fire, but his shot went wild when Norwood grabbed his arm and forced it up and away.

The free-for-all began all over again. It ended suddenly when another gunshot rang out. Donnelly twisted the knob on his cane and ejected a shell, then slid another in. With a solid click, he closed the breach and cocked the weapon. He pointed it straight at the captain. "Give me one good reason I shouldn't kill you, Norwood."

"You're a yellow-bellied coward with no

spine. You won't kill anyone."

"Mr. Donnelly, let the marshal handle this," piped up a deputy.

"Yeah, let him. He's still sucking wind." Norwood tried to punch the lawman and lost his balance. They piled onto him, their considerable weight pinning him on the floor.

He tried to fumble out his pistol, but the marshal plucked it from his grip.

"To the hoosegow. Right now. You're under arrest, Norwood."

"A moment, Marshal. Wait." Donnelly hopped up and used the desk for support as he came around to perch on one corner. He looked at Norwood the way a buzzard eyes a choice hunk of carrion. "He's not going to bother us anymore. He's been transferred. Up north. Far up north. When do you have to be at your new post, Captain? Ah, yes, here it is." He picked up the crumpled telegram and made a big show of reading it. "Immediately. Your transfer is effective right now. Today. This minute."

"That mean you don't want him arrested, Mr. Donnelly?"

Norwood almost pulled free from the two deputies, then sagged. Never had he experienced defeat quite like this. He had faced Comanche bows and arrows, he had led the

150

charge against Confederate positions, he had even fought outlaws after the war. He thought of himself as a brave man.

Now he had to think of himself as a defeated man. His change in attitude showed.

"That's it, Captain. At least you weren't demoted. Get out of my office. And get out of my town. Immediately."

The deputies and marshal half dragged him outside and sent him stumbling down the front steps. The officer straightened, smoothed wrinkles from his uniform the best he could, rubbed the toes of his boots behind opposite pants legs to renew the sheen, then marched stiffly to his horse and mounted. He had to show honor, even in defeat. He rode from town and went directly back to camp to pack and be on his way.

CHAPTER 10

"Don't you like it when you see a young man so dedicated to his work that he burns the midnight oil?" Henry Hesseltine leaned against a post supporting a wall that threatened to topple into the street. He tested it, considered how easily displaced it was and the damage it would do if he kicked the post away. He shrugged off any such attempt as being too much work for no good reason. "Dedicated, I say. He will go far."

"He's a gunsmith." Rance Spurgeon spat a gob of tobacco into the street. "Not even that. He's an apprentice."

"Why do you say that?"

"The old man without legs said the kid's name was Seth Lunsford. That's the Yarrow Gunsmithy. Names don't match, so he works for the owner. He's too young to be anything but an apprentice, so I make him out to be a fledgling. Now, he might be a journeyman, even so young, but he came to

152

town with Knight. That sounds like a man drifting through the country and not one settling down long enough to learn a trade."

"You are a marvel of deductive ability, my friend." Hesseltine reached under his arm and touched the butt of his pistol. "Do you think the young man has time to look at my pistol? It's been months since I had it professionally oiled."

"Let him look at it. Down the barrel." Spurgeon slipped his Walker Colt from the cross-draw holster and cocked the gun. He took careful aim through the lighted window where Seth Lunsford bent over his work on a table. His finger tightened on the trigger, causing Hesseltine to intervene.

"No gunplay. We need to know where Knight went. If anyone knows, it's this apprentice."

"Whatever you say." Spurgeon lowered the hammer and slid his gun back into the holster. "Nobody's around. Let's ask those questions."

"You are right. The sooner we find out what he knows, the sooner we can find supper. It's been so long since I've eaten, my stomach is rubbing up against my backbone."

"We had breakfast."

"That was almost eighteen hours ago."

153

As they discussed the matter of meals, they crossed the street and never broke stride opening the shop door and entering.

Seth Lunsford looked up in surprise. He coughed and laid aside the trigger mechanism he worked on. "You gents startled me. I thought I'd locked the door. The shop closed at sundown."

"That was almost six hours ago," Hesseltine said. "We should have known, but we're only passing through town and just arrived. Buffalo Springs, isn't it? The town's name?"

"It is." Seth looked at his work, then back. "If your needs aren't too big, I can fix your gun and let you be on your way in two shakes of a lamb's tail."

"Lamb's tail," muttered Spurgeon. "Now isn't that about the sweetest thing you ever did hear?"

"Don't mind my friend. We are a tad nervy after being on the trail so long."

"You've come far, then?"

"All the way from Pine Knob." Hesseltine drew his gun and pointed it directly at Seth's face before the youth had a chance to react. "Don't go reaching for one of those weapons. I see you've fixed an entire rack of them. Today? You've been busy."

"What do you want? You're not lawmen."

"In a manner of speaking, we are," Hesseltine said, puffing out his chest. "We are Pinkerton detectives."

"Where's Dr. Samuel Knight?" Spurgeon drew his own revolver and pointed it at Seth's head, too.

"He's got an itchy trigger finger," Hesseltine warned. "Me, I'm more sedate in how I ask questions. But my partner has spoken plainly, and I must honor his impatience. Where'd Knight go when he left town?"

"You've been sent to arrest him?" Seth Lunsford shifted in the chair, obviously in pain at the thought of betraying his friend.

"We have been enjoined to return him to Pine Knob."

"Donnelly." Seth spat the name. "He wants Sam dead. Well, it ain't gonna do you any good. I don't know where he went. He left town and never told any of us he was going, much less where he intended to go."

"Not even his betrothed? I find this hard to believe."

"It's the gospel truth. Miss Parker — Amelia — is still hurt and angry over the way he didn't tell her anything. If he wouldn't tell her, he sure as hell wasn't gonna to tell me."

"I think that is an unwarranted conclusion since you rode with him. With the Milo Hannigan gang. Are you a desperado, too? Have you robbed banks or stuck up stagecoaches? Perhaps he trusted you more, having been a comrade in arms." Hesseltine looked to his partner. "We might get an added reward if we return with the only other surviving member of the Hannigan gang."

"Donnelly wouldn't pay spit for anybody but Knight."

"But the law in Pine Knob can be a different case. That marshal struck me as a man who carried a grudge. The Hannigan gang made him look mighty stupid."

"What do we care about that?" Spurgeon said. "Knight's the only one we were hired to bring back."

"Mr. Spurgeon has a point. We really don't care about you. There's not even a reward on your head, not that we know about. It will be easy for us to ride off after Knight if you tell us where he went. Why, we would leave Buffalo Springs with a clear conscience, and you can continue tinkering with your firearms. That strikes me as a reasonable way to continue our relationship."

"Tell us what we want to know and we forget we ever met you," said Spurgeon.

"Again, my partner has a knack for distilling the matter to its essence. Where's Knight?" Hesseltine trained his pistol on Seth's head, then slowly dropped the sights to a spot between his legs. "You use those balls to stand up to us and I'll shoot them off. Then I'll work up to other parts of your anatomy."

Seth swallowed hard and shook his head. He put his shaky hands on the table and leaned forward slightly. "I can't tell you what I don't know."

"You're not even going to try lying?" Spurgeon sounded amazed at this.

"That's not the way I do things. I was raised to be truthful."

"An honest crook and possibly a murderer, too. Fancy that." Hesseltine fired.

Seth jumped a foot, but the bullet only creased his thigh before embedding in the chair seat. He bent over and grabbed the wound. Blood trickled between his fingers.

"I missed the thighbone on purpose. I'm a very good marksman. Unless I hear what I want to know, a second shot might shatter the femur. That's what Dr. Knight would call it, isn't it? Where is he?"

"That hurts like hell."

"I'll see that you get a shot or two of whiskey to deaden the pain. If you tell us

157

what we want to know, that is. Otherwise, the pain is only beginning. Tell us what became of Knight."

"I don't know! He didn't tell —" Seth Lunsford shrieked when Spurgeon fired. His bullet tore through the young man's shoulder and spun him around, knocking him to the floor.

"You hit the collarbone, Rance. You need to practice more. All you should have done was shoot through the shoulder. Have the bullet come out on the other side without doing so much damage. See? This is the way." Hesseltine took aim.

Seth held out his good hand and groaned. "Please, it hurts. You want me to lie? I will! He rode north. Is that good enough? He went south or west. For all I know, he went back to Pine Knob to kill Donnelly. That's what I woulda done if he set my friends against me."

"We've not been wasting our time, Seth. No, not at all. You haven't gone back to Pine Knob and you've had a chance to avenge the man who set your brother against you. And Milo Hannigan and the others in that gang, the gang you rode with, were recruited by Gerald Donnelly. If Knight thought as you claim, he would have turned up already."

"If I had to bet, I'd say he's fed up with being chased. He wants to vanish." Spurgeon moved the muzzle of his Colt around in lazy circles, as if undecided where to shoot next.

"My partner's talking about Knight, I suspect, but he also reads your intentions pretty well."

"You leave and I'll forget all about you, you and your partner." Seth winced as he tried to lift his right arm. "You done me more damage than Milo ever did, and I've put him behind me."

"From accounts you put him in the ground. Or perhaps your friend Sam did. Yes, that's what happened. Knight saved you, so you feel an obligation to protect him." Hesseltine moved around the table, grabbed Seth by the injured shoulder, and lifted him off the floor. "I do believe you, though, that you don't know where he went." Hesseltine shoved his prisoner toward the shop door.

"Where are you takin' me? If you believe that I don't know squat about Sam and where he went, why are you takin me?"

"There might well be others in town who do know. Move." Hesseltine shoved hard and sent Seth stumbling ahead of him. He lowered his pistol to his side to hide it should anyone be out on the street, but a quick look around revealed that Buffalo Springs was sound asleep.

In twenty minutes they were outside town, near a stock pond and a grove of cottonwoods. Spurgeon pulled a groggy Seth Lunsford from his horse and dumped him on the ground.

"There's a good place," Hesseltine said. "Go on, Rance. You enjoy this so."

He watched his partner drag Seth to his feet and over to a tree. Working with practiced skill, Spurgeon tied their prisoner spread-eagle between two trees. Seth passed out from the pain of his injured shoulder being pulled up and at an angle.

"He's not going to die on us, is he? That won't do." Hesseltine walked to Seth and lifted his chin.

The youth groaned softly.

Hesseltine let Seth's head drop and roll about. "He's in no danger of dying, though the shoulder wound is far more serious than the one I put in his leg."

"You want me to patch him up?"

"There's no need. We really do need to find some food. Do you think anywhere in town can accommodate us? The hotel, perhaps? With a saloon running in the sitting room, they might have something to

160

eat stored in a jar under the bar."

"I want more 'n pickled pigs' knuckles or hardboiled eggs."

"You echo my sentiments exactly, Rance. Come along. Let's leave our friend here to ponder the choices facing him and then return when we've had something filling." Hesseltine rubbed his ample belly.

They mounted and rode away, heading back toward Buffalo Springs. Hearing the receding hooves caused Seth to stir. He moaned and began tugging on the ropes, trying to free himself. Spurgeon had lashed him too securely to the trees. He sagged down, only to cry out in pain as weight tore at his wounded shoulder. He got his feet under him and turned as much as he could to take pressure off the broken collarbone.

The moon had risen and begun to sneak across the sky when soft footsteps approached him.

"Help me," Seth croaked out. "Help!"

"Don't say anything, Seth darling. I'll get you free."

"Marianne! How'd you find me?"

"I heard the gunshot in the shop. I worried you might have accidentally fired off a gun you were working on, so I snuck down to see. I didn't wake Papa." She moved closer, her fingers worrying at the knots fastened so tightly around his wrists. "When I heard the second shot, I knew there was trouble."

"Did you wake your pa then, tell him?" Seth groaned as she ran her fingers over his wounded shoulder.

"I didn't dare. I worried you had been careless. I didn't want him chewing you out or even firing you if the accident was serious enough." She muttered under her breath when she broke a fingernail tugging at the ropes.

"I've lost a lot of blood from where they shot me. I don't think I can even stand."

"You poor dear. Why'd they do this to you?"

"Get me down. We've got to tell . . . somebody."

"Who? The marshal's dead. Hannigan killed him. Or one of his men did. Most of the men have left for New Mexico Territory to prospect for gold. The old men left behind are like my pa. You can't expect them to stand up to killers."

"They did against Hannigan."

"You know that was you and Dr. Knight who stood up to them all by yourselves. If you hadn't been there, the two of you, Hannigan would have robbed the bank and then burned the rest of the town down just because he was so cussed. And him and his men would have . . ." Her voice trailed off. What the outlaw gang would have done to the womenfolk was obvious.

"Do you have a knife to cut the ropes? If you don't get me free, I'm gonna pass out. I swear it, Marianne."

"I'll see what I can do." Marianne Yarrow stood on tiptoe and gave him a quick kiss.

"That'll keep me goin' for a while." Seth tried not to sag and put pressure on his wounded shoulder.

The woman vanished into the dark, only to reappear a second later. A knife gleamed, a silver streak in the moonlight as she waved it around. "It's dull. I keep meaning to sharpen it, but I never get around to it." She started sawing at the rope. The blade proved even duller than she hinted.

"They'll be back soon. They went into town to eat. I don't know if they'll get drunk, too, but countin' on that's not a good bet."

"Oh, Seth, the rope's too tough."

"Keep tryin'. Keep at it." He shook himself to keep from passing out. He blinked hard as tears of pain welled. Then he squinted. "What's that movin' around in the dark?"

"A dog or coyote or something. I'm about

163

halfway through. Brace yourself. I can't hold you up when I cut through the rope."

"That's all right, Miss Yarrow. We'll be happy to."

"Thanks. I —" Marianne Yarrow spun to face Henry Hesseltine. "You!" She lunged with the knife, trying to drive it to the hilt in his gut.

He batted away her thrust and caught her wrist. She cried out as he twisted her arm and forced her to drop the knife.

"You should have come armed. With one of the firearms your pa sells. Or are they all waiting to be repaired by your beau? He looked very competent the way he worked on that pistol when we entered the shop."

"Sh-she's not my girlfriend. She just works in the shop, cleaning and sweeping up. No more 'n that."

"Miss Yarrow is more than that. We heard, didn't we, Rance?"

"We heard. We weren't that far away."

"You only pretended to go to town for food." Seth sobbed, as much in frustration as in pain.

"It was a crude trap, I admit. We prefer more elaborate ways of capturing those we seek. However, time is working against us. Every minute Knight is on the trail, he's a few paces farther away from us apprehend-

164

ing him."

"He . . . he might be in town. When he hears of what you done to me he'll —"

"He's not in town. We made sure of that. Amos Parker certainly would have a score to settle, if he were. And if Amos wasn't in on such an elaborate scheme, Knight would have let Amelia Parker in on it. Her bitterness at being abandoned wasn't feigned. She would cut off his balls using this dull knife, given the chance." Hesseltine picked up the knife Marianne had dropped.

He ran the dull blade along Seth's jawline.

"Stop. You'll hurt him!" Marianne struggled in Hesseltine's grip to no avail.

He was stronger and had the advantage of leverage. He twisted in the other direction and forced her to her knees.

"I promised Seth that we would ride away, and he would never see us again if he spilled the beans on his friend, Dr. Knight. I'll make you the same promise. Tell us where Knight went, and we'll be on the trail and twenty miles from Buffalo Springs by dawn."

"How do I know that?" Marianne winced as Hesseltine twisted her wrist back and forced her to sit on the ground at Seth's feet.

"We don't lie. We keep our promises," Spurgeon said.

"My partner's right. What possible reason could we have to return if our assignment takes us away from Buffalo Springs and you two lovebirds?"

"She doesn't know. I don't know. *Nobody* knows. Sam's too smart. If any of us did, Amelia would have found out and gone after him. He wanted to make a clean break because Donnelly sent so many after him. He cut down Hector Alton and then Milo. Sam's a smart fella. He had to know Donnelly would send someone else."

"Us," said Spurgeon. "Donnelly sent us."

"There's a never-ending string of killers, and Sam didn't want Amelia or anyone else in town to have to deal with that." Seth shuddered as pain wracked his body.

"He's right," Marianne said. "We lied to cover for him when the cavalry came through. The soldiers left thinking he had been in town for years and that we didn't know anybody named Sam Knight."

"So, Miss Yarrow, you admit that you lied to protect him, when the bluecoats were hunting for him?"

"We knew then. He was in town. We protected him for everything he had done for us, but he saw how it was and left. He didn't expect us to keep lying, not when men like you two were going to follow. He didn't tell anybody where he went. That's the truth."

"I think they're telling the truth, Rance. How about that?" Hesseltine stepped back and looked at the man and woman.

"A pity. Now we have to depend on guessing."

"Our gut instincts need working on, I suspect." Hesseltine paced back and forth a few times, then stopped in front of Seth Lunsford. "Why're there so few men in this town?"

"Gold fever. It hit before I got here."

"He's right," added Marianne. "I never saw anything like it. The lure of getting rich drained the men from Buffalo Springs like water through a hole in the bottom of a bucket. They heard stories of the rich strikes in western New Mexico and packed up and took anything that had four legs to carry them and their supplies."

"Western New Mexico Territory?" Hesseltine stopped. "So there'd be a steady stream of strangers going there?"

"Boomtowns," Marianne said, rubbing her wrist.

"Do any of these boomtowns have names?"

167

"I don't know. I heard tell of Ralston City being on a stagecoach line. Some of the men from here talked about it as if it were the biggest strike in the history of the world."

"Do you think Knight headed there, figuring to blend in with the other prospectors?" Hesseltine looked to his partner for an answer.

"It's worth a look," Spurgeon said.

"You're going? You won't be back?" Seth Lunsford gasped out the words through the red-hot pain filling him to overflowing.

"I promised you both that you'd never see us again." Hesseltine drew his pistol and dispatched Seth with a single shot to the heart.

Marianne Yarrow cried out in anguish until Spurgeon put her down, two rounds to her breast and a final one through her forehead.

"Really, Rance, three shots? You need to practice your marksmanship."

"Shut up. We got to find this Ralston City."

The two Pinkerton detectives mounted and took the horses used by Seth and Marianne as spares so they could make better time by switching mounts when the ones they rode got tired. Sam Knight had a big start on them, and they needed to catch up

168

before he vanished forever into the vast
frontier.

CHAPTER 11

Dr. Samuel Knight yawned, stretched, and almost toppled over. It had been a long, exhausting few hours since he and Wilcox had arrived at the mine. More miners had been pulled from the collapsed shaft. Tending them had been difficult because of their broken bones and some with injuries even more devastating. Several had been mashed flat by falling timbers.

He looked at his bloody hands and resisted the urge to wipe them off on his trousers. Limbs had been hacked off using an axe blade that had started out rusty and ended up polished smooth with the flesh, blood, and bones of too many good men, reminding him too much of the battlefield surgery that had been necessary during the war.

Sever a limb, save a life. That had been required when he saw the condition of too many miners. It had taken even more energy and determination out of him getting Doc

Murtagh to tend the patients afterwards so he could move on and dispense whatever surgical skills he had to the most recent patients. The drunken doctor had, at one time, possessed a modicum of ability. Somewhere, for some reason, he had burned it out with too many bottles of whiskey over the years, but he still had enough knowledge to keep some of the men alive until Knight returned to tend them.

"How's it looking?" Dave Wilcox came in, covered with dust. He steadfastly eyed Knight, his neck stiffly not turning either left or right as he stood just under the tarp.

Knight didn't blame him for not wanting to stare at the injured men. It turned his own stomach, and he had gone through more than one battle and seen more than one severe injury in his day.

"Let's go outside." He steered his friend out of the crude tent into the cold dawn. With shaking hands, he fixed a cigarette, rolling it with precision in spite of his nerves being shattered.

"Are you scared, Sam? Your hands are trembling something fierce."

"Cold. I lose circulation in my hands when I operate like that." He jerked his thumb over his shoulder to show what he meant. He let Wilcox light the smoke since he didn't trust himself with a match. A deep draw filled his lungs. Warmth, soothing warmth filled him. Then he began to revive a little. Working as he had tuckered him out both physically and emotionally.

"I wasn't wrong, was I? About you being a doctor, I mean?"

Knight refused to answer. He still had a faint hope of putting his past behind him, but Wilcox now knew for certain he had been a surgeon. The cowboy-turned-miner wasn't dumb, and the way he had come begging for medical help showed he'd more than suspected before tonight. Now there could be no doubt. More than one man inside the tent owed his life to Samuel Knight.

"Where am I?"

"What? What do you mean? You haven't gone loco from all that blood and cutting, have you, Sam?"

"I meant, what mine is this? You brought me here, and I never thought to ask."

"That peak behind us. See it? That's Red Mountain. The reason Sierra Rojo got named the way it did. In the sunrise it turns a dull red. Sunset really sets it afire with color."

Knight nodded, puffed a few more times and reached the end of the cigarette. He

172

ground it out between his fingers. The hot coal at the tip felt good for a moment before he extinguished it. "I can see other reasons why it got named that. What's the red rock? Granite?"

"Danged if I know. What I do know is that it shines the most awful red color in the setting sun. Doesn't look that way at sunrise, only sunset. Bloody red sunset."

"There's a fair amount of blood that's soaked into the ground." Knight looked at his own boots. They had been well polished when he rode into the mining camp. Now they were sticky red and covered with dirt clinging to the blood that had sloshed onto them as he'd hacked off arms and legs.

"This here's the Lucky Draw mine, the biggest and best producer anywhere on the slopes of Red Mountain. I landed the job as shift supervisor first thing," Wilcox said.

"The owner must have seen something in you nobody else did to give a man without any mining experience such a big job." Knight chuckled. "Then again, you probably sweet-talked your way into the job."

"Hellfire Bonham owns the Lucky Draw and has the reputation of being the hardest, foulest-mouthed mine owner anywhere on the slopes of Red Mountain, and there must be two dozen other mines boring into this very rock. The strikes here — damned near all of them — make those Billie Ralston claimed look like pocket change."

"What aren't you telling me?"

"I got the job because Hellfire chews up men and spits 'em out. The supers that aren't killed, either on the job or by the miners, quit or get fired. Hellfire Bonham claimed the supervisor before me lasted almost a week, and he beat the record by two days."

"Did you have anything to do with the cave-in?"

"That happened in a stope started by my predecessor. Truth is, I've never been in that section of the mine." Wilcox turned somber. "But I will have to get in there. Likely a half dozen miners died there."

"Leaving them buried might be for the best," Knight said. "Put a gravestone on the cave-in and dig somewhere else."

"I can't do that. They have families. Hellfire wants a decent burial for them, too, so it'll get done."

"Bonham can't be too bad, then, doing the right thing by the miners."

"There's constant fighting going on between us and the owner of the Blue-Eyed Bitch. That's the next biggest mine on the mountain. I've heard how Jefferson Avery operates." Wilcox shook his head. "His miners are all in debt to him because he charges them for room and board at exorbitant rates, and he keeps them in virtual slavery. If they try to sneak away and they still owe him money, he's got a posse that goes after 'em. He's set up his own court and will sentence them to a year or two extra working in his mine."

"The Blue-Eyed Bitch?"

"That's what he calls his mine."

Knight had heard some crazy names for mines in his day, but that was the strangest. Prospectors spent long, lonely hours hunting for their big strike. Few actually got rich, but all were a little loco and had big dreams not shared by most men.

"Wilcox! We're ready to start digging out the miners trapped in the new drift." A ragged man dressed in canvas miner's trousers and a filthy denim shirt waved from uphill. "Come on. We need you to keep the gang working."

"Time for me to earn my pay," Wilcox said. "Come on up. You can see what we're up against."

"There might be miners who need patching up, too. Only the worst injured must have made it to my field hospital. I've seen men with minor wounds keep fighting until

175

infection sets in and they die when there wasn't any call for it."

"I see you're fitting right in, Sam."

Knight sucked in his breath and held it, realizing how much of his background he had given away. He knew medicine. He knew how to set up a hospital and decide who to save and who to let die. Such decisions always hurt deep down in his gut, but saving the greatest number of the injured forced him to make such choices. It went with the job.

But he wanted to walk away from being a doctor. He wanted to be anything other than a doctor. Circumstances refused to let him.

"I don't want to leave Murtagh alone with them too long." He looked over his shoulder. Doc Murtagh sat with his back to a rock, sipping the last drops from a whiskey bottle.

"You've patched them up real good, Sam. They'll be fine for a few minutes."

"Wilcox! Are you still workin' here or do I get your job?"

"For two cents, Sampson, I'd let you have my job. Only trouble is, Hellfire would chew me out and I'd be out that two cents." Wilcox nudged Knight with his elbow and said in a low voice, "Sampson's the best damned miner working at the Lucky Draw. He ought to be the super, but Hellfire wanted me instead. Who knows why?"

"Let's go." Knight was bone tired from working all night and found climbing the steep slope to the mouth of the Lucky Draw difficult. He was gasping for air before he reached the level area in front of the mine, the altitude only part of his exhaustion.

In the midst of all the confusion he saw a thread of logic. The man Wilcox had praised, Sampson, got his work teams into order while Wilcox climbed over piles of material destined to go into the mine. Knight went to the base of a pile of cut wood supports used to shore up the tunnel walls and roof.

"You must have cut down damned near every tree on the mountain to get this many beams." Knight kicked one. Something sounded wrong. He looked closer. The wood beam intended to support the mine roof had a section on one end that had been glued on. "What's this?" He ran his fingers around the seam and held up his hand, covered with the sticky substance.

"Get on outta the way, mister, or help us. We got timber to move." Sampson pushed Knight away and started loading the beam and others onto a cart to move them to the mine.

"Sam, over there. Come take a look, will you?"

Knight thought Wilcox was ordering him out of the way, then saw two men supporting each other. They were covered in blood. One hobbled and the other held his arm, which dangled at an odd angle.

"On the job," Knight called, ignoring the feeling something was wrong with the beams making their way into the mine to replace those that had already failed.

"You comin' to tell us to get back into the mine?" The miner with the broken arm shook his head as he spoke. "We ain't up for it."

"Do as you please, but you need to get patched up first. That arm looks to be in a bad way."

"You're not the new super, are you?"

"Dave Wilcox is my friend. He fetched me from Sierra Rojo to help with the wounded. That's you. Sit down so I can look you over."

"Your name's not Murtagh, is it?" The miner edged away.

"Sam Knight. Now sit down or I'll have to knock you down to set that arm."

"It hurts something fierce."

"That's a compound fracture. I see the bone poking through your skin. It's going to hurt even worse, but not right yet. Give me a minute to get ready." Knight took a firm hold on the man's wrist and elbow. "First I want to —" Suddenly, he yanked hard, taking the miner by surprise. The man let out a howl of utter pain, then sank back. Knight followed him to the ground, fingers probing the wound.

"You said not yet. You lied. You went ahead when I didn't expect it."

"How's the pain?"

"I . . . not too bad. I hardly feel any now. More of an ache." He tried to stretch it in front of him, but Knight held it firmly to prevent that.

"Don't move it around too much. I need to put a splint on it, but your friend needs me more right now." Knight motioned to the other man, who hobbled over and eased himself down to a pile of cinders. He held his leg out straight.

After cutting away the man's pant leg to reveal a nasty gash in the thigh, Knight began cleaning the wound the best he could.

"I need to clean it better, then sew it up. Do you know if there's any thread and needle around the camp?"

The man looked sheepish and fumbled in his pocket. He pulled out a tiny spool of thread that gleamed in the morning light.

179

Knight held it up, unrolled a few inches and frowned. "What is this?"

"Silver thread. Will that do to sew me up?"

"I've never used metal thread. Do you have a golden needle, too?" He laughed in spite of himself.

"Mostly silver comin' outta the Lucky Draw. I worked in a mine on the other side of the hill where they dig out hunks of gold the size of my fist, but I never had a chance to make either thread or a needle out of any of it."

"That might be just as well. Can you stand?" Knight helped the miner up and let him put his arm around his shoulder to make their way down to the field hospital.

"Wait up. I'm comin'. Slow but sure, but I'm comin'." The miner with the broken arm made his way down the slope of loose rock, sliding and slipping but getting to the tent before Knight and the man with the gashed leg.

"Sit here. I'll be right back." Knight made sure the two were comfortable and not likely to get themselves into trouble, then went to see how Doc Murtagh fared. As he crossed the tent, he glanced left and right, taking in the condition of the severely injured miners. All but one dozed. The one who had not fallen asleep had died. Knight knelt, made

180

sure the man had passed on, then pulled up the thin blanket to cover his face.

"He cain't breathe if you do that."

Knight held his anger in check. He spun, grabbed Murtagh by the throat, and lifted. The man's breath was almost enough to knock over a grizzly. Two quick steps forced Murtagh back. "You let him die."

"I didn't know he was dead. Sneaky bastard, dyin' when I wasn't lookin'."

Knight's anger exploded. He had started to strangle the drunken doctor when he felt vibration coming up from the ground through his boots. The rumble grew and then he was thrown to his knees.

"The mine's collapsed again!" The cry from the two miners he'd just brought in merged with the deep rumble. Seconds later a dust cloud washed through his hospital, choking him and making his eyes water.

All he could think was, "Wilcox!" His friend had gone into the mine to rescue others. Now he was trapped.

CHAPTER 12

Victoria Donnelly stared at the food on her fine bone china plate, then looked up to the far end of the table where her husband's meal had been placed. She pushed away and called, "Matty, come here, please."

The black maid came in, looking defiant. She clutched a towel and twisted it around in one direction, then reversed the motion.

"Whatever it is, I didn't have nuthin' to do with it."

"You're not in trouble, Matty."

"You ain't touched the food. What's wrong with it?"

"Nothing, nothing, I assure you. I wanted to know where my husband is." She looked at the empty chair, then back to the maid. Victoria held back the tears that threatened to spill down her cheeks. She clutched her linen napkin in the same way Matty did, but she forced herself to drop it on the table. "Do you know where he is?"

"No, I don't. He don't tell me nuthin'."

"You may clear the table." Victoria stood and turned away. The tears trickled down her cheeks and she hastily brushed them away.

"You want me to put a plate aside fo' whenever he comes home?"

"Throw it to the pigs." With that Victoria left the dining room and went to stand on the front porch, cool night breeze drying her tears. She leaned on the railing, remembering when Samuel had spent the entire week building it. They had worked on this house ever since they were married but didn't have the money to hire carpenters to help. But that was back then, what seemed a thousand years ago.

He had worked a full day at his office in Pine Knob, then come home and worked for another hour or two doing the finishing on the house. Painting, putting up the porch railing, even hanging the windows. She went to the window in the parlor and ran her fingers around the frame. It was out of square. No matter how Samuel had tried he hadn't been able to get it square. Rather than waste another day after he had struggled with it over a week, he had used caulk to hide the gaping crevices. Huge chunks were still there, dried out now and threatening to fall off to let in cold winter air. She kicked at one piece that had dried out and fallen to the porch. It went spinning off and fell into a flower bed.

When the second story had been added, at Gerald's insistence because he had lived in a two-story house back in Boston, the house had settled and almost brought the window frame into alignment. It took time and mischance to correct what Samuel had done wrong. Somehow, she saw her life running parallel to that.

Victoria still saw the differences in the construction, both small and large, and remembered how she and Samuel had worked when building the house. As newlyweds they had been happy. They had been together, and that was all that mattered.

Then the war came, and he had to go off to Virginia as an army officer. For a few months, she had written every day. The mail had become sporadic and eventually she had stopped receiving any letters from him. No matter where she inquired, no one knew his fate. After the Battle of the Wilderness, she pored over newspaper reports. The journalists tried to put a good slant for the Confederacy on the battles, but she read the truth between their highfalutin words and glowing patriotism. Her anxiety turned to bitterness, and then Gerald Donnelly had come to town after the war ended.

She smiled weakly. What a dashing man he had been. Well dressed and commanding, he had come into Pine Knob to make certain Reconstruction went according to the plans laid down by Washington. He was so different from Samuel. He never asked what she wanted. He seemed to know and gave it freely without her asking. Although many in town looked askance at her when she began seeing Gerald, she had ignored them.

If Samuel had abandoned her and was dead somewhere in Virginia or Pennsylvania or another battlefield she could not name, Gerald Donnelly had swept her away with money and position. The courtship had been a whirlwind that swept her up and left her giddy with fresh love.

"I thought he loved me," she said softly. She wiped away more cold tears.

He hadn't wanted anything more than a lovely local woman on his arm. And she had obliged him. In exchange for a fine house and fancy clothing from New York and Paris, she had crawled into bed with him to keep from being alone, to improve her station in life.

Victoria realized the terrible decision she

had made when Samuel had come back, emaciated and looking as if he had one foot in the grave. Any chance she had of renewing that relationship was long gone, along with him turning into some kind of outlaw and fleeing with a terrible gang of desperados.

"How would I have ever made it right, even if I had chosen him?"

Gerald had used his political connections to annul her prior marriage and give the full force of the law to theirs. She had cut herself free from Samuel and treated him horribly.

It was her turn to be punished for her behavior. Gerald seldom came home, always protesting how he had to work late. When he did come home, he smelled of liquor . . . of liquor and cheap perfume. She suspected he did more than frequent the dance hall in town with its painted women. He rejected her sexual overtures. All she could think was that the whorehouse he had allowed to open in Pine Knob — in Pine Knob! — saw more of him than she did in her fine two-story house.

Matty lit a lamp in the front room. Victoria knew she ought to go inside and finish her chores. She had the household books to keep and a letter to write, but such work could be postponed until tomorrow. As she thought on it, she knew those trivial tasks could be postponed forever.

She went into the house and told her maid to go to bed. When Matty disappeared into the kitchen, heading for her attached quarters just beyond, Victoria climbed the stairs to the second floor. One foot after another, slow and painful, she climbed. She had never noticed before that there were thirteen steps. The same number that a condemned man climbed up to the gallows. She went to her bedroom and found a carpetbag in the wardrobe. She stared at it and reflected on the irony as she packed. Her husband was a carpetbagger.

Choosing carefully from her clothes, she packed until the bag almost failed to latch. Then she began on a second bag, this one containing her jewelry and any other valuable item she could cram in. Only then did she take off her fine dress she had chosen for dinner with her husband, hang it in the wardrobe, and don rougher clothing intended for travel.

Victoria stood a final time in front of a mirror brought all the way from Italy, smoothed out wrinkles, and settled a hat at the proper angle. Without a backwards look, she picked up the bags and went downstairs

187

and outside.

She considered telling Matty she was leaving, then decided against it. The less of a trail she left, the harder it would be for Gerald to find her. Or would he even try? She sighed, knowing that he would. He thought he owned her, and he was a possessive man. And one who carried a grudge. She knew how he still sought Samuel to exact revenge for all he had done to him.

Victoria took no comfort in how Samuel had sliced Gerald's Achilles tendon or even shot off his index finger. They had been locked in life-or-death struggle. Gerald was lucky to have survived either encounter, much less both.

She made her way in the dark to the barn and hitched up her buggy. The horse protested at being awakened. It wasn't used to going out at night. Soothing it the best she could, she led the horse around to the front of the house, the buggy creaking and rattling behind. Both bags dropped into the buggy and she got in. The horse neighed in protest, then settled down to pulling.

She drove to the road Gerald had ordered plowed to their house, then cut through town and hesitated. The saloons were filled with boisterous music and the voices of drunken men. Gerald Donnelly was in one of them . . . or in the two-story house next to one music hall where every window blazed with a coal oil lamp. She couldn't see what went on in each room, and the sounds were drowned out by the piano player banging away in the saloon, but she knew.

Gerald was more likely in one of those rooms than leaning against a bar, drinking beer or whiskey or whatever men drank. She sighed. Samuel had never had more than a single drink of wine at Thanksgiving. Never had she even suspected him of imbibing. The worst had been him coming home with the pungent smell of ether and carbolic acid on his clothing.

The horse tried to rear. She kept it under control, turned its face out of town, and snapped the reins. Moving prevented the horse from getting ideas of its own. When she saw the army encampment, she slowed, expecting a sentry to challenge her. She saw soldiers gathered around campfires but no one walking patrol. Another snap of the reins got the buggy moving toward the tent where she knew Captain Norwood made his headquarters. She pulled around to the side, stepped down, and fastened the reins around the brake handle.

She walked hesitantly to the front of the

tent, wondering if she ought to get an orderly to announce her. None of the soldiers took notice of her, so she called out for the captain.

"Captain Norwood?" She got no answer at first but heard movement inside the tent and repeated the summons. "I would have a word with you."

"Enter." The mumbled command worried her that she had the wrong tent. Norwood always barked out his orders.

She pushed back the tent flap and saw him sitting on a stool, a map spread on a low table. To one side shined an oil lamp and to the other stood a half-empty whiskey bottle. The light caught the amber contents and rippled strangely.

"You've been drinking." The accusation slipped from her before she realized it.

"You. Mrs. Gerald Donnelly. You've come to gloat? It's not enough your husband has me transferred to the devil's own armpit, but he has to send *you* to pour salt into my wounds?"

"I had heard Gerald talking about sending the letter to the War Department. It doesn't surprise me he carried through with his threat to have you transferred. I am sorry, sir, and I apologize for him." She stood a little straighter and brushed her hat

190

on the top of the tent. "No, no, I do not apologize for him. Not at all."

"What do you want?" Norwood rasped.

"Your assistance, sir."

"That's rich. Your husband destroys my career by sending me to a post even a shave-tail lieutenant would consider punishment, and you come begging for a favor."

"It's not like that, Captain. I . . . I am leaving Gerald. I have had enough of him and his ways."

"You want to join the army? I can swear you in. Hell, I'll drink to that." He took a swig of the whiskey and carefully put it back on the edge of the map. "You see where I set the bottle? That's my new command in northern Montana. I will be in charge of ten men. Ten. I won't even have a sergeant under me. Nothing but privates. We are entrusted with keeping Crow Indians from sneaking into the country to do mischief." A hollow laugh came from Norwood, then he continued. "Ten men to stop an entire invasion? If the Crow swept down from Canada, there would be hundreds of them. But more likely, I will be ordered to prevent white men from selling firewater to them. I commanded a company during the war and distinguished myself. Unlike many of my fellow officers, I was not reduced in rank. I achieved a high ranking when I graduated from West Point, and I performed well in the field." His voice was filled with bleak despair as he went on. "Now I am faced with the end of my career."

"You can resign your commission."

"Is that what Donnelly wants me to do? Quit? Isn't he man enough to tell me to my face that's his scheme? No, he sends his woman."

"Let me make myself perfectly clear. He does not know I'm here. I am leaving him. It embarrasses me, not only what he has done to you, but his other dealings are also reprehensible. When he came to Pine Knob, he maintained order and did well keeping the townspeople in line. Somewhere he decided his job was to steal their land and their businesses and to do everything but imprison them." Victoria heaved a sigh of resignation. "I have no doubt he is planning to do that when enough begin to protest what he has done. Mr. Fitzsimmons at the bank is already talking rebellion again."

"I won't be here to quell any riots."

"Good. You should not be part of such blatant illegal activity. He is stealing land, property, things my neighbors clung to by the skin of their teeth throughout the war. It disgusts me what he does in the name of

192

law and order."

"Something else is eating you, Mrs. Donnelly. What did he do? What did he do to you?" Norwood took another drink, paused, then silently offered her the bottle.

Victoria recoiled at the idea, then stepped forward, took the bottle, wiped off the mouth with her handkerchief, and tentatively tipped it back. She choked. She hadn't expected it to burn like fire.

"Too strong?" Norwood mocked her.

She tilted the bottle back and took a longer pull on it. This time the whiskey slid past her tongue and down her throat. It burned on the way to her stomach, but it calmed her and focused the anger she felt toward Gerald.

"That's another count against him. He has driven me to drink." At that she smiled, then laughed, Norwood joining her.

"What do you want from me? I can't arrest him, not with his connections in the War Department. Believe me, I have sent telegrams of my own and there's nothing my allies can do. General Sherman's hands are tied in the matter." Norwood scowled. "More likely, he has to choose his battles, and I'm not worth fighting for."

"I am sure that's untrue. You have done a fine job getting these soldiers into fighting shape. I can tell by the way they march about."

"They hate me, but a commanding officer's job isn't to be liked. If we had gone into the field against the Comanches, we would have acquitted ourselves well. That's what matters, but I have failed at another duty of a commander. Politics. I had to get along with the federal administrator. In that, I have failed terribly." He took another drink.

Victoria joined him, but moderated the amount she swallowed. The first gulp already had turned her woozy and made her ears buzz. In spite of this, she felt more confident than ever that her plan was the proper one.

"When do you leave, Captain?"

"In the morning."

"I would consider it a great favor if you would escort me, wherever you go."

"Why do you want to go to Montana?"

"I . . . I don't, but you are traveling north. Escort me as far as Kansas City or perhaps St. Louis."

"I'm heading to Saint Louie. From there I'll catch a riverboat up the Missouri and finally head across country to my post."

"That is perfect, if you will. I can go with you as far as you will take me."

194

"You're really leaving that son of a bitch?"

"I am," she said, "leaving that son of a bitch."

Norwood took another drink, then passed her the bottle. They looked at each other.

"Where are you staying tonight?"

"Where are you?" Victoria Donnelly set aside the bottle and went to the captain.

Before dawn they rode from camp, she in her buggy and he on his stallion, sitting tall and putting Gerald Donnelly from their minds.

CHAPTER 13

The ground heaved and gave a final shiver. The rolling dust blinded Knight. He frantically wiped the grit from his eyes. He finally saw what had happened. The canvas roof on the hospital had fallen down, covering the men stretched out on the blankets. Some of them cried out in panic. Others couldn't summon even that much strength and only moaned in pain. A lump in the canvas showed where Doc Murtagh thrashed around, trying to get free.

Knight heaved and struggled out from under the canvas, joined by the two men he had just patched up. They huddled together as the dust settled.

"What happened?" Knight asked. "That felt like an earthquake."

The expression on the men's faces told him what actually had happened higher on the hillside.

"The mine collapsed again?"

"There's no other reason for this dust storm," said the one with the broken arm. "We got out of the mine before. The timbers creaked once, then snapped like thunder. It's the most frightening sound in the world, bar none."

"You got that right," said his friend with the wounded leg. "We got to get up there to help out. There's no way more men didn't get trapped, and they was the ones tryin' to rescue the others still down in the mine."

Knight grabbed them both by the collars and forced them to the ground. "You're in no condition to do anything but die yourselves. Stay here and do what you can for the others." He glared at Murtagh, emerging from under the canvas still holding his bottle in his hand. "Keep him from doing too much damage, and I'll be back to finish patching you two up."

"I'll hunt around for a needle," said the one. He grinned weakly. "I don't promise no gold needle to go with my silver thread, but I'll try."

Knight appreciated the attempt at humor, but the sight of the mountainside above turned him cold inside. For the mine to belch out that much dust and rock, the explosion deep down underground had to be incredible. If the entire shaft had col-

197

lapsed, getting anyone out alive would be impossible. Better to seal off the shaft and put up a grave marker for those caught in the collapse, no matter what Hellfire Bonham thought was proper.

As Knight trudged up the hill, his breath coming in fast, short gasps, he realized that Dave Wilcox had been taking a pile of the timbers into the mine. Had he delivered the load and made it out for another when the mine collapsed? Knight didn't see how that was possible, but Wilcox was a lucky galoot. If he hadn't made it, some of the others must have.

"Sampson. Name was Sampson," Knight muttered to himself as he dropped to help himself up the steep slope using his hands. Toes dug into the gravel. Inch by inch he made it up the steep slope until he came out on the level stretch in front of the mine mouth where the piled beams had made a criss-cross pyramid. More than half the pile remained. Most of the men had vanished into the mine.

Men wandered around dazed. He grabbed a couple and demanded to know who was in charge, if Wilcox was in the mine. When he failed to get a coherent reply, he scrambled to the top of the wood pile and looked around. His heart sank when he saw how the mine mouth was filled with rock and splintered timbers.

He jumped down, grabbed a pick, and joined two men at the side of the mine working to dig a new entrance. He worked for what seemed an eternity. Men came and went, bringing water, offering him jerky to gnaw on as he worked. He took it all without actually seeing anything but the chore ahead.

"Get back," the miner beside him said, taking his arm and steering him away.

"But we're almost through to the main shaft."

"Get back. We're gonna blow our way in. It's a damned sight faster that way, and time counts for them poor bastards caught inside."

Knight stumbled back, eyes watering from dust and his body aching from the exertion. Never had he worked harder — physical work. The long hours in the operating theater caused joint and leg pain from standing for days on end. That was more grueling from the point of view of exhaustion — mental and physical. Here his muscles hurt rather than his joints and his legs.

A small man dressed in a bright red shirt and canvas pants with a floppy brimmed hat pulled low over the eyes pushed past him. A bandana had been pulled up to hide most of his face so only bloodshot blue eyes peered out. Knight started to ask what was happening, but the man who had worked beside him dragged him back.

"Let Hellfire set the charge. Ain't nobody better at blastin'."

"What's that?" Knight pointed to a large glass tube in the man's gloved hands. A yellow viscous fluid sloshed about. It looked as if bubbles formed and popped on the surface of the liquid.

"That's nitro."

"Nitroglycerin? I don't know much about it, but you can't carry it like that. A shock and it'll explode!"

"That's what's gonna happen." The miner turned, dropped to one knee and covered his head with his arms.

Knight mirrored the stance and a few seconds later the ground lifted under his feet, then fell away. The rumble of the blast seemed to come seconds later, but he realized the time delay was because he was so on edge. The world moved like molasses around him, and that included the dirt and rock spit from the new mine shaft they had dug. The shock wave and pelting stone finally shoved him off balance. He fell facedown, and the rest of the blast raked along his back and down the hillside.

His ears rang but through the din he heard a high voice calling out, "That did it, boys. We blasted through behind the plug. Let's go get them poor souls outta there!"

Knight pushed to his feet and found his legs too shaky to walk. The miner who had been beside him braced him for a moment. "You ready to get to work?"

"What've we been doing?" Knight realized he shouted. He was almost deaf from the explosion. He followed the miner toward the new, raw, gaping hole in the side of the mountain. It had cut just behind the collapsed section of the original mine.

The miner laughed. "You ain't seen nuthin' till you put in a full shift underground." He slapped Knight on the back, staggering him.

Wiping dirt from his face, Knight entered the ragged hole, ducking to keep from banging his head against rock sticking down from the roof. In the main tunnel he found a half dozen men already at work. Lighting the candle on a miner's helmet took some doing, but he finally got a shimmery, shaking yellow glow from it. After putting the helmet on his head, a pry bar was thrust into his hands.

"This way. There're two men caught in a

side stope not ten yards from here."

He barely saw the miner who had carried the nitro and had set the charge in the murk. Dust choked everything, forcing him to pull his handkerchief out and fasten it around his nose, making him look like the outlaw he had once been. Whatever he looked like now in his fancy vest marred with bloodstains and dirt, it wasn't a tinhorn gambler. He wished he had put on his discarded coat, but it was back in the hospital tent, turned beige from the dust the last time he saw it. As he looked at his arms, he saw sparkles like he was on fire.

"Silver dust," a miner said. "That's how rich the Lucky Draw is." The man pushed past Knight and disappeared straight down the main shaft. The blaster pointed at Knight and gestured for him to follow.

He hurried to catch up. The smaller man ahead of him in the dimly lit tunnel smelled of explosives. Still wearing gloves and with hat pulled down and bandana up, he looked ready to do some more blasting.

"There's the rockfall. See how the boulders on top of the heap are balanced? Pry them loose, then get the hell out of the way."

"Do you know Dave Wilcox? Is he here?"

"Of course I know Wilcox. Is he a friend of yours?" The miner peered at Knight through the gloom. "I haven't seen you here before, and you sure as hell aren't dressed like a rock monkey."

"I'm a friend from Sierra Rojo. He said there were wounded and thought I could help."

"Hell, a rattlesnake could do a better job of saving the injured men compared to Doc Murtagh. You're not like him? No, I don't smell whiskey on you."

"How can you smell anything but the nitroglycerin?"

"Practice. I've blasted so much it's beginning to smell like fancy French perfume to me. Maybe better, considering. Now get to prying the rocks loose. Start with that one. I'll work on the other side."

Knight shoved the pry bar between the rocks and put his back to it. Even with the leverage gained from the long iron rod, he couldn't budge the rock. He looked over at the other miner. Already rocks matching the one he attacked had started tumbling down. A few seconds watching how the other man worked gave Knight the idea how to proceed more effectively. Before he knew it, his pile of rocks matched that of his companion.

He grunted, heaved, and bent the iron bar just a mite. A cascade of rock and dirt came pouring down over his feet. At the top of

203

the rockfall came a rush of air. A faint light flickered on the far side.

"We're through!" Knight scampered up the steep slope and poked his head through the opening to see who waited on the other side.

He recoiled. Inches away Dave Wilcox's face tried the same trick, only on his side of the rock pile.

"You're as ugly as ever, Sam, and I have never been happier to see anyone in all my born days. How much more digging do you have to do to get us out?"

"How many is there?" the blaster called from behind Knight. "Do we have to get more men or even use some nitro? I got some Giant Powder if nitro's too dangerous."

"I do declare, all you want to do is blow things up, boss." Wilcox wiggled around.

"Boss?"

"That's Hellfire Bonham, the owner of the Lucky Draw," Wilcox said. "You get hit on the head, Sam? Who else would it be?"

"Things have been confusing. I can still barely hear after I was deafened by the first blast to get into the mine again."

"You must have your head scrambled like breakfast eggs. Now get us out. There's two more behind me, one of them's in sorry shape."

"Broken bones or something worse?"

"You'll have to decide, Sam. All I want to do is see sunlight again, and you lollygagging's not going to get me out of this death-trap mine."

"That's no way for my superintendent to talk, Wilcox. You take it back. The Lucky Draw isn't a death trap, not by a hundred rows of apple trees. I don't know what happened, but it's no fault of the rock. That's solid. Sturdy solid, it is."

"Keep your apple trees, Hellfire. Get us out of here into sunlight."

"I'll pick 'em off your tree if you don't help out."

"Don't make promises you'll never keep, boss."

Knight slid down the steep slope and poked at the roof with his pry bar. No new rocks tumbled down. It was sturdy enough to support a larger opening at the top of the plug in the tunnel. He began gingerly removing rock until Hellfire pushed him aside.

"Don't mollycoddle that rock. Show it who's boss. Like this." A pickax rose and fell, sending sparks and stony debris flying. A dozen strokes tore away enough rock for

Knight to crawl back, grab Wilcox under the arms, and pull him through the hole to slide headfirst to the mine floor.

"Damn me, Sam. Tear all the skin off my belly, why don't you?"

A second man wormed through the opening and ended up beside Wilcox. He pointed a broken finger back up where he had been and said, "Juan's banged up bad. I don't think it's a good idea to move him till he's patched up some."

"I'll go see." Knight climbed the shifting slope and shoved himself halfway through the hole.

The light from his guttering candle provided all the light on that side of the cave-in. He moved to kneel beside the man on the rocky floor and probed as gently as possible.

The man still cried out. "You're killin' me. I got a leg pinned under a rock that won't move. Wilcox couldn't budge it."

Knight shifted position so his candle flickered closer to the man's legs. He shook his head, then regretted it when the light flickered and the flame almost went out.

"What's it look like, Knight?" Hellfire Bonham peered through the hole, holding a larger candle. "You need more light? I can have somebody fetch a carbide lamp."

"It's going to be just fine, even if it doesn't feel like it right now," Knight said to calm the miner trapped under the rock. He tapped a couple times with his pry bar, then inched it forward, caught the edge of the rock, and used another as a fulcrum. "Pull free when you can."

"There, there! I'm out from under it. And my leg's all banged up, but I can move it."

"Not even a broken bone. Just nasty cuts and bruises. Here." Knight helped the miner stand.

"I can walk. I limp, but there's feeling in my foot and it's not too painful."

"Get out of here." Knight looked around and felt as if the walls closed in around him. He had heard of people who panicked when caught in caves or other tight places, but he had never appreciated the gut-grabbing terror. The longer he stood, the more he felt as if someone had choked all the breath from his lungs.

He closed his eyes, then followed the miner through the hole into the main tunnel to find himself alone. For a minute, he stood and took in as much of the stale, dusty air as he could. His lungs strained, and his feet refused to move. Then he heard Dave Wilcox's voice coming from far down the mineshaft. Pretending this was the

Piped Piper luring him out, Knight let the sound lead him away from the collapsed shaft and into bright sunlight.

The autumn warmth erased his fears and returned him to the world around him. If he never went into a mine again, it would be three days too soon.

"Where'd Wilcox go?" he asked a nearby miner.

The man looked up, then pointed downhill toward the makeshift field hospital.

"Thanks." Knight slipped and slid down the hill past the tailings to the canvas-roofed hospital. Somebody had propped the canvas up again. Knight paused and glared at Doc Murtagh. The man had finally passed out and snored loudly on one of the pallets that had been used for a man who had truly needed it.

"Don't worry your head none, Sam," Wilcox said. "Murtagh didn't kill anybody whilst you were rescuing me. I rolled him onto the blanket when I got here. Sonny was feeling good enough to get back to trying to save the rest still in the mine. Good man, Sonny Trilby."

"You need to rest. You've been through hell in the mine."

"Damn me if I don't want to take your advice, but I'm not being paid to lounge

208

around. I need to get back to see if there are any more patients I can bring for your tender, loving care." Wilcox stared hard at him. "You're more 'n a gambler, aren't you, Sam?"

"I'm dog tired, that's what I am. But I ought to make one more round to see if there's anything else I can do for the men."

"You're a good man, Samuel Knight." Wilcox slapped him on the back and limped away.

Knight checked the two nearest men, then looked across the makeshift tent. He blinked, thinking his exhaustion was causing his eyes to play tricks on him.

A woman with short-cropped blond hair knelt beside a miner who had been severely injured. She rested her hand on the man's cheek and stroked gently. In a mining camp, a touch like that from a woman as good looking would bring a man back from the dead. Knight had to laugh when he heard what she told the man.

"You'll get your lazy ass out of that bed in a day or two, mark my words. If you don't, I'll take a blacksnake whip to you." She stroked his cheek again, then tweaked his nose. "And don't you forget it."

She saw Knight watching her, abandoned her examination of the other patients, and went to him. Knight didn't know who she was but had the feeling they had met before. When she got within arm's length, he took a deep whiff and knew where that encounter had taken place. "Nitroglycerin."

"The damned stench is impossible to get out of my hair. I changed clothes, but I need a decent bath to clean off the smell. Thanks for doing what you did for my men."

He stared at her, realization dawning on him.

She thrust out her hand and her blue eyes fixed boldly on his. "I'm Helene Bonham. But everybody calls me Hellfire. I'm the owner of the Lucky Draw." Her hand almost crushed his in a handshake meant to tell him exactly who was boss.

CHAPTER 14

"I don't think he killed nobody."

"Came close."

"But he didn't. I watched him real close."

"You just wanted a nip of his booze."

The two miners stretched out and propped up on their elbows were arguing about Murtagh. The doctor snored peacefully at the edge of the hospital tent.

"Nuthin' wrong with that. A man that far in his cups ought to know good whiskey when he sees it. All the work in the mine's made me powerful thirsty."

"You know Hellfire don't let anybody drink while they're workin'."

"A good thing 'cuz you'd be soused all the time."

Sam Knight had to smile at the byplay. These were the last two miners left in his field hospital. The others had been moved to the shacks and tents provided for their usual habitation. The men arguing over Doc

Murtagh had been the most severely injured, and he wanted to keep an eye on them for another day or two.

He tried not to be too apparent as he looked from the men to Hellfire Bonham. The woman sat on a stool just outside the canvas roof, arguing with Dave Wilcox. The way the sun caught her hair turned it to a silver purer than the metal she scratched from the mountain. The elegant lines of her face belied her language. She might have been a fine lady waiting to go to the president's cotillion if it hadn't been for the scratches and cuts on her face from rooting around in the mine, and the burn marks on her fingers. Two others working for her had experience as blasting engineers, but she preferred to do the actual demolition work herself.

From what Wilcox said, she was quite a chemist, mixing up the nitroglycerin herself in a shack set off a quarter mile from the mine. If anything happened, she'd blow herself to kingdom come, but the Lucky Draw wouldn't be in any danger.

He admired her spunk. She didn't have others doing a job she could do, no matter how dangerous it was. Her no-nonsense manner, the way she dared convention working alongside her men, the bravery she showed in handling the tricky explosive all appealed to him. And she wasn't bad-looking, not by a mile or two.

She turned from Wilcox and stared at Knight as if she had felt him looking at her. Her bright blue eyes sparkled. She had slept enough to get rid of the bloodshot. When she looked at him, it was like her gaze went right through to his very soul.

That made him a little uncomfortable, but it also made him think she understood him and what he had been through without having to hear one word of his history. Hellfire Bonham accepted him as he was and didn't much care what he had gone through reaching the mouth of the Lucky Draw mine.

"Sam, come on over." Wilcox waved for him to join them.

Knight found himself wishing that Wilcox would find some chore to tend to so he could be alone with Helene, just for a few minutes. "The men are healing nicely. I'd keep them out of the mine and away from doing any heavy work for another week, but there's no reason you can't give them lighter duty."

"You sound like a military man," Hellfire said. "Were you an officer?"

Wilcox said, "He doesn't talk much about his past, boss."

213

Her eyes bored even deeper into Knight's soul. She finally nodded. "I can live with that."

"No reason for you to live with it or not," Knight said, "because that's the way it is. When those two are up and about, I'm heading back to Sierra Rojo. There are scores of miners waiting to sit at my table and lose their hard-won pay to me."

"A gambler." She shook her head and pushed a strand of her bobbed hair out of her eyes with an unconscious, brusque gesture. "I saw how you patched up my men. You're ten times the doctor that old sot is."

"Wait, Sam, don't argue. Just take it as a compliment." Wilcox looked anxious about something, as if Knight might pack up and leave on the spot.

"I've been on the trail long enough to know how to take care of injuries."

"You used that silver thread to tie off an artery," Hellfire said. "That's surgical work. Wait, no, I apologize. If you don't want to fess up to being a doctor, I'm not going to call you a liar."

"That's mighty kind of you." Knight wasn't sure if he was pleased or irritated. Hellfire Bonham was nobody's fool. She had seen enough of the world to know a doctor when one came into her camp and tended men ten times better than the man who called himself a doctor.

"How much do you make gambling?"

"I never bothered to count the money. Enough to live on."

"I'll pay you fifty dollars a month to do nothing but fix broken bones and put iodine on cuts."

"I can make that much in a single hand of seven-card stud."

"I'll make it a hundred a month."

Knight blinked. "Why so much?"

"There's fierce competition for miners on Red Mountain. There's got to be a couple dozen mines, but the real fight's between the Lucky Draw and the Blue-Eyed Bitch. Jefferson Avery will hire away the best, just to keep me from putting them to work in my mine. I've got to keep the men I have, and letting a doctor keep them in good shape goes a long way toward keeping them happy."

"Yeah, Sam. If the men are happy, they won't quit and go to work for Avery." Wilcox looked at Hellfire out of the corner of his eye as if expecting her to contradict him.

"It works both ways. Promise of a doctor at the Lucky Draw might lure his best men away, as if he has any." Hellfire snorted in

215

contempt at such an idea.

"I'm not a doctor."

"Who the hell cares? Word's already out that you know what you're doing. That fellow you tied up with the silver thread's boasting how he's got precious metal in his blood now. It doesn't matter what you say, it's what everyone believes that counts."

"Well, Miss Bonham —"

"Hellfire. Call me Hellfire. Or Helene." She graced him with a bold smile.

Knight saw how Wilcox reacted. He guessed Hellfire Bonham didn't let just anyone call her by her given name. Somehow, that tipped him toward accepting her offer to work at the Lucky Draw.

"He's mighty quick with that revolver, too, Hellfire. I saw him throw down on a gun-slick and he cleared leather before the other fellow was half out of the holster."

"A man of many talents, eh? I'm glad you're taking my job offer."

"I never said I would."

"Reading men comes easy enough for me. You're doing more than thinking it over. You're fixing to say yes."

"And he's a damned fine marksman, too," continued Wilcox, oblivious to the undercurrent between Knight and Hellfire. "He saved my bacon out on the trail going into

Ralston. We were down to a few rounds each, and he never missed. Not a one of them Apaches trying to lift our scalps dodged lead slung by Sam Knight."

Knight wanted to point out that the fight hadn't gone that way at all. Either Wilcox's memory was faulty or he embellished the story to get Hellfire to hire him. Wilcox had missed the silent agreement that had already passed between them.

"You need a contract all signed and proper, or will a handshake do? Seventy-five dollars a month." Hellfire thrust out her hand.

"You said a hundred." Knight forced himself to remain motionless. He felt that the slightest move would be vindication for her. She drove a hard bargain. He had to match her.

"Did I? The sun must be giving me heat-stroke." Hellfire fanned her face mockingly with her other hand and made as if she were going to faint.

"It's autumn, and the sun's not that hot."

"You can't be too careful about sunstroke, not out here in the desert, not this far up the mountainside where the air's thinner than a whore's promise." Hellfire waited for him to grasp her hand.

He did. He shook. And said, "A hundred

a month and the mine owner gets a checkup for sunstroke."

She clung to his hand just a moment longer than necessary to seal the deal. Knight didn't mind, even if her hand showed scars and chemical burns.

Her laugh was musical. Dave Wilcox looked from his boss to Sam and back, not following half of what had been said — and what had gone unsaid between them.

"Now what are you doing sitting around on your asses? Get to work. The Lucky Draw will be puking out silver by the ton again by the end of the month. Go on, get."

"Come on, Sam. When the boss gives an order, she means it."

Knight hesitated a moment. This was unfamiliar territory for him to explore. He had never worked for anyone else before, anyone who wasn't wearing a uniform. And he certainly had never thought the moment would come when he worked for a woman. He touched the brim of his hat and hurried after Wilcox. He thought he heard Hellfire say something, but it was too low for him to understand.

He glanced back over his shoulder, but she had already dropped back to talk with one of his patients — one of her miners. Hellfire Bonham was unlike any woman he had ever come across before. She was a breath of fresh air blowing across a stale world.

Tramping upslope, he got to the mouth of the mine where Wilcox already ordered a team around, getting timbers from the pile and carrying them deep into the ground to shore up the tunnel. Knight went to the stack of beams and stared at them. Something had bothered him before. It still did. Knight pulled out a knife and dug out a knot in the closest beam.

Wilcox came over and looked at Knight's handiwork. "What are you doing? If you want to whittle, go find yourself a piece of pinewood."

"There's something eating away at me. Or maybe it's eating away at the wood."

"Looks fine to me. We've been having a hard time getting enough wood for mine supports. Most all the trees have been cut down. There's a whale of a lot of competition for wood in these parts, with so many mines working on Red Mountain."

"There's nothing wrong with this one. Or this one." Knight drove his knife blade down hard. The tip barely penetrated. "What caused the collapse?"

"Hard to say. Some of the miners aren't as good working with wood as they are pick-

219

ing away at hard rock. A poorly placed beam might have caused the roof to cave in."

"Do you think it could have been sabotage?"

"Listen to you, Sam. You take a job that requires you to use your gun as well as a scalpel and you start seeing trouble around every bend in the road."

"What aren't you telling me?"

"Damn me if Hellfire didn't say the same thing, but then she's in a constant fight with Jefferson Avery over at the Blue-Eyed Bitch. They don't get along one little bit."

"So this Avery might do what he can to destroy the Lucky Draw?"

"I've never seen hide nor hair of him here." Wilcox pursed his lips in thought. "But then again, I've never laid eyes on the man. Only heard what Hellfire says about him, and she hates him with a fiery passion that'll burn the hair off a bull's balls."

Knight pulled his knife out and found a beam similar to the one he had noticed before. He shoved the blade into the end where a short cap of wood had been glued on. A little wiggling broke the cap off. Sand poured down to the ground.

"What the hell?" Wilcox knelt and let the sand run through his fingers. "Never in all my born days have I seen anything like that.

How'd it happen?"

"If you put a support like that in the mine what would happen?"

Wilcox scratched his head. "Damn me if I know. The wood's all hollowed out. That'd weaken it. But why fill it with sand?"

"To make it feel as if it had never been tampered with. Pick up a hollow beam and even the laziest miner would notice. Keep it weighed down and all you get are the usual complaints about hard work and heavy wood."

"So somebody hollowed out the beam, filled it with sand, and then glued a wood plug on the end so we wouldn't notice?"

"That's what it looks like." Knight went through the pile and carved big Xs on four more beams. "You'd better see if any of those already used in the mine are tampered with and replace them with good wood."

Wilcox bellowed orders. Sampson argued a bit, then Wilcox brought him over and showed him the sabotaged wood.

"I'll get the men hunting for more of them down in the mine, Dave. If I get my hands on whoever done this —" Sampson balled his hands into fists the size of Mason jars and smashed them together. He spun and began barking orders.

Knight had expected sparks to fly from

those rocky hands. He turned to Wilcox. "Where did you get the wood? Do you send out a crew to cut the trees?"

"Miners are too scarce in these parts to waste their time sawing down trees. I'm not sure who does it, but Hellfire hires a bunch of locals to supply the wood. They bring in firewood as well as the supports that go into the mine."

"Firewood's not as important."

"It keeps us warm at night. These mountains are mighty tall and the temperature drops like a rock, if you hadn't noticed."

"I have. I need to get back to Sierra Rojo and get my gear if I'm going to stay here at the mine." Knight hesitated, then asked, "When's the next load of support timbers due?"

"Any time now. Hellfire ordered a special delivery since we have so much of the Lucky Draw to shore up again."

"I'll be out of camp, so no need to come hunting me down."

"What if someone needs attending?" Wilcox winked broadly. "You never can tell when Hellfire might develop a case of sunstroke and need some personal attention."

"Unless I miss my guess, she got that moniker for a reason. Anybody getting too close is likely to get burned. Bad."

Wilcox went off, laughing at this. Knight poked through the pile of timbers and found one more with a glued-on cap that had been hollowed out. Grunting, he moved those beams off the pile and stacked them some distance away, where he covered them with a tarp. He brushed off his hands, then climbed up above the mine to get a better look at the lay of the land. The Lucky Draw dominated that section of Red Mountain, but dark tailings from other mines were visible both east and west. He wasn't a mining engineer, but from the look of the discarded rock, those mines weren't as large and the coloration told him something other than silver came out of the ground there.

He looked down the winding road and tried to find Sierra Rojo in the distance. Haze blocked his view, but he figured where the town lay in its hollow amid the Big Burro Mountains. Blue Creek ran past it, giving needed water. Somewhere south of Burro Peak lay Knight's Peak. He tried to make out even a lump in the distance and couldn't. He had no idea who the mountain was named after. It certainly wasn't him or any of his family. None of the East Texas Knights had ever traveled that far west.

His thoughts drifted. Had he come far

enough west to avoid the troubles in Pine Knob? Nobody could track him there since he hadn't had any destination in mind when he left Amelia Parker back in Buffalo Springs. A catch came to his throat. Amelia had been so lovely. The type of woman he needed to settle down.

To settle down *then* . . . before he'd realized Gerald Donnelly would never rest until he hunted down the man who had blown off his trigger finger and crippled him with the single slash of a scalpel. As Knight looked at the mountains, he wondered at the type of woman he needed.

"Helene." The name came unbidden to his lips.

She had obviously taken a shine to him, but he knew nothing about her other than what he had seen. Running the mine, she was as good as anyone he could imagine. Brave, strong, willing to do whatever it took to keep her men safe even at the risk of her own life.

He pictured her carrying the volatile nitroglycerin into the mine herself, then working alongside him to free Wilcox and the other two trapped in a drift. It took a special woman to do all that.

Knight jerked from his reverie when a wagon rattled up the road to the mine. He shielded his eyes from the noonday sun and saw the load — freshly cut timbers. Two men rode in the back while the driver cursed and shouted at his lop-eared mules, occasionally resorting to cracking a long whip directly over the team. Despite the threat posed by that whip, the mules never changed gait, never pulled harder, never sped up. They moved at their own pace, no matter the driver's desires.

Knight made his way down the mountain to a spot where he could watch the wagon come to a halt by the stack of beams. The two men in the wagon bed jumped down and began unloading their cargo. The driver secured the reins around the brake handle, then went to the pile.

Knight smiled grimly. The driver examined each of the beams, even tugging at the end of one as if checking to see whether the end had been glued on. Finding none of the hollowed-out beams, he went to the wagon bed and lent a hand helping the other two men. When they finished, the driver disappeared, only to come back with Hellfire Bonham a few minutes later. She didn't examine the beams, only counted them to be sure the driver hadn't shorted her.

Money changed hands. She went back down the mountain in the direction of the makeshift hospital, and the driver turned his rig around and, with the two helpers in the back, started back down Red Mountain. Knight waited for the wagon to round the first bend and drive out of sight before he went to the newly stacked supports.

He marked three more with huge cut Xs before mounting and riding after the wagon. Solving part of the Lucky Draw's problems was a good day's work. Now it was time to complete the picture so he could tell Hellfire the source of all her troubles.

Keeping far enough back and letting the wagon roll downhill faster than he rode proved a problem. The driver kept the brake on and skidded along the slope most of the way. Knight impatiently waited more than once so the driver stayed far enough ahead, but eventually the wagon reached the base of the mountain and rattled away toward Sierra Rojo.

Knight picked up the pace and narrowed the distance between him and the wagon. He rode past the point where the two helpers were dropped off and kept after the empty wagon. It hardly surprised him when the driver didn't head for Sierra Rojo but took a side road. Cutting across country, Knight intended to cut him off from his destination, whatever it was.

The wooded area grew thicker, making riding difficult. Rather than duck constantly to keep from banging his head on low limbs, he dismounted and walked his horse for almost a mile. He was glad he did when he came upon a clearing. Not twenty yards away the driver stood next to his rig, smoking a cigarette and looking around nervously.

Knight stepped back into deeper shadow when a man rode from the far side of the clearing. His black hat was adorned with silver conchas that dazzled in the sun. He wore a fancy vest and a split-tail coat that was better suited for a fancy ball than riding around the New Mexico Territory countryside. Knight caught sight of a pearl-handled revolver tucked into his belt as he dismounted and went to the wagon driver.

Try as he might, Knight only heard snatches of the conversation, but he saw the fancy-dressed man reach into a coat pocket and hand over a wad of greenbacks. The driver gestured wildly, then held up his right hand showing three fingers. Three sabotaged beams? Knight only knew the man with silver conchas peeled off another sheaf of greenbacks, slapped the driver on the back, then mounted and rode away without so much as a backwards look.

The driver counted his money carefully, then tucked it into his shirt pocket before climbing into the driver's box and turning his wagon around to retrace his route to the main road.

Knight watched each of the men go. Following the driver was pointless. He was a hired hand, a flunky. The well-dressed man with the money called the shots, but Knight saw no reason to track him down now. Tugging on his horse's reins, he mounted and rode for Sierra Rojo to gather his belongings so he could return to the Lucky Draw.

To the Lucky Draw and Hellfire Bonham.

CHAPTER 15

"I thought West Texas was bad. I didn't think I would ever see anywhere worse." Rance Spurgeon spat the grit from his mouth and wiped his lips with his sleeve. He spat again and pushed his hat back. "I was wrong."

Spurgeon's sour tone worried Hesseltine. "Texas wasn't so bad. I liked Pine Knob." He shifted in the saddle, looking around the rocky landscape. Low sandy hills rose on either side of the road, perfect for Indians to hide before they ambushed unwary travelers. "They had trees and lakes there."

They had come far after Dr. Samuel Knight. Hesseltine felt in his bones they were close. He also felt Spurgeon might decide to quit the Pinkertons or simply disappear, leaving him by himself on the trail.

"Get the dirt out of your eyes and look. Ahead, Rance, ahead. Those are mountains unlike anything you will ever see in Texas.

From what I understand, you can find entire forests of pine and juniper and something called piñon. And a huge river called the Gila, after the poisonous lizard that lives in these deserts." He waited to see if any of that talk about trees or deadly animals perked up his partner.

It failed.

"That's a kind of pine. Piñon. Or fir or spruce or one of them evergreen trees. Think of the shade they offer. Sit beside that raging river or any of the streams that feed it, so cool, damp, peaceful." Hesseltine saw the mention of such scenery did nothing to brighten Spurgeon's disposition. He was at the point of giving up.

"I want to get back to Chicago. Hell, I'd even settle for going back to Baltimore. It's too lonesome out here for my taste."

"We're not far from Ralston City. Everything we've learned says that all the gold-seeking men from Buffalo Springs had to pass through there on the way to richer strikes."

"Billie Ralston? Isn't that the name of the miner who struck it rich?"

"I assume that Ralston the miner is the same as the Ralston the town's founder. They tend to have an inflated opinion of themselves once they have more money than Croesus."

"What difference does it make? Who cares about any of it?" Spurgeon sank down in the saddle, eyes ahead and looking glum.

Hesseltine knew that cheering his partner up wasn't going to happen until they got Knight in their sights. Only successful completion of their assignment would brighten Spurgeon's outlook.

Spurgeon pointed to the north where a cloud of dust moved along, paralleling the road. "We're in for a fight," he said, perking up. He tapped his fingers on the butt of his revolver slung in its cross-draw holster. "I'm in the mood to kill something. An Apache would be good. I've never shot one of them."

"That's a dust devil. The miniature tornado that whips along in the desert," said Hesseltine.

"No, it's not. Riders. A goodly sized bunch of riders. See?" Spurgeon pointed as golden flashes appeared in the middle of the cloud.

"You have sharp eyes, my friend. It's more likely an army patrol. The sun is reflecting off their brass buttons."

"The Apaches might have stolen the jackets of an ambushed patrol."

Hesseltine fell silent when he saw that Spurgeon only sought a reason to argue.

Being on the trail so long wore on both of them. Spurgeon wanted to kill someone, and Hesseltine wasn't sure if he didn't want to kill his own partner. Spurgeon had become unbearable since they had crossed the Rio Grande. Finishing the assignment quickly took on more importance for both of them, even if each had a different reason. Spurgeon wanted to return to Chicago. Hesseltine wanted civilized society again.

Moving on, he heaved a sigh of relief when he spotted a faded sign marking the edge of Ralston. The town had fewer than five hundred people living in it, if the number scrawled across the bottom of the sign was to be believed, but that was more than enough to satisfy Hesseltine that he had arrived in civilization again.

"Where do we start?" Spurgeon asked. "There's a saloon. Even if they don't know anything about Knight, we can use a drink."

"And food," Hesseltine said, patting his bulging belly. "One thing about being on the trail is missing so many meals."

He dismounted and went directly into the saloon, not waiting for his partner. Hesseltine considered having Spurgeon go his own way. The two of them could cover twice the area in the same time if they split up. Although he was the senior Pinkerton agent, he knew better than to actually give orders to his partner. Spurgeon didn't take kindly to being ordered around.

As he looked around the saloon, he saw that it didn't matter. The few men bellied up to the bar could be pumped in just a few minutes for any information they might have. A casual mention, a shot of whiskey, a friendly smile, those were the tickets to getting what they wanted.

"We don't even know if Knight came this direction. Just because the other men from Buffalo Springs came this way doesn't mean he did." Spurgeon rapped his knuckles on the bar and called, "Two beers. Make 'em cold. We've been on the trail."

"Coming right up." The barkeep drew the beers and set them in front of his new customers. "You gents passing through? Which direction are you heading?"

"Does it matter?"

"Only that I'd like to know what's happening west of town if you came from that direction. I got family out on a ranch and heard the Apaches are massacring any white folks they find. My damned fool brother-in-law insisted on taking my sister and her brood into the Sonora desert where God Himself ain't safe."

"We came from the east," Hesseltine said.

233

"We got separated from a friend a while back and are trying to find him."

"We get a fair number of drifters through here. And folks lookin' to be prospectors and makin' their fortunes with a gold or silver strike. Why, the gent this here town's named after, William Ralston, did that very thing. He got so rich he moved to San Francisco and has a fancy-ass house up on Russian Hill, or so I've been told."

"His name's Knight. Our friend. You know of him?" Spurgeon drained the mug and set it down on the bar with a click.

"Knight? Well, now — wait a second, gents. I just made my nut for the day."

Hesseltine glanced up into the mirror behind the bar. He heaved a sigh of resignation. A dozen black soldiers crowded in, nudging each other and looking like they could drink every drop of beer the barkeep drew all night long.

"There're other saloons in town. We ought to go." Spurgeon eyed the soldiers with disdain.

Hesseltine started to ask if his partner had ever served in the army. He knew so little about him, but the lack of respect he showed for men in uniform — or was it only blue-coats? — made him think Spurgeon might have sympathies more in line with the South than anyone else in Chicago. Still, the North had its share of Southern sympathizers. He had heard of the copperheads and marveled at how impractical their approach had been to reconciling with the Confederacy rather than bringing the war to a conclusion.

He and Spurgeon left. Questioning the barkeep didn't look too promising, not with him serving a saloon filled with buffalo soldiers. Out in the street Hesseltine looked around and nudged Spurgeon, alerting him to another saloon a few doors down. An officer, brass gleaming and saber dangling at his side, entered there.

"The enlisted men come here, the officers go there. If anyone has been entrusted with finding Knight, it would be a lieutenant of cavalry." Hesseltine's spirits rose. He enjoyed being a detective, piecing together small tidbits of information and tracking down a quarry. Spurgeon only cared for the actual arrest, especially if it included gunfire.

They walked into the other saloon. Hesseltine inclined his head, sending Spurgeon toward the back of the long, narrow room to be sure they were alone, then brushed dust off his fancy clothing and went to a spot at the bar a few feet from the lieutenant.

"Whiskey, my good man," Hesseltine

called to the barkeep. As the liquor was poured, Hesseltine paused and, as if seeing the officer for the first time, said, "A toast to you, sir, for protecting our frontier."

The lieutenant's eyes narrowed as if he thought he was being mocked.

Hesseltine moved quickly to allay such suspicion. "And one for our noble defender, bartender. Yes sir, one for the cavalry officer."

"You mean you want to buy him a shot, too?"

"I do, good sir. Hell, no. No, I don't!"

The lieutenant began to take umbrage. Hesseltine timed his response perfectly.

"Buy this man a bottle. He deserves it, patrolling out in the hot, dry desert, fighting savages, bringing outlaws to justice. Yes, give him an entire bottle." Hesseltine slapped a ten-dollar gold piece on the bar so hard it rang, the echo filling the empty saloon.

"You're not mocking me?"

"I am praising you, Captain."

"I'm only a lieutenant."

"But not for long, Lieutenant . . . ?" Hesseltine prompted.

"Lieutenant Billings, 25th U.S. Colored Infantry Regiment, Company B, 9th Cavalry Regiment."

"To you, Lieutenant Billings." Hesseltine knocked back his drink and almost gagged. Even used to frontier trade whiskey, this burned his gullet and choked him. "That's mighty potent liquor. I see why you drink here. Away from the darkies."

Billings bristled at that. "They're fine men, brave and loyal. Better than any other company I have ever commanded."

"All the better that they have a stalwart officer leading them." Hesseltine trod carefully, feeling out the officer. He saw the ring on the man's finger. "A West Point graduate inspires those under his command."

"How? Oh, this." Billings rolled the ring around. "I am a Point graduate, but I missed serving in the war by a few months."

"The fights on the frontier are as fierce as anything in Virginia or Pennsylvania."

Hesseltine got the man talking about Fort Bayard and a few of the excursions against the Apaches.

"Not a month back I led my men into Mexico, chasing down a band of Warm Springs Apaches. We lost them just over the border."

"You pursued into a foreign country? That's mighty brave. I've heard that the Federales don't take kindly to U.S. Army troopers coming across the border."

"I was in hot pursuit, but the Apaches know the mountains better than I know the back of my own hand. We got turned around in the Peloncillos and gave up. As luck would have it, we returned in time to rescue two white men beset by a smaller band."

Hesseltine poured him another drink. He stepped away to see that Spurgeon had taken a seat at the first table behind the officer. The Pinkerton detective listened intently, taking notes in a small notebook. When Hesseltine finished, Spurgeon would have a complete map to show of the countryside and where Billings had patrolled. From the mention of the two rescued by the patrol, he had hit pay dirt. All he had to do was keep the lieutenant's story lubricated with more rotgut whiskey.

"You did save them, didn't you? It would be a pity to think of two white men getting their scalps lifted."

"Not only did I save them, I took them to Fort Bayard to report directly to my captain. I thought they had information that'd be useful tracking down other Apache raiders."

"Did these two have names?"

"Why're you asking that?"

Hesseltine smoothly refilled the lieutenant's glass as well as his own. He lofted it

238

and smiled. "So I can toast them personally."

"Don't remember. It was in my report." The lieutenant spat toward a cuspidor and hit the splash plate nailed onto the wood bar. "One was Wilcox. Yeah, that was it." His words came out slurred. He had knocked back quite a few shots in a short time.

Hesseltine made sure he had another full glass in front of him, hoping it would pry loose the other name.

But Knight might have decided on a summer name as so many outlaws did. And who was the other man? Knight had left Buffalo Springs at midnight, riding alone.

"The captain gave you a commendation for their rescue, I am sure." Hesseltine saw how the officer tensed and closed in on himself. He clutched the shot glass in both hands and pulled it in close to his chest as if he hid a winning poker hand. "Didn't Wilcox and Knight testify to your bravery?" Hesseltine tossed the name out to see if Billings contradicted him. He held down his elation when the ploy worked.

"Knight kept his damn mouth shut. He let Wilcox do all the talking. Shoulda tossed both of them in the stockade. What were they doin' out on the road like that? Nothin' but targets. Injun targets, both of 'em."

"That Knight fellow sounds like a real scalawag, not speaking up for you."

"Like all the rest of them gamblers. Close-mouthed."

"Now where would a gambler be going along the road? Wouldn't it be here to Ralston?"

"Nowhere else along the road. The Ben Holladay Stagecoach Company keeps the road all open, runnin' 'tween here and El Paso, then over to Yuma."

"But Knight and Wilcox weren't looking to catch the stage, were they?"

Hesseltine looked up when the barkeep chimed in.

"I remember them gents. The Wilcox fellow told how they'd come in from Fort Bayard and how the army had tried to throw them in the stockade."

"What of Knight?" Hesseltine felt rather than saw Spurgeon behind him. He was like a pointer on a pheasant hunt, all alert and ready to go crashing through the brush to bring back the bird.

"Both of them had a drink, then said they was goin' on to Sierra Rojo. Knight was a gambler, he said, but Wilcox wanted to work in the mines."

"Not prospect? Either of them?"

240

"Naw, they wasn't dressed like prospectors. I could believe the one was a gambler. He had the quickness in his fingers to deal seconds and off the bottom of the deck. I offered him a job here, but he wouldn't have anything to do with it. He and his partner were bound and determined to go on to Sierra Rojo."

"Figgers. They were shady characters. Thass the right place for shady characters."

Hesseltine plucked the whiskey bottle and the half that remained off the bar, shoved the cork in it, and tossed it to Spurgeon. His partner caught it in one hand, turned, and was almost out the swinging batwing doors before the lieutenant protested.

"You b-bought me that b-bottle."

Hesseltine ignored the complaint. He mounted and trailed Spurgeon from town on their way to Sierra Rojo. The end of the trail was so close he could taste it.

CHAPTER 16

Sam Knight wasn't in a particular hurry to return to the Lucky Draw. He had too much to think over. After leaving Buffalo Springs, his plan to become a gambler had worked just fine — for a week or so. He was good at poker, but he realized he had played only miners with no sense of winning. They played for the release it gave them, the companionship that had nothing to do with swinging a pickax, and, he realized, the thrill of *maybe* winning. There were only a couple miners who had ever sat across from him that had any idea what to do with their money if they'd won. Most would gamble away a windfall until it was lost, buy a round or two of drinks for the house, or go off to find a lady of the night to steal the money from them.

In spite of the long and tiring hours, in spite of the smoky and noisy surroundings, Knight had enjoyed his stint as a gambler.

242

His nimble fingers handled the cards well, and he was a rarity among professionals. He refused to cheat, even when it was easy. Too many of the miners almost begged him to lie about what he held as he laid down the cards, being too drunk to see straight. Everything on the table before them was seen in pairs because of doubled vision. His code of honor was set in stone. He played to win, but he also played fair.

That notion rose repeatedly as he rode back to the Lucky Draw mine. All that he had encountered, all that he had endured, he always played fair. He wasn't sure he had come close to giving Gerald Donnelly his due back in Pine Knob, but he felt no guilt about crippling the man. If anything, Donnelly deserved more punishment than he had received. And Victoria? Knight's thoughts of his former wife were confused. She and Donnelly deserved each other, but he had real regrets about Amelia Parker. Leaving her as he had tore at his heart, and he knew it had hers, too, but it had been necessary.

Hector Alton had been a gunfighter intent on killing Knight and anyone near him. He had tried to match Knight's speed and accuracy with a gun and had fallen short. Milo Hannigan had been worse. He had once

243

counted Knight as a friend, and turning on him for a few dollars hadn't bothered him one iota. Gunning him down had been more self-defense and defense of others whose lives Knight valued than anything else, but it proved one thing. Gerald Donnelly would keep sending killers. Knight might be lucky a few more times in stopping them with a quick draw and accurate shot, but eventually one would end his life. Or worse, begin killing those Knight loved most.

Amelia Parker didn't realize it, but he had done the right thing by leaving without so much as a whisper in her ear. If she didn't know where he was, Donnelly's killers would ignore her.

His horse finally topped the long trail up the steep side of Red Mountain. He sat for a moment, studying the mine. The original mouth remained closed, with nobody even working to reopen it. The new way into the shaft that Hellfire Bonham had blasted had been framed in during his short absence, and ore cart tracks had been laid through it, vanishing into the hillside. The men worked diligently to burrow back into the rock and bring out tons of silver-bearing ore. A sizable pile of the black rock with silver highlights had piled up again.

"You took your sweet time getting back, Sam."

He looked down at Dave Wilcox. The man's face oozed blood in several places from shallow scratches. One eye was bruised and partially swollen shut. His clothing had seen better days — and he grinned ear to ear. For all the minor damage he endured being the mine super, banging around in the rocky shaft in near pitch black darkness, he enjoyed the job.

"I thought being a day or two late would help you out."

"How's that?" Wilcox held up his hand to forestall the answer, turned, and barked an order. Two men carrying a length of iron track worked their way into the new mine mouth and vanished. Wilcox turned back to his friend.

"You don't have to pay me," Knight continued. "That'll help out the payroll for this period."

"I'd as soon pay you as put up with numbskulls like those two." Wilcox shook his head. "They have one job: carry the track into the mine. They get turned around and would've gone down a drift not where I need the track the most. We blasted a new section this morning."

"I thought I heard the blast at the base of

245

the mountain."

"Sweetest work you ever did see. We drilled in eight holes, Hellfire poured in her nitro, and when it detonated, we turned a good ten feet of solid rock to gravel. Richest damned silver sulfide ore you could want spilled out all over the mine floor. All we have to do is use the mercury amalgam to get the silver out and —"

"Whoa. I know some chemistry but not anything when it comes to mining."

"Nope, your chemistry has to do with fixing up people. Should I start calling you Doc?"

"No need." Knight dismounted, still irritated that his background had come out in such convincing fashion. "I should find a place to sleep and stash my gear."

"The stable's around the side of the hill and —" Wilcox cut off his words when a loud cry from the direction of the mine interrupted him. "Damn me, I knew there'd be problems with those two." He ran for the mine where one of the men who had carried the section of track sat, holding his hand.

Knight dismounted and trailed behind his friend, a diagnosis already formed by the time he arrived. He pushed Wilcox out of the way, then took the injured man's wrist and tugged gently. The scream almost deafened him.

"You busted a couple fingers," he said. "What happened?"

"The rail slipped as I was lowerin' it. Came down hard on my hand."

"I'll get you splinted up and back to work before you know it."

"How long will he be out of the mine?" Wilcox glared at the miner.

"You're beginning to sound like you own the mine, Dave. Is the tent hospital still set up?"

"Yeah, Hellfire decided it was a good place to keep these slackers away from the workers. Don't want any of the others getting the idea to injure themselves so they can have a few hours off."

"This one's going to regret mashing his hand. Come on." Knight tugged again on the miner's wrist and got a squeal of pain more like a pig than a human.

Wilcox ordered the injured man's partner to tend to Knight's horse. Knight was pleased to see the canvas still in place and flapping lightly in the afternoon breeze. He worked for almost twenty minutes, setting the broken finger bones and then taping them all up using small wood splints he carved from a hunk of pine left in the

247

makeshift hospital. When he finished, he chased the man back to work.

Knight stood and looked around, wondering what to do. He decided to find where he would bunk down and see that his horse was properly tended. As he worked his way around the tailings, he saw a shack with its door open and someone moving around inside. The wind blew in his direction, and he gagged on the smell. In spite of that, he went to investigate.

He stopped in the doorway. Hellfire Bonham sat on a low stool, bent over a worktable filled with beakers and jars of chemicals he could not name. She had no problem finding the ones she wanted, in spite of the bottles lacking labels. She poured expertly, then rocked back from the table as her mixture began to bubble and spew noxious fumes.

She waved her hand above the beaker to disperse the fumes.

"More nitroglycerin?" Knight asked.

"Experimenting. This might be better, not as volatile." She sucked on her hand, then spat. "I spilled some, and it tastes like hell."

"Let me look." Knight went in and took her hand in his, turning it over and frowning at the burn. "You need some kind of salve to put on burns like this. You'll be scarred if you don't take care of any injury right away."

"You decide to join up? Be doctor for the Lucky Draw? I wondered if you would come back or just keep on riding once you got down the mountain."

"We shook on the deal."

She looked at the Colt Navy slung at his hip and then pointed. "Wilcox says you know how to use that. A gun might be more valuable than patching up men."

"Or women." Knight bent, scooped up some dirt from the floor and spit on her burn, then smeared the dirt over it until it was covered in a thin layer of mud. "That's not too sanitary, but you want to keep the air off it."

"You won't have the urge to patch up holes in men you shoot, will you?"

"Not if they're trying to plug me. What caused the feud?"

"Most everybody is out to do in the competition, but we do it with a smile. It gets nasty between me and Jefferson Avery over at his worthless hole in the ground . . . that he doesn't know his ass from."

Knight wondered at her bitterness. He considered that he worked for the woman now and ought to tell her some of his suspicions. "Did you ever think that the

249

mine collapse might have been sabotage? I showed Wilcox how some of the beams were hollowed out and filled with sand. Used in the mine, they'd hold up the walls and roof for a spell, then the weight would cause them to buckle and snap."

She frowned, thought on what he said, then exploded. Her arm swept the beaker off the table and smashed it against the cabin wall. It sizzled and hissed as it ate through the wood on its way to extinction on the dirt floor. "Son of a bitch. I should have checked the men doing the cutting and bringing me the timber. They work for all the mines, so I thought I was getting a fair deal."

"You might have gotten a great price since they wanted you to use the defective beams. I followed the empty wagon down the hill and watched the driver get paid by a dude. I was too far away to hear, but I'd bet all I own that the money was for selling you the defective wood."

"What did the dude look like? Tall, a handsome devil riding a stallion, small, neat mustache all gussied up and waxed with gum Arabic and a scented oil?"

"I couldn't see any mustache, and he never dismounted so I don't know how tall he is." Knight shrugged. "I can't say that he was handsome, either."

"You called him a dude. Why's that? His clothing was flashy?"

"He was a real fashion plate. The coat, vest, and trousers must have set him back a hundred dollars. And the hat, well, he had enough silver conchas on it to blind anyone catching a reflection."

"And his pistol? Did you see it?"

"He never drew, but his coat pulled back and I saw a pearl-handed piece. You know him, don't you?"

"You saw Jefferson Avery paying off the man who fixed the timbers so my miners would get killed. Yeah, I know him. Damned if I don't know him. Without a doubt, that is Jefferson Avery you saw."

"Your rival."

"My rival now. He owns the Blue-Eyed Bitch mine." She turned to Knight and batted her eyes.

At first he didn't understand, then he did.

"You figured it out real quick," she said. "*I'm* the mine's namesake."

"How'd that happen?" The words slipped out before Knight had a chance to swallow them.

"Me and Jeff were married. It didn't end well between us because of his philandering ways, but I shouldn't have to tell a bright

251

man like you that."

Knight wondered how he had gotten himself into a feud between two hard-edged mine owners who used to be married to each other. Family fights were bad. Between former spouses had to be worse.

Especially when one resorted to sabotage and the other relished the idea of mixing up nitroglycerin and blowing rock to hell and gone.

CHAPTER 17

"You're sure he's the one you saw getting paid off by Avery?" Hellfire Bonham stood with arms crossed over her chest, her blue eyes like chips of ice as she stared at the timber wagon driver.

"He's the one," Knight said. "Why are you still getting beams delivered by him?"

"No reason to tip off Avery we're on to him."

"I'll be sure to check the beams." Knight started to go to the pile, but Hellfire grabbed his arm and pulled him back.

He spun around and found himself facing her, their faces inches apart. She held onto him a second longer than needed, and Knight found that he didn't mind. But she was the owner, his boss. Anything but business between them only spelled trouble.

More trouble, he mentally amended. The Lucky Draw had an ocean of trouble lapping all around it. Acting on what he felt for Helene Bonham would only lead to difficulty sorting out his intentions. He was drawn to her as a woman, but those feelings had only meant trouble in the past.

"Wilcox is testing the beams. Don't get involved."

"But —" Knight wondered at how she'd phrased it and repeated, "Get involved?"

"Stay here with me."

He smiled just a little. "You don't need a bodyguard. Why?"

"Might be I'm feeling lonesome."

Knight saw emotions fleetingly cross her round face that convinced him she felt about him the way he did about her. There was a definite attraction, but it was a moth flying close to fire. The attraction led to danger.

He looked away, feeling as uneasy as a young buck asking the sweet young thing to a barn dance. He caught his breath when he saw Wilcox talking with the wagon driver. Money changed hands and a strongbox was heaved into the rear of the now empty wagon. Unlike before, the two men working for the driver stayed behind as the wagon pulled out and started down the winding road leading back to Sierra Rojo.

"My super just hired two new miners," Hellfire said.

Something in the way she said that put Knight on guard. "What if they helped sabotage the beams?"

"Then they won't want to go into the mine. Does it look as if they're hanging back?"

"They've picked up pickaxes and are heading into the mine," Knight said.

"Then they're innocent. They didn't have anything to do with hollowing out the beams."

Before Knight could say anything more, the ground shook. His first thought was another cave-in, but no dust billowed from the mouth of the mine. He looked over Hellfire's head in the direction of her shack where she mixed up the nitroglycerin. Nothing. Slowly, he turned and saw a cloud of white smoke rising from beyond the edge of the road. Hurrying, he got to a point looking down the side of the mountain. Not a hundred yards lower the road had vanished.

"Now that's a real shame," Hellfire said, her voice cold. "Get a crew down there to rebuild the road."

"The driver —"

"I don't think there'll be enough of him found to bury. Leave the pieces for the coyotes." She started away, but Knight grabbed her arm.

"What did you do?"

"Don't ask questions if you can't stand up to the answers." She moved closer, their bodies pressed together. She looked up at him. "Don't tell me you haven't used that iron slung at your side. I'm not as good with a revolver as I am other weapons." She stood on tiptoe and surprised him with a quick kiss. With that, she darted away.

"You two, get shovels!" Dave Wilcox formed a work crew to go down the road.

Knight joined him. "What happened?"

"An explosion. I gave Thomas a box to deliver for Hellfire. If we can find it, we'll figure some other way to get it delivered."

"But the wagon blew up," Knight insisted.

"Looks that way." Wilcox directed his men to work on fixing the road while two others peered over the verge.

As Wilcox worked, Knight joined the pair looking downward. Only splinters remained of the wagon. The driver was nowhere to be seen. Knight remembered what Hellfire had said about leaving the chunks for the coyotes. She knew what he'd find. Try as he might, he saw nothing of the iron box the driver had been carting to Sierra Rojo, and he had deep suspicions as to why the box would never be found.

The road's repair took form so the mine

wouldn't be cut off from town. Knight wandered around and finally found what he had been hunting for. He reached out and cut his finger on a sharp piece of metal embedded in the solid rock above the portion of road that had been blown away.

"What do you have there, Sam?" Wilcox leaned on a shovel and wiped sweat from his forehead. "Damn me if it doesn't look like a knife blade."

"It's metal from the strongbox. I saw land mines like that during the war. If you try to contain an explosion, it'll be even more powerful."

"Thomas put explosives in the box? You mean that son of a bitch tried to steal nitro from the Lucky Draw! Damn me!"

Knight had a different theory that fit the facts a whole lot better, but he didn't correct his friend. He remembered what Helene had said about fighting with different weapons. In a crude way, justice had been done since Thomas had been directly responsible for killing men trapped in the Lucky Draw when it collapsed.

He hiked back up the road, a coldness settling on him. War had been declared. Jefferson Avery had caused the first deaths, and Hellfire Bonham retaliated. Knight had seen such family feuds before, and they never ended well for either side. He rested his hand on the Colt Navy slung at his side. Worse than a blood feud, he had chosen sides. He doubted Avery would allow Thomas's death to go unavenged. Thomas was only a pawn and probably didn't matter one bit to the Blue-Eyed Bitch mine owner, but the loss of a pawn had to force a response.

The rest of the day passed quickly. Knight kept busy setting up a more permanent hospital but was interrupted when Hellfire came in.

She hardly looked around. "Come with me."

Knight bristled at her tone.

She saw his reaction and softened her words a little. "I need you to ride with me. As bodyguard. Please."

"You're the boss." Knight finished putting away the few instruments he had. He had found his very first medical bag back in Pine Knob and had brought it along with him. As much as he had wanted to cut his ties with the past, parting with it had been impossible when he rode out of Buffalo Springs. Those few instruments used when he had been a medical student were proving useful.

"Strap on your gun. It's that kind of ride."

Knight said nothing as he did as he was

told. The revolver rode easy on his hip, a weight he had come to accept as part of his life. He made sure it slipped in and out of the holster, then nodded. "Where are we going?"

"Just watch my back. I'm not sure meeting with Pedro Ramirez is a good idea."

"The Blue-Eyed Bitch's superintendent?"

"Yeah, I'm meeting with my mortal enemy's right-hand man." She smiled crookedly. "Life was getting too relaxed. This will shake up things."

"You want me along if you're riding into a trap?" Knight tried to catch her expression, but Hellfire turned from him as she stepped up into the saddle.

Astride her white horse, she pointed down the road. Knight hurried to catch up with her. They rode at a brisk clip, going past the spot where the wagon had exploded. He was pleased at the speed and skill shown repairing the road that was the mine's lifeline to Sierra Rojo. All supplies came up the winding trail. The part of rock that had been blown away was shored up with a small bridge. There would be hell to pay when the spring rains came. It would wash out after the first shower. It might even be difficult going when snow and ice turned the entire road slippery.

"Yeah, they did a good job. It's always best to have good men working for you."

"Is that why you hired me?"

"Sam, Sam," she said, shaking her head. Her blond hair poking out from under her hat swayed gently with the movement. "Don't go fishing for compliments. You're better than that. Now, I'd expect Dave Wilcox to want to hear more good things about himself. That man's got problems with how he thinks of his own abilities, but not you. Why's that? How'd you get so all-fired confident in yourself?"

"What I've been through is worse than anything I'll face from here on out."

"You lose a patient? Wait, don't give me that guff about not being a doctor. I've seen plenty of sawbones in my day and dreaded most of them."

"Like Doc Murtagh?"

"He was available. I sent him packing when you signed on. I'm afraid the marshal might come arrest me for turning that son of a bitch loose on Sierra Rojo or Ralston or whatever saloon he floats into."

"I didn't think Sierra Rojo had any law. I didn't see any in Ralston City, for all that."

"Just the buffalo soldiers from over at Fort Bayard, but they've got their hands full with the Apaches. I swear, if they don't do

260

something to get all of them back onto the reservation, this whole country's going to be locked in war that nobody can win."

"Like the fight between you and Jefferson Avery?" Knight knew he was on treacherous ground with that question. He needed to find out where he stood and what Helene expected from him. If it came to gunplay, he wouldn't turn and run, but he wasn't a killer. He had seen Hector Alton and how he showed such contempt for everyone else, and Milo Hannigan had come to think a few dollars outweighed anyone's life. And it hadn't mattered if it was man, woman, or child.

"That goes deep and that goes personal. I didn't mind him fooling around behind my back, but he should never have done it with . . . her."

Knight said nothing as he brought his horse alongside the woman's. They had reached the road into Sierra Rojo before he knew it, but she didn't ride for the town. She found a game trail that meandered around the base of Red Mountain.

They rode for almost a half mile before she finally spoke again.

"It was my sister he was cheating with. My own sister. She should have known better than to let a snake like Jeff into her bed."

261

"Is she still with him?" Knight saw the way her shoulders tensed.

She sat a little straighter and stared straight ahead. Her grinding teeth rivaled the clop-clop of the horses' hooves against the stony trail. "He claims she ran off with one of his miners. I think he killed her."

"Why?"

"If I knew for sure, I'd walk up to him and shove a bottle of nitro into his mouth just to watch him blow up. I'd want to see his expression before he was blown to kingdom come. I would. I swear." She took a deep breath.

In spite of himself, Knight watched the way her breasts rose and fell under her duster. "But she might be in some other boomtown living it up with the miner?"

"I got rich making crazy bets. Nobody thought the Lucky Draw was worth the eight-dollar bet I made in the card game, and nobody was all that upset when I made the inside straight. But I knew there was silver there, and I was right."

"And you know Avery killed your sister?"

"Something like that." Hellfire drew rein. The arroyo ahead had already turned inky as the sun set and shadows claimed the rocky ravine. She stood in the stirrups and shielded her eyes against the light. "There he is. Keep a sharp lookout."

"He asked to meet you?"

"Pedro is a snake in the grass, but he's more the back shooter kind of snake. When I asked to bring you along, he had no problem with that."

"That might mean there are snipers waiting to kill us both."

"He told me to bring my whole damned crew. I hinted I just might. You'd better be as good as the rest of my miners combined, Sam." Hellfire hesitated a moment and in a voice almost too low for him to hear, added, "I suspect you are."

She snapped the reins and made her way down into the arroyo where Pedro Ramirez waited patiently on foot. His horse tried to nibble at a mesquite bush without getting a nose full of thorns.

Knight rode along the crumbling dirt bank, weaving in and out between clumps of prickly pear cactus and the mesquite bushes. A few greasewood bushes dared the arroyo rim and clumps of buffalo grass poked up, showing there wasn't any grazing going on. If there had been, the cattle would have gotten succulent feed in an otherwise barren stretch of desert.

He rode back, watching carefully for any movement in the shadows. When he heard a rustling directly under him, he drew the Colt in one easy move, cocked it, and pointed it at the arroyo floor. A startled rabbit froze, its eyes glowing red-orange in the last rays of sunlight. He shifted his aim to cover Pedro Ramirez, but the Blue-Eyed Bitch's super posed no threat. He stood with his arms held out at his sides, away from any gun that might be in a holster or tucked into his belt.

"Hola, Pedro. ¿Que tal?" Hellfire dismounted and went to stand a few feet from him.

Knight jockeyed around to get a better shot at the heavyset man. Ramirez's face was entirely hidden in the shadow of a broad-brimmed sombrero. His dark clothing made him almost invisible in the twilight. All Knight could see were the arms held out at his sides.

Hellfire irritably told him to lower his arms. "You looked like a damned bird ready to fly away."

"I might fly, yes, but never away from you, señora."

"It's *señorita,* and you damned well know it, Pedro."

"Then there is still hope for me." He laughed.

"I've got a mine to run, so quit wasting

264

my time. Or does Avery give you all this time away from work to butter me up? As kind as that is of him, he can rot in hell."

"Ah, *sí,* yes, I understand that." Pedro Ramirez turned somber, all joshing aside. "He says the same things of you."

She said nothing, waiting. Knight took another look around, saw nothing, and urged his horse down the crumbling embankment. Dirt flew and rocks came loose, but his horse slid down easily. He remained in the saddle as Ramirez looked in his direction.

"What I have to say, do you want him to hear it?"

"I haven't any idea what you're so all-fired anxious to tell me, so how do I know if I don't want him to hear it?"

Pedro Ramirez shrugged eloquently. "So be it . . . señorita."

Hellfire waited, saying nothing until the evening desert sounds became loud again and the animals, hunting and hunted, settled into their twilight routines. Knight felt the tension rising but kept his hand away from his revolver. A mistake would carry dire results. What that might be, he didn't know, but he obeyed his gut instinct. Hellfire was in no danger from Avery's superintendent, not physical danger. But whatever he wanted to tell her was another matter.

"*A ver,* I will tell you of a great danger."

"From Jefferson Avery?"

"He is very angry that you killed his friend Thomas." Pedro Ramirez held out his hand to forestall argument. "It does not matter if you blew him up or it just . . . happened. Señor Avery blames you."

"He should talk. Thomas sabotaged the timber he delivered."

"In retaliation for Thomas's death" — Ramirez went on as if he had not heard her — "he is hiring an army."

"You mean he's getting the soldiers at Fort Bayard to come after Miz Bonham?" Knight couldn't restrain himself from asking. He had no love for the Union army, not after being in their military prison and watching so many of his comrades-in-arms mistreated and die.

"Not that kind of army." Ramirez shook his head even harder. "He recruits mercenaries. He finds outlaws and offers huge money to come to Sierra Rojo and fight for him. Soon, he will have a dozen men. Two dozen. More! Then you will be attacked."

"Why are you telling me this?" Hellfire motioned for Knight to keep quiet. She didn't have to warn him against speaking.

The question she had asked was on the tip of his tongue, too.

"I owe you nothing. You will never come to my bed, yet I do not want to see bloodshed on Red Mountain. Many times I have warned Señor Avery not to do this thing. He ignores me. After Thomas's death, he thinks more of killing than he does of mining."

"Maybe the Blue-Eyed Bitch has petered out," Hellfire said.

"That is so. Maybe it has and he wants to jump your claim."

"That'll take some doing."

"He is a determined man. I do not wish to see such fighting. Now I must return to the mine before he wonders where I have gone."

"Tell him you were in Sierra Rojo getting *muy borracho* like you always do."

"Do not insult me. I bring you a warning. He sends an armed posse to kill you and your miners. Be wary." Pedro Ramirez tugged on his horse's reins, vaulted into the saddle, looked down at Hellfire Bonham for a moment, then let out a wild, bloodcurdling yell and galloped off.

In seconds he was gone, but the feeling that the danger had only started lingered like a bad smell.

CHAPTER 18

"Tell him to stop shutting his eyes." Hellfire Bonham threw her hands up in disgust. "He couldn't hit the broad side of a barn if he was locked inside."

"Wilcox isn't that bad," Knight said. "He at least scares the bottles. The others are worse." He cringed when Sampson hefted a rifle to his shoulder and fired, missing the rock balanced on top of another by a country mile. A second shot went even wider.

"Tell him, Sam. Show him how it's done." Hellfire stood with arms crossed on her chest.

Knight found this distracted him. He forced himself to concentrate on getting the miners to shoot the few rifles stored at the mine. "Look with both eyes open. Don't squint. Let your body move the rifle around, not your hands." He took the rifle from Sampson and showed him how to snug the stock into his shoulder. "Look at your target and the rifle will shoot where you're looking like this." He squeezed off a round. The top rock went sailing. The sound of the lead ricocheting off the stone filled the air. He handed the rifle back. "Try again."

The more Sampson tried to hit the target — any target — the worse he became. As upsetting was how bad Dave Wilcox was using either rifle or pistol.

"You did a hell of a lot better when we were pinned down by the Apaches. You hit one or two of them. Why's your aim so rotten now?"

"Sam, it's not my aim, it's my eyes. Being in the mine so many hours a day, dust makes my eyes water and everything turns blurry. I'm looking at the targets you put out there and I see two. Four. Damn me if I don't see a whole mess of them."

"Shoot at the one in the middle." Hellfire stalked over and yanked the rifle from Wilcox. "Like this."

Her aim was as good as Knight's. She started to shoot again, then lowered the muzzle. She seemed to sag in on herself.

"Is something wrong, Hellfire?" Wilcox went to her, but she handed the rifle to Knight.

"Every damned thing is wrong. I have twenty men working this mine for me. The

269

best miners in all of New Mexico Territory and not one of them handles a gun worth beans."

"They'll do better if Jefferson Avery sends his gunmen up the hill. We can even roll rocks down on their heads. We don't have to match them gun for gun." Wilcox sounded proud of his strategy, even if he hadn't thought it through. If they started an avalanche and the road went out, they would be trapped on the mountainside.

Worse, all Avery had to do if he didn't want rocks dumped on his head was blockade the bottom of the road. Trapping them at the Lucky Draw until their food ran out was as deadly as making them face armed gunmen, even though it was much slower.

"Dave, you're one smart man — in most things. That's the stupidest plan for defending the mine I've heard in all my born days. There's another way." She threw up her hands in disgust and said to Wilcox, "Keep the men working. I can use the silver."

"What are you going to do, boss?"

"Don't fret. You and the others won't have to shoot it out with a small army of gunslicks. I'll see to that." She motioned to Knight.

"I can't hold off a dozen men all by myself . . . even with you firing alongside . . ." Knight's thought trailed off. With more determination, he continued. "Even using nitro won't hold that many men at bay."

"Nitro's good for blasting in a mine — and other things. But for fighting a war like Avery is promising, it's not enough. I like the idea of blowing up some boulders to roll down on their heads, but that traps us on the mountain. All they'd have to do if we take out the road is wait us out. It's getting cold. In another couple weeks we'll be up to our chins in snow and cold so bitter your nose'll fall off if you touch it."

"You have something in mind," Knight said. "What is it?"

"Get our horses. We're riding to Sierra Rojo."

"We can't be back before dark. It's dangerous out on the trail at night."

"There's a hotel in town. We'll stay. Maybe we'll stay for a day or two. Wilcox can run the mine without me."

"What's waiting for you in town?"

"The horses, Sam. Get the damned horses. I've got a hankering to see me some civilization, and Sierra Rojo is as close to it as I can get. And go to my office. Take a couple hundred dollars from the cash box.

271

We're going to buy some expensive supplies."

"A couple hundred will buy a case of rifles and plenty of bullets," he said. "Should I get the wagon?"

"No need."

Knight was puzzled by the orders, but he did as she said. He found the tin box with more than a thousand dollars in it under Hellfire's cot. Dutifully counting out two hundred dollars, he made sure the rest of the cash was securely hidden under the bed then joined her. She was already mounted and gave final instructions to Wilcox. Knight mounted, patted his vest pocket to let her know he had the money, then trotted after her when she completed her instructions.

She rode fast as they made their way off the mountain. When they reached the bottom of the road she headed for Sierra Rojo.

He urged his horse into a quicker gait to ride beside her. "What should I look for?"

"You're doing a good enough job of looking at my rear end bouncing up and down as I ride."

Knight considered what she said and couldn't deny it. So he didn't. "I do appreciate a nice view. I also appreciate not risking my neck — and yours — by riding into trouble without knowing what I face. What's in Sierra Rojo? That is where we're going?"

"It is. I have business to conduct that doesn't concern you. Not at the moment. You've got most of it figured out anyway. You're a clever man, Sam. A real smart one who plans ahead and watches for trouble. Just don't go seeing trouble where none exists. If you start doing that, you'll drive yourself loco." She glanced over at him and added, "And you'll drive me crazy, too. That's not something you want to do."

They rode in silence the rest of the way into Sierra Rojo. He might not be the clever man she thought him, but he wasn't stupid. All the marksmanship training he had tried to give the miners had been wasted. Wilcox did the best of any of them, and he did nothing but waste ammunition. In spite of his spirited defense when the Apaches attacked, Wilcox shied away from firearms. Working in the Lucky Draw mine was the best thing that had happened to him. He did a good job, and the men respected him for his level head and willingness to take their complaints to Hellfire Bonham when others before him had been afraid of her.

"Should I stake out a table in the saloon?"

"Why'd you want to go and do a thing like that, Sam? You thinking on being a gambler again?"

"You have business in town. That's a central meeting place."

"You just want to get me drunk and take advantage of me. I know your kind, Samuel Knight."

"If you think that —"

"Oh, cool off, Sam. I'm joshing you. I can tell that you had a sense of humor once, but something happened to freeze it inside you. We're going to a central meeting place, but not at a saloon. I have the town's lone meeting room reserved. All you have to do is sit and watch or, if you want, go to the saloon and get roaring drunk. That might be what you need to get some of the starch out of your collar."

"I'm not stiff-necked."

"Sam," she chided.

"You're joking."

"Only a little." Her attention drifted to a small clapboard building where three men already waited. She put heels to her horse and trotted forward. With a quick move, she swung her leg back and off, dropping to the ground in a graceful movement. Not saying a word, she went inside, the men trailing her like ducklings behind a mama duck.

But the three men were anything but ducklings. They wore their revolvers slung low on their hips. The swagger and arrogance showed how these men were used to being in charge. Knight wondered how they would respond to working for a woman.

Worse, he knew now why Hellfire had come to Sierra Rojo. She wanted an army to match the one Pedro Ramirez said Jefferson Avery was recruiting. Dealing with owlhoots like these led to big trouble. He tethered his horse and went into the small room where Hellfire already sat at a desk at the far end. The three gunmen stood in front of her like unruly students waiting for their schoolmaster to dish out punishment or praise.

He went to the front and stood to one side to give the three a good look. One of them was walleyed, and Knight wondered how good a shot he could be. The other two had the look of men on the run. Before Knight could ask about who was on their back trail, the door opened and another man strode in.

None of the others dominated the room like this tall, thin man. His bushy mustache twitched at the waxed tips as his upper lip rose in a sneer. All in black, he pushed his duster away to show the gun hanging at his hip, as if this was all he needed to get any job Hellfire had to offer. Aware all eyes were on him, he walked forward making his spurs jangle. "I'm Kilgore, and I'm here for the job."

"Miz Bonham is talking to the others," Knight said. Something about Kilgore set his teeth on edge. He had been around dangerous men before, but his reaction to them had never been as powerful.

Kilgore whirled in like a force of nature, demanding that everything stop so he could take charge. Knight knew he would be in for a shock if he thought he could boss Hellfire Bonham around.

But it was Knight who got the shock.

Hellfire's tone was sweet as she responded, "Pleased to make your acquaintance, Mr. Kilgore."

"Hellfire, you were talking to these men," Knight said. "He can wait his turn."

"This ain't grade school," Kilgore said, not looking in Knight's direction. He ignored everyone in the room but Hellfire.

To Knight's dismay, she returned the attention. "He's the type of gent I'm looking to hire."

"Of course I am. You won't find nobody faster or more accurate with a gun than me. And I ain't no gentleman. I'm the worst nightmare you ever had — doubled. Hire me and that nightmare becomes your enemy's. From the word goin' around, you want me to" — he drew and fired, shooting the eye out of a picture hung on the back wall — "take care of Jefferson Avery. I'm your *man.*" Kilgore smirked, then shot Knight an insolent glance daring him to put up an argument.

"You handle your gun pretty well," Hellfire said. "Shooting a picture's different from shooting a man."

"I've taken down more men than you can count. Don't matter to me. White man, red, black, skin color don't matter — met and bested them all."

"What? No Chinese?" Knight didn't try to keep the sarcasm from his words.

"Never had the pleasure. That who I'm up against, who this Jefferson Avery hires? It would be a pleasure to take out some to bolster my reputation." He spun the gun around his finger using the trigger guard, then slammed it back into his holster, his hand hovering in anticipation of another quick draw.

"A dollar a day," Hellfire said. She held up her hand to silence Knight's objection. "You got the moves, you got the look of a gent — a man — able to do the job ahead."

"In advance," Kilgore said. "I want a month's pay in advance. And a bounty on each of Avery's men I put in the ground."

"How much?"

"It don't sound like much of a chore. Five dollars."

"Done. You're hired." Hellfire looked pleased with herself.

"Us, too? The three of us?" The walleyed man stepped up. "We want the same pay."

"You'll take fifty cents a day," Hellfire said.

They argued, but she was adamant and the trio finally hired on.

"We get the same bounty? Five dollars a kill?"

"Yes," she said. "But the money's only for those who work for Jefferson Avery at the Blue-Eyed Bitch mine. I don't want you bringing me scalps from people who don't have any dog in this fight."

"You want me to bring you a scalp? Or something else?" Kilgore scratched his crotch. "That's assumin' those I gun down have balls to cut off."

"I'll know. Avery will let me know. Now, all of you get on your horses and go to the Lucky Draw. Tell the super I sent you. He'll fix you up with a bunk and chuck."

"What about my pay?" Kilgore didn't budge.

"Pay him, Sam. Give the others a week's pay so they can get whatever they need here in town."

"Yeah, Sam, pay me." Kilgore grinned, his mustache twitching.

Knight made a point of paying the trio who had been in the room first. Only then did he fork over the thirty dollars for the arrogant gunman.

The three hurried out, but Kilgore took a little longer to leave. He ran his eyes over Hellfire, from the floor to the top of her head. Knight's gun hand twitched just a mite at such impertinence. He had seen how fast Kilgore was. Whether he was faster wasn't something he wanted to find out, but he knew they would lock horns sooner or later. The gunman's attitude showed that.

The spell broke when two more men came in.

"This where the hiring's goin' on?"

"Come on over, gents," Hellfire said. "I've got a couple more jobs to fill." She asked them more questions than the others. Their answers were all lies. Knight heard it and wondered if Hellfire did. Or if it even mattered to her. She had taken Pedro Ramirez's warning to heart and was preparing for a full-scale war.

When Sam had paid them their salaries and they'd left, he asked, "How many more are you going to hire? That's five."

"Six," she corrected.

"Six, with Kilgore."

"You don't like him, do you? You two bucks looking to lock horns?"

"He's trouble. I've seen his like before. They enjoy watching men die, and it doesn't matter to them who's on the receiving end of their bullets."

"As long as he keeps his gun pointed in Avery's direction, he'll earn his money. Besides, you can keep him in line."

They left the community hall and walked across the street to the hotel. Knight stewed over what Hellfire had done. Hiring an army of killers to fight Jefferson Avery was one thing, but having Kilgore as one of them was playing with fire. She enjoyed living dangerously, making and using nitroglycerin. Knight hoped Kilgore didn't prove more explosive than the yellow gel.

"Two rooms," Knight said to the clerk.

The man shook his head.

"What's wrong? We've got the money."

"It's not that, mister. We only got one room left."

"We'll take it," Hellfire said. She looped her arm through Knight's. "As long as it's got a bed, we'll be just fine."

Knight started to say something, then saw

Helene's expression. "Yes, it'll be just fine," he said.

And it was better than fine.

CHAPTER 19

"There is no doubt, Señor Avery," Pedro Ramirez said. "She killed the man who bored out the beams for you."

"She blew the poor bastard up?" Jefferson Avery shook his head in disbelief. "I knew she was a ruthless bitch, but that's just cruel. There wouldn't be any big enough pieces left to give a decent burial."

"I heard her orders were to leave the chunks for the coyotes. She is not going to stop until she has killed you and stolen your mine. She sees this as a good time to make her move against you."

"She wants the mine, that's true. But she'll take it first, then taunt me with losing it before she kills me. I know her. I was married to her." Jefferson Avery looked at the mouth of his mine boring into the side of Red Mountain. If the shaft went deep enough, it would come out on the far side of the mountain, where the Lucky Draw scrabbled to pull bits and pieces of ore from the rock.

"My spies tell me she has hired many killers. They ride in a gang like those who made Kansas such a hellhole during the war. They want to be Quantrill. They will be Jesse James. This is what my people in Sierra Rojo say."

"You keep them talking to you, Pedro. Pay them whatever it takes. I need to know every move she makes."

"I will do this for you, Señor Avery. I am your superintendent, *es verdad,* but I am also your friend. The men who work here are to be protected."

"They will be," Avery vowed. "I'm not giving an inch, not to her. This is a war and only one of us will come out of it alive, I swear that to you."

"I believe you," Pedro Ramirez said solemnly. He pointed to a dust cloud moving slowly in their direction. "Your army arrives. They are killers, one and all. Will only five of them be enough for this fight against all her outlaws?"

"You haven't met them. I recruited them from Ralston and was lucky that Jessup happened to be there."

"Carl Jessup? I have heard of him. He is a dangerous hombre and does not care who dies by his gun." Pedro Ramirez shifted uneasily. When he had urged Jefferson Avery to find guards for the mine, he hadn't thought Avery would actually find any who could put up much of a fight. "He is a wanted man, one with a big price on his head."

"Not in New Mexico Territory. If he's in trouble over in Texas, what difference does that make?" Avery settled his flashy coat about his shoulders and smoothed unseen wrinkles in the fine fabric. He hooked his thumbs in his vest pockets and waited for the gang to ride up and draw rein in front of the mine.

"So where's this bitch we have to kill?" Carl Jessup spat out the words without so much as a howdy. "I got places to go and things to do, and the quicker we're finished here, the sooner I move on."

"I appreciate your dedication to the task at hand," Avery said.

Jessup slapped leather and had his revolver out, cocked and aimed at the mine owner. Pedro Ramirez stepped between them, pushing his palms outward in the gunman's direction as if to hold back the hail of bullets being promised.

"We do not fight each other. Save your gunplay for Hellfire Bonham."

"Who're you, greaser?" Jessup shifted the gun from Avery to the super's chest.

Ramirez fixed a steely eye on the gunfighter. "I am Señor Avery's right-hand man."

"*Man,* ha." A sneer twisted Jessup's ugly, rawboned face. "You're a Mexican. I eat Mexicans for breakfast."

"This one will stick in your throat and choke you to death," Ramirez said. "Do not cross me."

"Enough of that, Pedro." Avery stepped around him, reached up, and pushed Jessup's pistol away. "I don't care if you get along with my men, but consider this. You are on *my* payroll. You have to please *me.* Do your job and we'll all be happy. Fail and you'll wish you were never born."

"Those are mighty bold words, Mr. Fancy Pants."

Jefferson Avery didn't back down an inch. "All I've gotten from you is hot air. Why don't you show me what you can really do? Or is your reputation nothing but a lie?"

Ramirez held his breath. Jessup wasn't the sort of desperado to accept such an insult without reacting, probably violently.

"For two cents, I'd ride on out of here."

Realizing he had to gain some control over the situation, Pedro reached into his vest pocket, fished out a coin, and tossed it toward the gunman. Jessup reacted with the speed of a striking rattler. He fired, blowing the spinning coin to hell and gone.

"What in blazes are you doing, greaser?" Jessup demanded as he sat there with a wisp of smoke curling from the barrel of his gun.

"That was a two-cent piece, Jessup." Ramirez turned to Avery and said, "He will do. Send him out to stop the shipment."

"That's a real good idea, Pedro." Avery cleared his throat and said loudly enough for all the gunmen to hear, "The Lucky Draw sends a load of silver to Sierra Rojo once a week. The wagon ought to be on its way down the mountainside about now. If you ride hard, you can intercept it."

"What becomes of the silver when we do?" Jessup kept the revolver in his hand but laid it across the saddle in front of him.

"Throw it in the river, for all I care. Now get going. If it reaches Sierra Rojo, you'll have to rob the bank to get hold of it."

"You don't care about the silver as much as us killing the driver and guards, is that it?"

"Go!" Jefferson Avery bellowed.

Jessup signaled his men and turned around. They retraced their way from the mine. Avery waited for them to get out of sight, then said to his super, "Follow them and be sure they do as they're told." He stalked off, grumbling to himself.

Pedro Ramirez smiled, then bent and picked up the two-cent piece he had tossed in Jessup's direction. He held it up and studied it. A rounded chunk the size of a bullet had been cut from it.

"Ah, Señor Jessup, you are not as good as you brag. You did not hit it dead center." He tucked the coin back into his vest pocket and went to get his horse. It would be a long day for him. Very long, indeed.

Trailing Jessup and his gang proved easier than Pedro Ramirez thought. They made no attempt to cover their back trail or worry about anyone behind them. That meant they were either confident or stupid. Ramirez decided stupid covered much, that and overwhelming arrogance. Carl Jessup was not as good as he thought. Ramirez grinned broadly at that idea since it made his plans so much easier to achieve.

The clanking of a wagon coming along the road alerted him that Hellfire Bonham's silver shipment was almost on top of him. He rode from the twin ruts that passed for a road into Sierra Rojo, found a thick-boled cottonwood tree, and watched from behind it. The twilight hid much of the details. He heaved a sigh. Avery should never have told Jessup to keep the silver. A few ounces would ride so nicely in the Blue-Eyed Bitch mine superintendent's pocket. Those were ordinary outlaws, back shooters and cowards with guns. They did not deserve so much silver.

From all he had heard, Bonham's claim was richer by far than the Blue-Eyed Bitch. To his mind, the blue-eyed bitch was worth more than the Blue-Eyed Bitch mine. That thought amused him. Hellfire Bonham was an attractive woman, but then every woman had a certain appeal out on the frontier. He had seen prettier down in Guanajuato and even in Chihuahua. He had taken to bed prettier *señoritas,* even in the United States of America. But in western New Mexico Territory, there were few women and of those, Hellfire Bonham stood out. He would possess her until he grew weary of her, then he would discard her.

The wagon passing by on the road interrupted his fantasies. He touched the gun in its holster but did not draw. There was no need. Jessup and his men would soon attack. Let them get filled with lead as they stole the silver shipment.

Ramirez frowned at the thought. Something was not right. The wagon belonged to the Lucky Draw mine. Of that he was certain. More than once he had noticed how the rear wheel wobbled as this one did. But details were wrong. At the same time it occurred to him that the wagon bounced along as if it were not laden with many pounds of silver.

Jessup and his men swooped down from both sides of the road not fifty yards closer to Sierra Rojo. Ramirez was lucky he had not ridden through their ambush. Hiding when he did kept them from noticing him. He tried to count them but the darkness veiled them. He thought three on this side of the road, perhaps four. Which of them was Jessup was concealed by the gathering nighttime.

To stop the shipment, Jessup and his men fired a few warning shots. The yellow flash from their gun muzzles dazzled Ramirez's eyes. As expected, the driver immediately surrendered, fastening his reins around the hand brake, but he did not stand in surrender. He dived for the wagon bed. Jessup shouted for him to get out. Then all hell broke loose.

The rear of the wagon sprouted a half dozen rifle barrels and all opened fire. Foot-long tongues of orange flame spurted out.

Bullets whined into the night. A horse shrieked in pain. Ramirez saw one of the dark riders jump from his mount as it collapsed under him, the bullet lodged fatally in its chest.

Confusion seized control of Jessup and his gunmen. They circled the wagon, firing into the bed. From the way the bullets sang away, metal plates had armored the back where the hidden riflemen hunkered down and fired.

"Get back! Get outta there!" Jessup called.

His men were slow to obey, costing one of them his life. He threw up his hands and flopped backwards off his horse as a bullet ripped into his body.

Ramirez kept his horse from bolting. He made what sense of the fight that he could. The wagon remained stationary on the road. Now and then a rifle barrel poked up, as if to shoot at the moon, only to drop back down.

To his surprise, a new attack surged from the far side of the road. Ramirez thought Jessup led it but could not tell then saw the tactic employed. The assault came with the outlaws in a widely spaced line, each man firing as he rode. Splinters flew from the wagon. Jessup and his men reached the vehicle and fired directly into it. Ramirez saw no way for the defenders to survive such an attack.

They didn't. The shots echoing through the woods died down. Quickly the normal night sounds replaced the gunfire.

Jessup jumped from his horse into the back of the wagon. He kicked viciously at a body, then emptied his revolver into his victim.

"Somebody toss me a rifle," he ordered. "I'm gonna shoot off the lock."

One of the robbers obeyed. Jessup reared back, fired, and cursed a blue streak when the bullet ricocheted back and grazed him. He tossed the rifle back, knelt, and opened the strongbox. Ramirez wanted to ride over and claim it for himself, but only one of Jessup's men had been killed. Others might be wounded, but they outnumbered him and he carried no authority with such cut-throats. Bonham's silver was lost to the out-laws.

Or was it?

"Son of a bitch!" Jessup roared. "The box is filled with rocks. They ain't even silver ore rocks. They're just . . . . rocks!"

"What are you sayin', boss? You mean we ain't gettin' rich?" The riders edged closer and peered into the wagon bed. "You sure that's not silver?"

"No, you numbskull!" Jessup threw the rock at the man who had asked the question, hitting him in the head. His tall-crowned hat took away the sting of the rock but caused him to jerk and almost fall from horseback.

"You mean they cheated us? Bennett got his head blowed off for nuthin'?"

"We were set up. This was a trap from the instant we rode away from Avery's mine. I'm gonna make him pay for this. I —"

"Reach for the sky," came a cold command. "If you don't, me and my boys'll cut you to bloody ribbons."

"What?" Jessup looked around wildly, then saw men coming from the woods behind him.

Ramirez tensed when sounds in the bushes behind him warned of someone advancing. But it was only a squirrel flushed from its hiding place by all the noise and nearness of humans. Ramirez shrank back when he saw three men moving behind Jessup.

"You killed two of my men in that wagon," said the same icy voice.

"Who the hell are you?" Jessup lifted his revolver, tried to fire, and had the hammer fall on an empty chamber.

"I'm your worst nightmare. Name's Kilgore. You heard of me? No? Too bad. You should have since I'm the man who caught you with your pants down."

"What are you going to do?"

Ramirez caught his breath and held it. He knew the answer. As Kilgore had found out, Jessup was a fool, but him getting killed so quickly and easily did not fit Ramirez's plans. There were any number of outlaws in this part of the territory, but when they heard how Kilgore had slaughtered Avery's men, none would hire on at any price. Without guards, Avery could never keep his mine from falling into the hands of his ex-wife. A thousand things raced through Ramirez's mind. All he knew was that his plans were ruined if Avery didn't have a small army to fight Bonham's killers.

The first *grito* left his lips before he knew it. Screaming at the top of his lungs and kicking hard at his horse's flanks, he rocketed forward. His revolver came up, and he fired at the first dark figure he saw creeping along on the ground. Jessup and his men fought to control their horses in the new roar of battle. Ramirez thundered past the wagon and saw three silhouetted figures ahead. He tried to make out which was Kilgore. Cut the head off the snake and the body dies. Then he realized that picking off the leader did not matter. Sowing confusion did.

He cut between the men, firing left and right until his revolver came up empty. Then he blasted past, bent low, and let the chaos expand behind him. Some of Jessup's men found their courage and began shooting.

Staying bent over, Ramirez left the fight far behind, though he looked up and saw his sombrero had several new holes shot through the brim. He cursed as he rode. It was his favorite sombrero given him by a lovely dark-eyed young *novia* before he left Mexico to make his fortune among the gringos.

It was small price to pay for rescuing Jessup, even if the man did not know who saved him and if he guessed, would be contemptuous of it. He was a man Ramirez would enjoy shooting down, but only when he had outlived his usefulness.

CHAPTER 20

"And I thought Ralston City was a hole in the ground." Rance Spurgeon spat in the direction of the small boomtown's signpost. The wind caught the gobbet and carried it away in a looping curve to splat against a rock in the road.

"We do seem to go from bad to worse," admitted Hesseltine. He brushed dust off his coat, wondering if he would ever be clean again. Even getting a decent hot bath in Ralston had been difficult, not that they had lingered once the drunken lieutenant put them on the right path. There would be time for proper bathing and sartorial excellence after they captured Dr. Samuel Knight.

At the moment, Hesseltine tended toward the idea of shooting the fugitive on sight and saving a great deal of trouble returning him to East Texas. The only problem with that, as he had discussed with Spurgeon at some length on their ride to Sierra Rojo, was the smell. A dead body draped over a packhorse began to rot after a day or two. Being followed by carrion beasts made the trip back hazardous, not to mention the smell soaking into every stitch that Hesseltine wore. More than once he had burned his clothing after a mission because of the death stench.

"But if he's not deader than a doornail, we'd have to feed him," he muttered.

"Are you going on again about whether we shoot him down or take him alive?" Spurgeon asked. "We settled that. We kill him. That's the way to get out of New Mexico Territory fast and without him yammering the whole way."

"We went over that scheme, yes, I know we did, but do you remember the bank robber we apprehended in Minnesota?"

"You shot him."

"I did," said Hesseltine, "and that caused us no end of problems since it was a four-day ride to get to a railhead before we delivered the body for shipment back to Chicago. Even wrapped in blankets, the odor caused me to puke."

Spurgeon muttered an insult about Hesseltine's weak stomach.

"You were green around the gills, too, as I

296

remember it. This time the trip will be much longer, almost a thousand miles, and all of it on horseback. There is no train to place the body on, not one going where we need to send it."

"It's getting colder, almost winter."

"It's still fall. While it freezes at night in the mountains, we will be crossing most of Texas where the weather has yet to turn so cold."

"We shoot him."

Hesseltine hid his exasperation. His partner got an idea fixed in his thick skull and nothing budged it. Yet, Spurgeon had a point. They would save themselves a great deal of trouble guarding Knight, even with iron wrist and ankle shackles on.

"We can see how it plays out," Hesseltine said finally. He snapped the reins on his horse and walked it into Sierra Rojo.

The pair was alert for any sign of Knight, though they didn't expect to find him in the town itself. A boomtown held the lure of sudden riches from swinging a pick and striking it rich and had enticed many a prospector in the past six months.

"A saloon," Spurgeon said, reining in as they came to a drinking establishment. "Remember what they told us back in Buffalo Springs about Knight setting up a surgery at the back of a saloon?"

"The barkeep in Ralston thought Knight mentioned something about becoming a gambler. That's a more dangerous profession than being a doctor, but he is a shrewd one, and hiding his past to throw us off the trail can show resourcefulness."

"Doesn't matter. I'm thirsty from all the dust." Spurgeon stepped down, looped his reins around a hitch rail, made sure his horse could drink from the water trough, and climbed the steps leading to the saloon's swinging doors.

Hesseltine followed him. He had lost several pounds on the trail from lack of food. If the saloon sold beer, they also served free lunches. He was ready for several beef sandwiches. Maybe with a pickle. Patting his belly to quiet the growling, he trailed his partner inside.

His nose wrinkled at the smell. He decided to skip eating in this place since he didn't want to end up with a bellyache or worse from spoiled food. The bread on a tray at the end of the bar grew fuzzy blue mold, and the slabs of roast beef had a curious green tint.

"Beer," Spurgeon told the bartender. "And gimme a sandwich."

"You will die eating that." Hesseltine

watched in disgust as his partner bit down on the tough meat and ripped a piece off like a feral wolf with a fresh kill, only there was nothing fresh about the meat.

"See that I'm buried in the Elks section of the cemetery."

"You don't belong to the Elks or any other society."

"I know," Spurgeon said, swallowing. He chased the food with a healthy draft of beer, belched, and worked on another bite. "I don't want to end up in a potter's field, and the Elks always stake out a decent section of every cemetery I've seen. I think I'd like to be on the top of a hill with a nice view. If I'm going to be there for eternity, I definitely want a good view."

"I'm not sure the neighborhood's not better in a potter's field than in the Elks or Masons' cemetery."

"What do you think?" Spurgeon directed his question to the barkeep. "Where's it better to get buried, with the paupers or with the Elks?"

"When I'm dead it won't matter," the man said.

"Lots of folks feel the same way," Hesseltine said, picking up the thread. "With so many newcomers, it's hard to keep up with who'd be buried where."

"There's a small cemetery outside town, up on a hill. Mostly prospectors." The barkeep drew himself a beer and sipped at it.

"How about gamblers? They get buried there, too?" Spurgeon belched again and wiped his lips. He pointed to get another beer.

Hesseltine couldn't stand it anymore and asked for a sandwich, too, green and blue or not.

"The town undertaker don't care who gets buried where, so long as he makes a dime on it." The barkeep topped off the glass he had drunk from and slid it to Spurgeon.

"That's the problem with newcomers to a boomtown. Most are penniless, unless they're a doctor. Then they have a profession that'll keep them rolling in the clover until they die." Hesseltine nibbled at the sandwich and decided it wasn't too bad. He ate faster, thinking it might not poison him as bad if he swallowed whole chunks without careful chewing. "Does the town have a doctor?"

"Nope, no sawbones anywhere I know about."

"Not even somebody who just got to town?" Spurgeon rubbed his belly. "I need a doctor."

"Don't die in here. Go somewhere else."

"It's always good to find a charitable man on the frontier," Hesseltine said. "We can offer a doctor a decent fee for a day's work."

"How decent?" The barkeep looked up from his work. "I can set bones."

"More than that's needed."

"Ask that gent who's coming this way," the man said as he looked past the batwings into the street. "He rode into town a couple weeks back with a gambler."

"Going to most doctors is like getting odds in a poker game," Spurgeon said. "Mostly odds against you living." He turned and nudged Hesseltine as a young, dark-haired, medium-sized man came into the saloon.

Hesseltine gulped down the sandwich and gave the newcomer the once-over. He shook his head. This wasn't Knight. He looked nothing like the picture they'd been given, although wanted posters notoriously lacked detail.

"Mister," Hesseltine called to him. "The barkeep here says you know a doctor. We have a partner stranded out on the trail in need of medical attention."

The young man came over and leaned on the bar. Before he ordered, Hesseltine pointed so the barkeep knew the beer was on him.

"Much obliged," the man said with a grin. He drank down half the beer in a gulp. "Name's Dave Wilcox. Damn me, I don't run into such generous gents as you boys too often. Most in these parts don't want anything except to get rich." He drained another inch from the mug. "I'd offer you a job, but you don't look like miners."

"Just passing through," Hesseltine said. "Our wagon broke down outside town and injured the driver. That's why we're looking for a doctor."

"There isn't one in town. A friend of mine's capable enough at patching up common injuries, but he's a ways off."

"We're from Texas. East Texas," said Spurgeon. "We heard tell that a neighbor of ours had come this way."

"What part of East Texas?" Wilcox rocked back and looked the two over.

"Pine Knob. It'd be really good to find a friendly face out here on the frontier," said Hesseltine. He shot his partner a look to shut him up. Being so blunt about where Knight hailed from could scare off a skittish source of information like this man. He dressed like a miner but sounded more educated.

But he wasn't Dr. Samuel Knight. That didn't mean his friend wasn't their quarry.

"You and your friend been in town long?" Spurgeon showed no subtlety asking such a question. Hesseltine wanted him to go back to eating the terrible sandwiches and drinking the bitter beer so he could conduct the interrogation without spooking the miner.

"What my friend means is that we're looking to settle down and want to know how long it takes to get a feel for the people here."

"We're like most folks," Wilcox said. "Just want to find work and earn a few dollars."

"Weeks? Days since you blew into town?" Spurgeon was pressing too hard. Hesseltine wanted to take him aside and tell him, but their fish would slip off the hook if he did that.

"It's hard to remember since one day's so much like the next," Wilcox said. "Much obliged for the beer." He backed away and almost ran from the saloon.

Hesseltine scowled. He downed what was left of his beer, getting his anger under check. "You scared him off," he told Spurgeon. "You need to cozy up to somebody you want to get information from."

"I'm tired of the way you pussyfoot around." Spurgeon reached over the bar and grabbed the barkeep by the front of his shirt. He yanked hard and dragged the man half over the bar. "The man who just left. When did he blow into town?"

"T-two w-weeks ago. Him and his friend came in from Ralston."

"What's his friend's name?"

"I don't know. Him, that's Dave Wilcox, like he said. He asks around town to hire miners for the Lucky Draw mine. He's the super there."

"Thanks." Spurgeon released the man, who staggered back. He turned to Hesseltine and said, "See?"

Hesseltine sighed, considered getting another beer and finally decided it was likely to be poisoned. The barkeep hadn't appreciated being assaulted.

"It's time to get back into the saddle," Hesseltine said. "If Knight's his friend, he'll make a beeline to tell him."

"Mission accomplished." Spurgeon led the way out.

Hesseltine trailed behind, keeping an eye on the bartender to be sure he didn't grab a scattergun and blow his two worst customers to hell and gone.

CHAPTER 21

"He won't be able to use that arm again." Knight did nothing to keep the bitterness out of his voice. "I warned you about doing this."

"You aren't going to amputate the arm. He can use it for something." Hellfire Bonham was clutching at straws. He heard it in her voice.

"What about the three who are dead? The two in the wagon were miners and never thought they'd be involved in a gunfight. The other, Kilgore's man, shouldn't have died, either. It was foolish trying to attack in the dark, on foot."

"Everything went well until one of Jessup's killers attacked from the far side of the road."

Knight stood and began to pace in the small space of the Lucky Draw mine office. He tried to put his concerns into words. She hadn't listened before the attack when he had warned against it. Kilgore had been too confident. Even though Knight had no military training for such fighting, he had seen the problems with the ambush when Kilgore laid it out for Hellfire's approval. If the wagon had stopped at a spot too far away, Kilgore and the men with him had to run on foot to give any kind of support. As it was, Jessup had someone waiting in ambush at the same place.

"Call it off."

"Call what off?" Hellfire looked at him curiously. "This is war, Sam. I didn't start it. Avery did. If I send a message to him that I want it to stop, that means I lose."

"Lose what? The mine's not involved in this shooting war. What you'll lose is the chance of more men getting killed. You saw how badly your workers were handling rifles and revolvers and yet you sent two of them into the middle of the ambush as bait."

"The silver got through. That's what matters."

"Wilcox got it through on pack mules, and you lost lives. Was it worth it? Ask the men who got killed. Ask the man who'll never use his arm again if it was worth it getting your silver into Sierra Rojo."

"I don't know what's eating you, Sam," Hellfire said. "I really don't. Avery caused the roof collapse that killed my men. You were there when Pedro Ramirez warned me he was recruiting gunmen for an all-out fight. I had to get gunmen of my own."

"Kilgore isn't too bright, and he's more inclined to shoot men in the back."

"Good." She stood up and slammed both hands down on her desk. "Shoot them all when they don't know what hit them. If I had Jefferson Avery in my sights right now, I'd pull the trigger. Barring that, I'll cram nitro up his ass and blow him and his murdering ways into next week."

Knight stood stock still for a half dozen heartbeats as he came to a conclusion. "I can't be part of this. Not a war where men get killed for no reason."

"Avery started it. I intend to finish it."

Knight headed for the door.

Hellfire came around and grabbed him by the arm. Her blue eyes flashed angrily. "You walk out that door and you don't come back."

He pried her hand loose. There was nothing more to say. Knight felt the loss deep down, but he had been too well trained as a doctor to see lives wasted wantonly. He saved those he could. Taking a life when he faced a rabid dog like Hector Alton was another matter. Feeling the gun buck in his

307

hand and knowing a man died as a result had not bothered him, and it went farther than killing before he was killed. Taking down a murderer saved lives, others' lives. It had been the same with Milo Hannigan.

Knight left with Hellfire shouting for him to go to hell. Given everything he had done, that might be his eventual destination, but in the here and now he wasn't going to add to the number of men being buried. The one whose arm he had been unable to save was worse off than the two who had died. What good was a one-armed miner? Whatever that man did from now on to keep body and soul together, it wasn't going to be swinging a pick or using a sledgehammer against a drill to plant explosives.

Knight went directly to his bunk and gathered his tack. He ought to say good-bye to Dave Wilcox before he rode on. It still gnawed at him that he hadn't told anyone in Buffalo Springs he was leaving, though that had been for their benefit. Amelia Parker would likely hate him for the rest of her days. Missing Seth Lunsford was bad, but the boy would understand. He had other things in his life. Knight hadn't wanted to put any of them in jeopardy.

He slung his gear over his shoulder and headed for the corral and his horse. Finding

Wilcox wouldn't be hard. The man spent all his time in the mine. With a heave, he got his saddle over the top railing and turned to head into the mine. He almost ran into Hellfire, who still glared at him.

"He's in town," she said when he asked about Wilcox. "I told him to recruit more miners."

"Miners? Or gunfighters?"

"I know how you feel about this, Sam, but the bad blood runs deep. And that river's not a silent one. It sloshes around and soaks others who get too close."

"It's one thing to defend yourself. It's another to set out to murder."

"Avery didn't have to send his bully boys to rob the silver shipment. That was a trap I set, pure and simple. If they weren't inclined to steal what I'd pulled from the ground, no one would have died that night." She took a deep breath and let it out slowly. "Or lost the use of their right arm. I'll take care of him, Sam. I will. He can read and cipher. There's a job working in the office tallying supplies."

"So Wilcox is in town? I'll say good-bye to him there."

"Sam, wait." She took his arm again. This time her touch was light, hesitant, her fingers shaking. "Don't go. Not like this.

Let's get away from the mine so we can talk. One last time, if that's the way you want it."

Knight hated himself for the emotions welling inside. He admired Helene, and other, different feelings had blossomed. It wasn't smart for him to fall for another woman, but he had. The night in Sierra Rojo after hiring Kilgore and the others had shown him that she felt the same about him. They made a better pair than they did separate people when they were apart. She gave him ambition he found missing since the war, and he held her down in her wilder moments. Or at least he had until the fight with her ex-husband took on such bloody consequences.

They walked side by side past the mouth of the Lucky Draw and around the side of the mountain, not saying a word. When they got far enough away that the sounds from the mine were muted and no one could see them, Hellfire spun around and pressed close to him, looking up into his eyes.

"Everyone says I'm too forward, but that's the only way I know how to do things, Sam. Nobody interested me until you came up that road. You've got a past you want to hide. I can understand that. I've done things I hope never get talked about by anyone. That might be one reason the fight with Jeff is so bitter. The stakes are higher than our mines. It cuts all the way down into our souls."

"You're trying to destroy each other for personal reasons. Let it go, Helene. You don't have to do anything but get rich from the silver." He put his arms around her.

She fit perfectly against him. It became harder to remember he intended to ride off when she pressed warmly against his chest and laid her cheek over his heart.

He felt his pulse accelerating. The night with her in town had been a prelude, but for any more he had to accept things beyond his ability. Running from his oath to never take a life, to first do no harm, trumped his emotions.

"I don't need you in my life, Sam, but if you go there'll be one hell of a hole that will never be filled again." She hugged him tighter. "How are we going to work this out?"

"You won't give up your fight with Avery. More will die because of that. And how can I be a part of a fight that's not mine?"

"What if I send him a letter asking for a meeting to talk a truce? Would you come with me to negotiate? I hate like sin to walk away when he's done so much against me, but I will. For you, I will." She moved back

311

and tipped her face up to his. Her lips looked so kissable.

He bent to taste them when a sharp crack echoed along the side of the mountain.

Hellfire jerked in his arms, then sagged. Her face went slack for a moment, then contorted into pain. "Damn, that hurts."

He swung her around, taking her off her feet as a second shot whined past his ear. A piece of his hat vanished when a third bullet tore through it. Knight lowered her to safety between two rocks as the bullets came fast and deadly every few seconds.

Rolling her over, he saw where the bullet had struck her. He let out a lungful of air he hadn't known he had been holding. His strong fingers ripped away her coat and pressed down into her shirt. Blood oozed out.

"You watch it, mister. Don't you go trying to take off my clothes." She grinned weakly. "Again."

"It's not serious. The bullet's still in you but was almost spent so didn't dig in too far. Don't go running off." He lowered her to her side and drew his gun.

"No, Sam, let it go. Get help from the mine."

He laughed harshly. Memories of how he had worked with the miners to become marksmen mocked him. For a bunch who lived on the frontier, they had been piss-poor shots.

"Stay here." He pushed her down as she tried to get up. "Stay here or you'll get spanked."

"Promise? That sounds like fun. If you're the one doing the spanking."

He got his feet under him, then drove forward, reaching a larger rock for shelter. Colt Navy in hand, he waited for another shot aimed his way. When it didn't come, he picked up a stick and put his hat on it. Lifting it just a bit so the crown showed over the top of the rock drew furious fire. Knight counted the shots. When he got to eight, he moved. Fast.

That should have emptied the attacker's rifle. He quickly found out how dangerously he had miscalculated. There were two snipers. Toes digging into the thin dirt along the game trail he and Hellfire had followed, he dived forward. He landed hard on his belly and scooted along almost a foot. He rested his elbows on the ground, steadied his revolver with both hands, and fired the instant a gunman showed himself from behind a rock twenty yards down the trail.

Knight was quick on the draw. He was an even better marksman. His slug caught the

313

gunman in the chest. His target straightened, dropped his rifle, then sat down and slumped forward. The sniper's partner behind the rock yammered for him to get to safety. Knight waited. The man doing all the shouting wasn't going to stand pat. He'd either try to help his wounded partner or run like a scalded dog. Either way, Knight was ready.

If he'd had to place a bet, he would have laid money on the hidden man hightailing it. Instead, the bushwhacker lunged into the open and tried to drag his friend to safety. Knight's second shot found its target in the arm reaching out. A spurt of blood and a fountain of cursing told Knight how accurately he had fired. The man threw himself back behind the shelter of the boulder where he'd been hidden.

Knight got his feet under him and started forward, keeping low so he could dive to either side of the trail if necessary. Watching for the man behind the rock almost did him in. The one he had hit in the chest proved to be the greater danger. He fumbled out his gun and fired wildly. One errant slug sent a sharp pain through Knight's left arm. He jerked away, got behind a rock closer to his assailants, and checked his wound. A crease. It hurt but wasn't serious.

A quick look let him take in the scene ahead. The wounded man had been pulled out of the line of sight. Since Knight had a clear look along the trail, he knew both snipers still hid behind the large boulder. Wounded as they both were, they'd never have enough speed to get away in the short time he had probed the bloody crease on his left arm.

A frontal attack would be dangerous. He decided against sliding over the edge of the trail and going down. Attacking uphill, even against a wounded enemy, took away any tactical advantages. He had heard enough about tactics and strategy from the wounded officers he had operated on during the war to know his best chance lay in getting above the two killers.

Working his way uphill proved easy, since the large boulders dotting the mountainside provided plenty of cover. Carefully putting each foot down to be sure he didn't slip before moving the other proved painstakingly slow, but he made no sound and eventually got to a point above where the two men waited.

He didn't have a clear shot. With only four rounds left, he had to be sure of a clean kill.

"He's mighty quiet. You think I killed him?" The question was punctuated with a groan that told Knight the first man he had wounded was the one who spoke.

"You mean you shot him through the heart and he's out there drawin' flies?" The second man scoffed. "He's waitin' to finish the job he started. Oww, be careful. You're pullin' the bandana too tight."

"Got to if you want the blood to stop spurting. That's what a tourniquet's for."

Knight took grim pleasure in severing an artery in the second man's arm. That wound might be more serious than the round he put into the other's chest. He picked up a pebble, judged distances, then awkwardly threw it side-armed with his left hand. The stone clattered in front of the rock where the two hid.

Then there was only one. As the man with the bullet in his chest rose to get a shot at what he thought was Knight creeping up, Knight found a perfect shot. The round went through the man's hat crown and into his skull. He kicked straight, twitched once, and died.

Provoked, the one with the wounded arm swung around and began flinging lead all around. Knight threw himself flat. When he chanced a quick peek, he saw the man running for his life down the trail. Knight got off a shot — too fast, not aimed, well wide.

Cursing, he scrambled to his feet, then slid down the mountainside to land beside the man he had cut down. The man lay on his side, his mouth open and blood leaking from it. The bullet had gone smack into his brain.

Knight scooped up the man's rifle and holstered his Colt. Making sure a round rested in the chamber, he gripped the rifle in both hands and then set out after the fleeing killer.

"I'll show you not to ambush me." Knight felt hot fury building inside him when he realized these men had shot Helene in the back. *She* had been their target. They must have been sent by Avery, but he wanted to hear it from the still-living man's lips. He wanted the confession.

Then he would kill the son of a bitch.

He knew better than to run pell-mell along the path. The man ahead of him was likely weakening from loss of blood if the severed artery still spurted. He would probably try to find another spot for an ambush. Knight had to avoid getting killed if he wanted vengeance. Back shooters were a fact of life on the frontier but to shoot a woman in the back made the crime even more heinous.

Drops of bright crimson blood on the trail

warned him he was getting closer to his quarry. When they grew to the size of silver dollars, he knew the man wouldn't be able to run much farther. Slowing, Knight chanced a quick look around a bend in the trail. He jerked back when a bullet tore off a bit of greasewood growing from a crack beside him.

"Your partner's dead," he called to the bushwhacker. "If you toss out your rifle, I won't kill you."

"Why should you give me a break?"

"I want you to confess. We'll go to Fort Bayard, and you'll tell the commander who hired you and what you did."

"The army would hang me. And if they didn't Avery would scalp me."

Knight moved fast, knowing what was going to happen. He retreated, found a safe place to cover the trail, and saw movement above where he'd been. The sniper had wanted to keep him talking so he could get a clean shot. Knight had outsmarted him and turned the tables. As Avery's henchman stood, Knight got a bead on him and squeezed the trigger.

The rifle jammed.

The click alerted the man, who whirled around, looking frantically for Knight, who'd dropped the useless rifle and stepped out of hiding as his hand flashed toward the gun on his hip.

He might have pulled iron faster on some occasion, but he couldn't recollect when. The Colt leaped from his holster and he fired. The first bullet took the man square in the middle of the chest, just as Knight had wounded the first man. Three more rounds followed in the space of as many heartbeats. Knight had fired a tighter pattern before, but all the slugs slammed into his target within a hand span, tearing out the man's heart.

Toppling like a felled tree in the forest, the bushwhacker crashed to the ground, rolled, and gathered speed. He rolled across the game trail and over the side of the mountain. Knight listened. No cry. The man had died before he took the plunge.

Knight went to the edge and looked over. A bent, broken body lay fifty yards lower down the mountain. Disgusted, he flung the man's rifle after him. It clattered and slid down and came to rest not far from its former owner. Knight took the time to reload his Colt, then quickly retraced his way along the path.

The first man he'd shot was already worm food. Insects crawled over him, nibbling away. Before long, bigger carrion eaters would strip the carcass of meat. Knight shooed off the flies, got his hands under the man's arms, then heaved and sent him sliding down the mountain, too. He didn't want any evidence of the fight to remain this close to the mine. Jefferson Avery might send others. Knight didn't want to scare off any would-be killers.

He wanted to cut them down first.

"I heard so many gunshots," Hellfire said when he got back to her. "Thank God you're all right, Sam."

She sat propped up against a rock. She looked a little pale but otherwise none the worse for the bullet in her back.

"Let's get back to the mine. I have to pluck out the bullet lodged in you. It won't hurt much."

"Not with you doing the surgery." She let him help her along, but he suspected she didn't need to lean on him as much as she did. "What now, Sam?"

"It's war . . . and I'm on your side." He knew the commitment he made. And it felt right.

CHAPTER 22

"He's leading us into an ambush. Nobody leaves a trail this easy to follow." Spurgeon pointed to the hoofprints in the soft dirt along the road. "He might as well be marking the trail for us."

Hesseltine worried about that, too. Once Wilcox had hightailed it from the saloon, they had agreed to track him back to wherever he hung his hat. The chances were good that Dr. Samuel Knight would be there, too. The barkeep had about confessed up to that. Hesseltine didn't like the way Spurgeon had gotten the information, but Sierra Rojo didn't have a marshal. The sheriff's office was far off in the county seat, and the cavalry only came through whenever they were chasing Apaches. The chance that the bartender had friends willing to come after the men who threatened him was small.

Wilcox was another matter. The man hadn't seemed stupid. How could he be so

321

careless as to leave a trail a blind man could follow when he had to realize Spurgeon's questions were meant to uncover Knight? Hesseltine kept a sharp eye out as they rode along. He estimated how fast Wilcox rode. The man moved at a trot, which was puzzling. If he was worried enough to warn his friend, why not gallop?

"He'd wear out his horse too soon," Spurgeon said.

"Are my thoughts so obvious?"

"I'm working on the same problem. Up ahead is a big mountain with plenty of mines. That's where he's going."

"Red Mountain, I heard it called. Sierra Rojo means that in Spanish, or so it seems. William Ralston discovered silver down south on the main road, then others swarmed to the region and discovered even richer deposits."

"Gold, too, but that's over on the Mogollon Rim."

"You sound as if you want to try your hand at gold mining, Rance. Does being a Pinkerton detective bore you now?"

"I'm paid good." With that he fell into stony silence.

Hesseltine knew what ate at him. They were taking too long to catch Knight.

The man had quite a head start on them,

but they should have nabbed him in Buffalo Springs. Having to kill the witnesses there undoubtedly had provoked the law, although like Sierra Rojo that town lacked a marshal, although for a different reason. In Buffalo Springs the marshal had been murdered by the Hannigan gang. Sierra Rojo simply grew too fast and sent too many miners into the hills for anyone left behind to spend money hiring a lawman.

Hesseltine felt a touch of pride at doing his job so well. Without the law in so many frontier towns, the Pinkerton Agency kept the peace and caused the criminals they sought to flee rather than holing up.

Knight had tried to make Buffalo Springs his home. They had chased him out. If they had been quicker to show up, they would have saved another few weeks on the road, but they were close enough now to taste victory. Wilcox might be an accomplice, but there wasn't a wanted poster for him. No poster, no mention, no reward.

"We can catch a stagecoach back once we capture Knight," Hesseltine said. "That will make the trip easier."

"It won't be faster. We need to decide whether he goes back dead or alive."

"I know how you vote. Rather than waste a bullet, let's try to capture him alive. The

323

situation dictates what we do." Hesseltine touched the pistol under his right arm. Spurgeon was gun happy, but Hesseltine felt the same growing urge to shoot something. The months they had dedicated to pursuing Knight required some release. "It would be a shame if he simply gave up, though."

"Yeah, a damned shame. Look, ahead." Spurgeon pointed to where the road forked. Wilcox had walked his horse along the left-hand branch.

"According to the sign, that road leads upward to the Lucky Draw mine. Wilcox did ask if we were miners. He does work as superintendent. Fancy that."

"Do we take him now or later?" Spurgeon asked.

"We are making the assumption that he's leading us to Knight. If he isn't, he knows where our fugitive has holed up. No, we let him run free until we see what we're up against."

"He can see us if he's far enough up that winding road." Spurgeon shielded his eyes against the sun. "Or maybe not with the sun in his eyes."

"Not once has he slowed. He isn't worried about us being on his trail. Rather, he hurries along to warn his friend. That has made him careless. We have no reason to fear an ambush, so let's press on, close the distance, and trust that if he does see us, he'll discount the notion we are after him or Knight."

"You think he's that stupid?" Spurgeon spat, wiped his lips, then answered his own question. "Yeah, he's that stupid." He raked his heels along his horse's flanks and sped up.

By the time they reached the base of the mountain, Wilcox was two switchbacks ahead of them, higher up the road. He paid no attention to anyone else on the trail. Hesseltine exchanged a look with Spurgeon, then started up the slope. They had nothing to lose and everything to gain by showing some daring. The way Wilcox rode told them the man was oblivious to the threat they brought to Red Mountain.

"Should we take him before he reaches the top?" Spurgeon strained to look out and up.

"Let's see what he does first. We might still have to shoot it out with him."

"Good." Spurgeon touched his revolver, itching to trade lead with Wilcox. Or anyone else.

Hesseltine was aware how the pressure built up in his partner to kill something. At times it was annoying. At others, perhaps soon, it proved to be the best way out of a nasty situation.

After a fifteen-minute climb, Hesseltine called out, "He disappeared over the top. He's at the mine."

Spurgeon kicked at his horse's flanks to get it the last hundred yards past two switchbacks. Hesseltine joined him on the level stretch in front of the mine in a few minutes. He looked around for Wilcox but couldn't spot the super. No one appeared interested in asking who they were, so Hesseltine decided boldness once more gave them the advantage. He called out to a miner who was struggling to do something to a coil of chain using only one arm.

"You need help?" Hesseltine asked. "You've got your hands full. Your hand."

"I'm practicin' usin' one hand. Got the other all mashed up the other day. Thanks for the offer, though." The miner peered up at them. More than his arm failed to work right. His eyes looked foggy. "You the new rock diggers? The super said he was bringin' some recruits in from Sierra Rojo to replace those we lost."

"That's what we have to talk with him about. Knight's his name, right?" Hesseltine watched the reaction.

"Naw, that's the man what fixed me up. Saved my life, you betcha."

"Did a poor job of patching you up if you lost your arm," Spurgeon said.

"Don't you go sayin' nuthin' against him. He's a real fine fellow."

"So where do we find Knight? He's the head man, isn't he?" Hesseltine waited.

"If this is the first time you been up to the Lucky Draw, I can't see how you got that idea. Him and the boss are thicker 'n thieves now, that's for sure, but Dave Wilcox is the super. He does the hirin', but Hellfire does the firin'. She's the owner."

"So Knight and the owner are, shall we say, very good friends?" Hesseltine tried not to laugh. How easy it was to find the most intimate secrets after a short conversation. These men were starved for someone to listen to them. Feeding them a few falsehoods brought out their feelings of superiority as they explained what they thought he didn't know.

The miner chuckled and bobbed his head. "That's the rumor. But you want to talk to Wilcox about a job. The boss and Knight are holed up over in her office."

"That way?" Spurgeon pointed to the west.

"Around the hill *that* way." The miner

327

pointed in the other direction. "You boys need to get better directions. Wilcox went that direction. He just got back from town."

"Much obliged." Hesseltine shrugged his shoulder and moved his fancy jacket out of the way to get his shoulder rig settled down. Spurgeon reached across his body and tugged at his gun in his cross-draw holster. They were ready to finish their mission.

"There's Wilcox," Spurgeon said.

"And he's going into what just might be the office for the entire operation. What do you think the owner's like? Good looking or a face like a mud fence in the rain?"

"I don't care." Spurgeon slipped his gun free as they drew rein in front of the office. "I can buy me a good-looking dance hall girl with the money we're going to collect."

Hesseltine appreciated such optimism. He swung down from the saddle, drew his own gun, and went to the office door, which stood open a few inches. He saw Wilcox pacing, coming into his line of sight every few seconds. Another man in the cabin tried to calm him, but Hesseltine couldn't get a good look at him.

Then Wilcox said, "I tell you, Sam, something was wrong about them. They were all polite and well-mannered and friendly, but they gave me the fantods."

328

Another man asked, "Do you think they were the law?"

That was the first time Hesseltine had heard the voice . . . but he knew who it belonged to.

Hesseltine kicked the door open and let his revolver swing across the room. He swept the barrel past Wilcox and centered it on the man behind the paper-littered desk. It was Dr. Samuel Knight for certain.

A broad smile appeared on Hesseltine's round face. "No, sir, we're not the law. Not exactly. We're Pinkerton detectives — Hesseltine and" — he nodded at his partner — "Spurgeon, and we're taking you into custody, Samuel Knight."

"Don't!" Spurgeon added, pointing his gun at Wilcox to keep him from going for his iron. "We don't have a quarrel with you, mister, but I'll lay you out if you try anything."

"Sam, they must have trailed me!" Wilcox exclaimed in startled despair. "I'm sorry!"

"That you are, my friend," Hesseltine said. "You are very sorry as a trails man. We were close enough the entire way from town to pick your pocket and you never noticed."

"I was in a hurry to tell you, Sam, I —"

"Shut up." Spurgeon emphasized his command by cocking his pistol. The harsh

329

metallic click sounded like a thunderclap in the small room.

"You don't want to shoot," Knight said. "You really don't."

"Why, because all those miners will come running to help you?" Hesseltine laughed. "It won't matter by then because you'll have a bullet hole in your head."

"Your orders aren't to bring me back alive?"

"My partner and I have discussed this at some length. Dead or alive is what Gerald Donnelly said. It makes no difference to us which way you prefer to return to Pine Knob."

Wilcox frowned. "Sam, what's this all about?"

"Be quiet," Hesseltine said. "We have no intention of harming *you* unless you get in the way."

"Then I get to shoot you," Spurgeon finished.

"I warned you about shooting in here. And it's got nothing to do with everyone in the mine coming to help." Knight placed a bottle filled with clear yellow liquid on the desk with exaggerated care. "This is nitroglycerin. One shot in here will echo and that will set it off."

Hesseltine pursed his lips, then stepped

closer and reached for the bottle.

"You'll blow us all up!" Knight backed away from the bottle on the edge of the desk.

"I've worked up a powerful thirst coming up the mountain." Hesseltine grabbed the bottle, flicked the cork out with his thumb, and took a long drink. He smacked his lips. "That's mighty fine corn squeezings."

"And a mighty poor bluff," added Spurgeon.

"Dave, these men will kill me and you, too. They can't let you identify them."

"Donnelly said you weren't too bright, but friends in Buffalo Springs said different. Yes," said Hesseltine in response to the look on Knight's face, "we stopped by there to get on your trail. What were their names? Oh, yes, Seth Lunsford and some fine-looking filly named Marianne."

"Seth would never tell you a damned thing," Knight said.

"You're right. He didn't. Neither did the girl."

"You killed them." Knight's hand twitched.

Hesseltine reacted instinctively. He cocked his pistol and put the muzzle against Wilcox's forehead. There wasn't any need to spell it out. Their fugitive understood what would happen if he went for his gun. Donnelly had said Knight was quick and accurate, but there wasn't any way he could clear leather before his friend died with a bullet through his head.

"Where's the woman? The mine owner he's sweet on?" Spurgeon moved to get a cleaner shot at Knight.

"How'd you know about that?" Wilcox blurted out the question, tried to move away from the cold steel pressing into his head, and found himself forced to his knees in front of the desk. Hesseltine took special pleasure in seeing how the man knew his fate was sealed.

"We asked around," Spurgeon said. "Should we hunt for the woman?"

"There's no reason to do that," Hesseltine said. "She is only a distraction." He grinned like a wolf. "Do you find her to be a distraction, Dr. Knight?"

"You *are* a doctor," blurted Wilcox. "I thought so!"

"How is it you hide your identity from your closest friends and yet we had no trouble crossing a thousand miles to find you?" Hesseltine laughed again. "It must be that we are very, very good at our job."

"Take their guns, Henry. Stop taunting them."

"I shall do that very thing, Rance. Keep your pistol trained on Dr. Knight. He is a slippery one." He bent, plucked Wilcox's revolver from its holster, and tossed it into the corner of the cabin. Keeping his gun trained on the super's head, he inched around the desk, bent at the knees, aware of the aches in his joints from so much time in the saddle, grabbed Knight's Colt and threw it after Wilcox's gun. "There. That pulls your fangs."

"Now what?" Knight looked forlorn.

Hesseltine relished that expression. Too many men kept up a façade of bravado. He always waited for the resignation, the firm knowledge that there was nowhere to run, no way to escape justice. If Knight wasn't quite there yet, he was close.

"Why, Dr. Knight, you should know. You are the only one we want." Hesseltine stepped back, straightened his arm, and aimed for Wilcox's head. "It's time for us to tie up loose ends and return you to Gerald Donnelly."

The fear on Wilcox's face fed Hesseltine's delight in the cruelty. His finger tightened on the trigger.

CHAPTER 23

"Wait!" Knight tried to stop Hesseltine from murdering his friend. "It's me you want, not him."

"He knows what happened to you. From what I hear, everyone at the Lucky Draw thinks you walk on water. We don't leave behind any way to track us." Hesseltine grinned. Knight looked around frantically for a way to stop the killing.

It came from an unexpected direction. A shotgun blast ripped away the wall immediately behind him. A pellet struck Knight in the cheek, causing him to wince. More of the double-ought load hit Hesseltine. The Pinkerton detective recoiled as he jerked the trigger. His shot missed Wilcox by a hair's breadth.

Knight wasn't sure what he did next. He seemed to be in the corner of the cabin in one instant and wrestling with Hesseltine the next. He drove the detective backwards

334

until he slammed hard into the wall, knocking loose a few planks. Behind him he heard Wilcox shouting and Spurgeon firing. And from outside came more buckshot, followed closely by rifle and pistol reports. No lead from those weapons ripped away the walls, but the confusion was enough for him to get his hand around Hesseltine's wrist and twist viciously. The revolver went flying.

Knight rolled over and snatched his Colt from the floor. He came up onto his knees and fanned the hammer, spraying lead all around. He hoped to hit Hesseltine. He missed, but what mattered most was that he sent both Pinkerton detectives scurrying out of the cabin.

Knight slid the other fallen gun in Wilcox's direction. With a clumsy grab, Wilcox recovered his pistol and flopped around, back against the desk and his gun held in both hands.

"What's going on, Sam?" he panted.

Wilcox had barely got out the words when several more shotgun blasts blew new holes in the thin planking. They were lower than the initial one and intended to kill anyone sitting at the desk.

"We can find out later. We've got to corral those two. They'll stop at nothing to kill me — and you. They mentioned Helene, too.

They'll cut her down if they get a chance."

"Helene? Oh, yeah, Hellfire." Wilcox flopped onto his belly and crawled to the door to thrust his pistol out. "What did you do that someone sent those snakes after you?"

"Let's get out of this death trap and then we can talk about it." Knight had no intention of ever letting Wilcox or anyone else know why Gerald Donnelly sought him. All he wanted was for Wilcox and Helene to be safe.

Two more shotgun blasts tore away most of the back wall. He swiveled around and saw a man rise up to let loose with another blast from a double-barreled Greener.

Knight made sure he never got the chance. His first bullet caught the man in the chest. He grunted, bent over slightly, then as he straightened, the shotgun's twin barrels wobbling around, Knight finished him off with a well-placed round to his head.

"I don't recognize him," he called to Wilcox. "Whoever's so intent on ventilating us isn't one of our workers."

"You thought they would?" Wilcox fired four times as fast as he could cock and pull the trigger. "Got one! He's wearing a mask. They might be robbers thinking we're easier to rob than a bank. Hellfire's got almost a week's worth of silver stored up here."

Knight doubted that Wilcox was right about the shotgunners being bandits. He scrambled to the back of the office, chanced a quick look around, and leaped out through the gaping, buckshot-torn hole. Immediately, he found himself looking down a rifle barrel. The man who held the rifle was even more surprised than Knight.

He died surprised. Knight got off three shots before the man squeezed the trigger on his rifle even once.

Tucking his Colt Navy into its holster, Knight scooped up the fallen rifle and went back to the cabin. Wilcox struggled to reload while stretched out on his belly.

"I'll cover you while you reload. And you can use Hesseltine's gun, too. He dropped it."

Knight kicked the Pinkerton's gun to him, then stood guard as Wilcox reloaded his own gun. Only once did someone poke his head up from behind a rock, but Knight held his fire. He recognized the man as one of the Lucky Draw miners. He was armed with a pickaxe. A pickaxe against rifles and shotguns. It wasn't a fair match.

Knight charged out to even the odds. He bent low and ran, skidding to a halt beside the miner. A quick peek showed where the gunfire came from.

"Mighty good seein' you, Sam," the man said. "I thought I was a goner. I was headed to the office to meet with Hellfire and them varmints started shootin' at me."

"Stay down." Knight went the other way, rose, and got off a well-aimed shot. He didn't hit the sniper but drove him back under cover. He levered a new round into the Winchester and remained exposed. The miner tugged at him to take cover. Knight ignored him. Cool, calm in spite of the risk, he waited.

He fired when the sniper showed himself. Knight's marksmanship proved perfect again. The attacker fell silently over a rock, then bonelessly slithered back. His rifle remained in front of the rock. As if no danger existed, Knight walked forward, grabbed the rifle, and returned to where the miner clutched his pickaxe so hard his knuckles had turned white from strain.

"Here. Use it the best you can. Don't shoot our men."

"I can do that, Sam. I can."

"You said Hellfire told you to come to the office? Why?"

"I was meetin' with her to talk over how to blast a new drift. The current vein's peterin' out and —"

338

"Where is she? She's not in the office."

"Last I saw her, she was headin' into the mine to look over the situation with the new drift, but that was fifteen-twenty minutes back."

"Get into the office and back up Wilcox. Wait for me there."

"What about Hellfire?"

"I'll make sure she's all right." Knight waved and called out to Wilcox, letting him know he was getting help in defending the office, and pushed the miner in the direction of the cabin. When he didn't hear any shots coming from that direction, he reckoned Wilcox had understood and not fired on an ally.

Knight hunkered down and reloaded his Colt Navy. With it heavy at his hip and the Winchester in his grip, he felt ready to take on a wildcat and spot it two bites. As he started toward the mine, his optimism faded. Four miners lay dead in front of the entrance. Two others returned the bushwhackers' shots from just inside the tunnel's mouth, but their field of fire was limited since they were too far back to see the men pot-shotting them one by one. Knight hunted for any trace of Helene, but she was nowhere to be seen.

If he waited too long, the men in the mine

would be killed. But he had the two Pinkerton detectives to hunt down, as well. He decided to go after Hesseltine and Spurgeon later when he spotted a man worming his way toward the mine. The attacker clutched a bundle of dynamite in one hand and a lucifer in the other. His intention was clear — blow the mine and trap a dozen men inside. Since most were down in the bowels of the earth, there'd be no one outside to rescue them.

Knight drew a bead on the man, not liking the idea of shooting him in the back but seeing no way around it. The man struck the match. It sputtered to life and he lit the fuse. The waxy black miner's fuse burned precisely one foot a minute. He let it burn down until only a few seconds were left, then reared up to throw.

Knight squeezed the trigger and his bullet shattered the man's spine. The attacker let out an inhuman screech. The bundle dropped from his suddenly nerveless hand and a second shriek of fear blended with the earth-shaking blast. When the dust settled there wasn't even a wet spot left on the ground.

Knight waved to a miner who appeared at the mouth of the mine and motioned him back. If the man had any sense he wouldn't retreat too far. The narrow mine shaft forced attackers to silhouette themselves and become easy targets, even for the poor marksmen among the defending miners.

Jessup stood and got his men's attention. "Get back, damn you. Don't try to go into the mine!"

If there had been any doubt who was attacking the Lucky Draw, it was all gone with Jessup revealing himself. Jefferson Avery had sent his bully boys to kill and destroy.

While it wasn't an easy shot, Knight tried it anyway. He fired twice, as fast as he could, at Jessup. The first round went high. The second scraped the rock in front of the man's face. Jessup recoiled and ducked out of sight. Knight tried to send a third round Jessup's way, but the rifle mechanism jammed. He swung around and worked to clear the bent cartridge in the receiver.

Before he could clear it, he saw Hesseltine running for cover off to one side. He wanted the Pinkerton detective dead, but Jessup presented a greater immediate threat to the mine and the men inside. Giving up on the rifle, Knight slid his Colt free and headed for a spot where he could get Jessup in his sights.

Only a few yards toward Avery's henchman he came upon two men with rifles taking random shots into the mine. They didn't see him as he crossed behind them. It wasn't good tactics letting armed men remain behind him to cut off possible retreat, but he had already shot one of the attackers in the back. His conscience told him that man wouldn't have died if he hadn't lit the fuse on the dynamite and blown himself to kingdom come. That was a lie, but it helped him believe he hadn't done anything wrong.

One man rolled onto his side, did a double take, and then shouted a warning to his partner as he swung his rifle around to shoot Knight. Two shots ended his life. Knight took some consolation in the fact that he had been facing the man when he killed him.

The other man understood that death stalked him and never tried to get a shot at Knight. Digging in his toes, he launched himself forward as if making a frontal assault on the mine.

Knight took aim but never fired. Someone in the mine took care of removing the sniper for him. The shot wasn't clean, and Jessup's crony wasn't dead, but he was in no condition to continue fighting. Knight left him where he lay. If the fight ended soon, he could tend to the man, maybe save his life.

If Jessup fought on, then his man's death was on his shoulders.

Knight circled, hoping he was far enough behind Jessup that he wouldn't be seen until it was too late as he attacked from the rear. Moving slowly, he got closer. Then he froze. Two of Jessup's men held Hellfire Bonham between them. Jessup stood in front of her and leveled his pistol, ready to put a round through her head.

Knight reacted without thinking. He ran forward, firing. The fusillade startled Jessup and gave Helene the chance to jerk free from her captors and bolt.

Knight dropped behind a rock, taking time to reload. Helene had gotten away, but for how long? As he started to renew the attack, a hail of bullets hammered at him from behind. He dived between two low rocks for cover but was caught between Jessup ahead and his men behind.

But the shooters behind him weren't Jefferson Avery's men.

"Give up, Dr. Knight," Hesseltine called. "We promise we'll get you back to Pine Knob alive if you throw down that gun and give up."

That was a lie and Knight knew it. He took a quick peek and saw where both Pinkertons waited for him to surrender.

Even if he believed Hesseltine, Knight had seen the kill-crazy look in Spurgeon's eyes back in the cabin. The man needed spilled blood to feel alive. Spurgeon was smiling and anticipating the death bullet through his adversary's heart.

"I can't move," Knight said, trying to make his voice sound full of pain. "I took a bullet through the knee. I can't even stand up."

"We're not stupid," called Spurgeon. "You want to shoot us."

"No, no, I'm wounded. I'll give up if you promise not to harm Wilcox or any of the others."

"Even that lady mine owner?" Hesseltine shifted position, intending to get Knight in a crossfire between him and his partner. "We saw her. She's quite comely. I see why you're sweet on her. But I have to wonder . . . whatever does she see in you? Perhaps she doesn't know all the terrible things you did back in Texas."

Hesseltine harangued him, trying to make him mad and distract him so Spurgeon could move in on him. Knight held his fire, caught sight of Spurgeon, and fired. The Pinkerton yelped as a bullet tore away a chunk of his forearm.

Knight swung around and got off a couple

rounds in Hesseltine's direction to pin him down. He whirled back to Spurgeon, but the detective had already dropped flat on his belly. Knight fired until his revolver came up empty, sending dust billowing up in front of the man.

That didn't accomplish anything except to blind Spurgeon, but for the moment that was good enough. Rolling onto his back, Knight worked to reload. Before he finished, he looked up and saw one of Jessup's killers standing on a rock above him. The man grinned, raised his rifle, and fired — but the man wasn't aiming at Knight. From the way he stood, he might not have even seen him. He fired at Hesseltine, taking him for one of Hellfire's men.

Knight finished reloading, but there wasn't any need to take out Jessup's confederate. Spurgeon did that for him. As the Pinkerton fanned off a few rounds that ripped through the bushwhacker and knocked him off the boulder, Knight fired. Spurgeon yelped again and grabbed his arm. Shot twice in the right arm, he began squirting blood all over the ground. He drew back before Knight could finish what he had started.

"I'm hit pretty bad, Henry," Spurgeon called. "Cover me while I get out of here."

"Wait. Don't, Rance. We have to get him

now." Hesseltine sounded a little desperate. Things weren't going as he and his partner had planned.

"There's a damned army behind him. We have to get out of here *now.*" Spurgeon kicked up a little dust as he took his own advice and lit a shuck toward the horses.

Knight pivoted back and forth, wanting to shoot both of them but having nothing in the way of a shot at either. Then he heard boots against rock behind him. He ducked low and fired without completely turning around. Three shots roared from his gun before he came up empty again.

He had dropped one of a trio of Jessup's men. The two still on their feet stared stupidly at the one he had killed. All they had to do was aim and fire. Knight was empty. The time it would take him to reload was plenty for them to saunter over and put a bullet through his head half a dozen times. When faced with such an impossible situation, a colonel he had patched up during the war had given him some simple advice. *When you're going to die anyway, do it attacking.*

His throat aching from the rebel yell, Knight surged up and waved his empty revolver above his head. The two men's eyes got wide and their mouths dropped open.

Then they turned and fled. Knight grabbed the fallen man's Henry rifle and fired a couple times after the two he had bluffed. He hardly believed his crazy attack had worked.

A look over his shoulder revealed nothing but an empty stretch where Hesseltine and Spurgeon had lain in ambush for him. If they were smart, they'd hightail it away from the Lucky Draw. And he had the feeling they were just that — smart. Tracking him down the way they had might have required an element of luck, but from what they'd said, they had pieced together hints he'd left and hadn't even realized at the time.

He went cold inside, remembering their boast of killing Seth and Marianne. They had never mentioned doing anything to Amelia Parker or her pa, but he wouldn't put it past them. Either way, there was no reason for him to return to Buffalo Springs. If they'd left Amelia dead, he could only put flowers on her grave or, if she still lived, he'd be put in one himself when her rage boiled over at all the misfortune he had caused.

Working his way to the flat area in front of the mine, he saw that Jessup was pulling his men back. Knight held off taking a shot at a couple. Having Hellfire's men trapped in

347

the mine escape safely was good enough for the moment. Or so he thought until he heard her voice over the din of horse's hooves and random gunfire.

Heedless of being shot, he ran across the open stretch to a spot around the curve of the mountain where Jessup had left his horses. Several mounts stood riderless, a tribute to Knight's marksmanship. But he saw one rider and went cold inside.

Hellfire Bonham sat astride a horse, her hands bound behind her back. She fought to fling herself off, first to one side and then the other. Jessup rode on one side of her and one of his henchman guarded her on the other. Sandwiched between them she could do nothing but let them lead her horse away from camp.

If they couldn't seal the mine with the miners inside, kidnaping the owner had to rate second best. For all Knight knew, Jefferson Avery wanted to kill her with his own hands. The animosity between the former husband and wife ran deeper than most blood feuds.

"Stop!" Knight shouted to draw their attention.

None of Jessup's men heard him, but Helene did, twisting her neck to look back over her shoulder at him. She tried once more to escape, and again they held her in place.

Knight took a deep breath, lifted the captured rifle, and started forward. A frontal attack had worked once. It had to again. He had a loaded Henry rifle, even if he dared not take out Jessup for fear of hitting Helene.

He took off at a run when the raiding party wheeled around and trotted away, heading for the road down the mountain. If he missed them there, he always had a second chance by looking down the slope to where the road doubled back. If he missed then, he was out of luck — and so was Helene.

Jessup vanished over the rim and started down the road. Knight had almost reached the top of the road when a flurry of bullets kicked up dust all around him. One came close enough to his ear that he instinctively jerked away from the wind-rip of its passage. This caused him to lose his balance and fall to one knee.

He looked up to see Frank Kilgore, the man Helene had hired to protect the mine, galloping past. As he drew even with Knight, he kicked out and caught him on the side of the head. Knight fell backwards, the rifle spinning from his hands. Stunned, he lay on his back, watching as Kilgore joined Jessup and the others in their escape.

CHAPTER 24

Pedro Ramirez completed the chore of sending men into the Blue-Eyed Bitch for the new shift and found the owner pacing outside the mine's mouth. "Why are you so nervous?" he asked Jefferson Avery. "Is something wrong?"

"It's nothing for you to worry over." Avery said the words but obviously expected something to happen. He kept glancing toward the road leading from the mine and into Sierra Rojo.

"It is my job to worry for you, Señor Avery. I am your superintendent. I should know of any trouble so I can deal with it. This is dangerous work, pulling the silver from the ground." Ramirez looked around, then frowned. "Where is the man you hired? What is Jessup doing?"

"I said it's none of your business." Avery spun and walked away.

His broad back presented an easy target.

351

Ramirez forced himself to keep from pulling the gun at his hip and firing. One shot. Two. Such would end the life of his boss.

"Wait," he said as he followed Avery. "You must tell me. Where has Jessup gone?"

Angrily whirling on him, Avery poked a finger into his super's chest and pressed hard. "He's doing what needs to be done."

"No." Ramirez's eyes widened in disbelief. "You cannot have sent him to kill your former wife."

"Don't act so shocked. It has to be done, and you know it."

"No, no!" Ramirez threw his hands up in the air and cried out in frustration. "She cannot die. Not yet."

"She has to, and Jessup has to be the one doing it. You pulled his fat from the fire when he tried to rob the Lucky Draw silver shipment. He wasn't smart enough to figure out that was a damn trap."

"I did not know it was a trap, either. I suspected, but did I know?" Ramirez shook his head. How was it that this fool found new ways to confound him? "You should not trust Jessup. He is an outlaw, and not a good one. He will ruin everything."

"What do you care about Hellfire? You work for me." Avery stalked off, leaving Ramirez standing there still half-shocked by this development.

Ramirez chewed his lip, thinking hard about what to do. Jessup succeeded only in making every plan a shambles. The worst thing he could do was kill Hellfire Bonham too soon. Ramirez intended to kill her, but only after he killed Jefferson Avery. That order was important if he was going to be successful in his plan to pin the crime on her. Avery being obviously murdered by his ex-wife had to happen first.

Ramirez looked at his departing boss and knew he would have to rely on Jessup failing once again. Avery might have sent his henchman to kill his ex-wife, but Jessup had not shown he was good at following orders. In this, too, he might fail. Ramirez smiled widely at the thought of Hellfire turning the tables on Jessup and shooting him. That would work well. That would work even better. It would provide yet another reason for Hellfire to kill Avery. He had sent Jessup to kill her. When Jessup failed, Hellfire would seek revenge and murder Avery.

But that still required Jessup to fail. If he didn't, if he again meddled and destroyed Ramirez's plans, the cavalry would have to conduct an investigation. He had seen Lieutenant Billings in Ralston. Ramirez knew the young officer sought a better command elsewhere and considered his post at Fort Bayard as punishment. With the right clues, Billings would jump to whatever conclusion Ramirez suggested. But the clues had to be laid before Avery died and while Hellfire Bonham still lived.

Ramirez veered away from the mine and climbed a steep slope to a point above the tunnel mouth. Moving a few rocks revealed a gunnysack filled with items he had stolen from the Lucky Draw's owner over the past month.

He sat on a rock and opened the sack, pawing through the contents. He had a scarf. Would anyone remember Hellfire wearing it? He stuffed it back and pulled out a pistol. One gun looked like another, but many people had seen her with this one. He laid it aside. He would use Hellfire's own gun to shoot Avery.

"In the back," Ramirez muttered. "He must be shot in the back to make the crime worse." He continued rummaging in the sack.

He held up a scrap of cloth with a brooch pinned to it. One of her miners had stolen this from her. Ramirez had paid a pretty penny to get it, lying to say he wanted it for a *novia*. The notion of a gift for a girlfriend had pleased the thieving miner almost as much as the five dollars Ramirez had given him.

Even better was a sheaf of love letters from Hellfire. Stealing those had been difficult since Jefferson Avery kept the letters in the company safe. Ramirez had seen them there and finally figured out from comments Avery made that the man's former wife had written them.

More than a month passed after Ramirez realized the letters were from Hellfire before he'd been able to get the combination to the safe. He had replaced the missives with blank sheets, leaving only the top and bottom letters to fool Avery, should he bother looking. They would provide another motive for Hellfire to enter the camp and murder Avery. She wanted the love letters back. If Ramirez hinted to Billings that she wanted to destroy them, that might be all it took to frame her.

Her gun, the brooch, the letters. Those were the clues he would strew about after he gunned down Avery. Then, and *only* then, would Hellfire Bonham die.

With both of them dead, the lawyers in San Francisco would look to Pedro Ramirez to run the mines. What a shame if neither appeared to be profitable and for sale at a price so low even a superintendent might buy them.

Both of them.

Ramirez stashed the sack back in the hole and covered it with rocks. He had what he needed to set his plan in motion. All he wondered about was his counterpart at the Lucky Draw mine. Dave Wilcox had only recently taken the job. Hellfire went through supers at her mine at such a frantic rate, Wilcox might be gone, too. He would present no threat to Ramirez making his claim to buy both mines. And who else on Red Mountain would enter a competing bid?

He had free rein to become very, very rich.

Kill Avery. Frame Hellfire. Show that the pair of mines were not producing much silver at all, making them almost worthless. Then he could put in his offer to buy them. From their lofty perches in far-off San Francisco, the lawyers would take a quick buck to be rid of the distant properties. If the lawyers sent out someone from their office to investigate, Ramirez had no doubt such a dangerous place as New Mexico Territory would provide a new resident in a boneyard.

That would never occur if he dealt quickly enough with the lawyers. More immediate concerns were that fool Jessup and the doctor Hellfire had hired. Rumors had them as lovers. And she had hired a man to fight Jessup. *Frank Kilgore.* Dealing with hired killers was not a trifle, but Ramirez knew money convinced such men to desert their employers. All it took was *enough* money.

After he killed Avery, he would have that. He shook his head sadly.

"He caught her robbing him. He protested. She shot him in the back and fled. She left behind the letters, jewelry, and her gun because I chased her off. That is a good story. Then I tracked her down and killed her at her mine? Or should I notify the army?" Ramirez chewed on his lip as he thought it through. Hellfire had to die. Should he kill her at her mine or lure her to the Blue-Eyed Bitch after Avery was dead?

Ramirez had accumulated the evidence against her. How he used it to the best advantage was a question he had to answer. He hefted the gun he had stolen from her, and knew first he had to kill Avery. No matter what Jessup did, Avery had to die.

Making his way down the hill and worrying that Jessup would turn up, Ramirez looked around. The mine was quiet, and the shift wouldn't change for another couple hours. The miners not down in the tunnel were still asleep or only just getting up. They'd eat before hoisting their pickaxes and shovels, so he had time.

He went to the office and kicked open the door, Hellfire's gun swinging around as he hunted for his target. Jefferson Avery was nowhere to be seen. Cursing under his breath, Ramirez went to the desk and tossed the packet of love letters into the kneehole. A quick look around identified the best place for the brooch. He ripped part of the cloth holding it and hung it on a protruding wall nail at shoulder height. Everything else was in place, so he broke a chair to make it look like a fight had raged through the office and went to the safe. He knew the combination, but he had to be certain everything was in place.

He quickly opened it and found the partnership papers. The temptation to steal the document so he could present them to the lawyers was irresistible. If Hellfire had gotten the love letters, she would take the partnership papers, too. If the agreement wasn't in the safe when she looked, she couldn't take it. He worked through the details and encountered too many things that might go wrong.

"Damn you, Jessup." The hired gun had turned everything on its head with his incompetence. Ramirez came to a quick decision and took the partnership agreement. He would figure out how to get it into the lawyer's hands later. He crammed it into his coat pocket and went to set his plot in motion.

He left the office, clutching the stolen revolver in his hand. Jefferson Avery frequented only a few places at the mine. He had little to do with the everyday operation down in the tunnels, and he never spoke to the miners unless it was to fire them. That left only a couple places, and Ramirez thought his boss would be in the livery.

He went to the corral behind the small barn. A few horses frolicked in the corral, but Avery wasn't there. The man had to be in the barn. Ramirez went in and saw his target at the back stall, examining his horse's left rear hoof.

Avery looked up. "When's the farrier due to come by?" he asked with his usual arrogant impatience. "My horse is about ready to throw this shoe. Only two nails are holding it on —" He stopped and stared as he saw the pistol leveled at him. "What the hell are you doing, Pedro? Put that down."

"It is the gun of your wife. She is going to kill you." Ramirez walked to the stall.

Avery dropped the horse's hoof and leaned against the animal, causing it to stir nervously. He stared at the pistol clutched so firmly in his super's hand. Ramirez never wavered as he lifted the gun and pointed it at his boss.

"You're working for her? That's why you were mad that Jessup went to kill her?"

"I don't care if he kills her, but she'll die when *I* want, when it will fit everything I've done. I'm taking over both mines."

"You'll never make it, Pedro. You're a loser." Avery suddenly kicked up a rock in Ramirez's direction, ducked, and darted away.

Ramirez smiled broadly, drew a bead, and fired. The first bullet hit the owner of the Blue-Eyed Bitch mine in the shoulder, causing him to stumble and fall. As Avery thrashed around, trying to get to his feet, Ramirez stepped closer, cocked the gun again, and took careful aim.

The shot struck Avery in the back of the head. He slammed forward, twitched once, and then lay still on the ground.

"Now for the blue-eyed bitch herself," Pedro Ramirez said. He tossed the gun to the ground near Avery, turned away from the corpse, and went to complete his plan.

CHAPTER 25

Samuel Knight stumbled, kept his feet, and got off a shot at Kilgore before the man disappeared over the rim of the mountain and galloped down the road. He ran hard until he reached the head of the trail. Kilgore had disappeared around the first bend. Two switchbacks down the road Knight saw Jessup and two of his henchmen herding Helene between them, keeping her moving and unable to escape. He lifted his aim from Kilgore and got off a shot at Jessup. The range was too great for a handgun.

Knight reversed his direction and headed for the corral, panting harshly, a stitch in his side almost doubling him over in pain. By the time he had thrown on the saddle and mounted, Wilcox and three others had come from the mine. All clutched rifles.

"Where are you going, Sam?" Wilcox came up beside him. "You're not running away, not you!"

"Jessup," he gasped out. "Jefferson Avery's gunman. He's got Hellfire. Kidnapped her."

Wilcox swore and motioned for the men with him to get horses. They'd be a poor posse but better than nothing.

"What do you think they intend doing?" Wilcox asked. "Avery can't ransom her. I don't have the combination to the Lucky Draw safe."

Knight had the combination, but getting into a discussion of the matter with Wilcox wouldn't do anything to rescue Hellfire. He pulled the rifle from his saddle scabbard and pointed with the barrel. "Follow me when you get saddled up. I'm not waiting."

"Sam, you can't go it alone. We have a better chance of saving her if we all go together." Wilcox's words faded behind Knight as he galloped off in a cloud of dust.

He rushed past the mine and hit the road, his horse kicking up gravel as it skidded around the first sharp bend. Head down and urging the horse to even more speed, he galloped along the trail, occasionally catching sight of Jessup far lower on one of the switchbacks. Knight lifted the rifle to take a shot at Kilgore when the treacherous hired gun appeared, but he had to give up the chance when his horse cut back along the road, taking him in the wrong direction.

Knight settled down to ride hard. The time to fight was coming up fast. He had to get to the bottom of the road before Jessup had a chance to set up an ambush. One sniper would be all it took to bottle up everyone from the Lucky Draw since the road was so narrow.

He rounded the last bend and saw Kilgore on the ground, taking cover behind his horse. What Knight feared most had happened. Jessup had a sniper waiting for anyone foolish enough to follow, but why was Kilgore pinned down after obviously having his horse shot out from under him? Kilgore had knocked Knight down in his haste to join Jessup.

Knight gripped the saddle tightly with his knees as he used both hands on the rifle. It bucked as he squeezed the trigger. He missed the sniper hidden behind a thick, tall clump of prickly pear cactus. Juice and bits of thorny pads went flying. He levered the rifle and triggered again.

Kilgore responded in a way Knight hadn't expected. He got his feet under him, vaulted over his dead horse, and rushed headlong toward the sniper, his gun leveled. Knight's bullets occupied the would-be killer a second too long. Kilgore got close enough to fire through the cactus. Mixed with the juicy pulp blown off the plant, blood flew in the air.

Kilgore kept running, vaulted over the cactus, and landed hard behind the sniper, rolling as he went to the ground. Twice more he fired as he came back up to his knees.

Jessup's henchman threw up his arms and crashed into the prickly pear. From the way the sniper lay still, not moving a muscle, Knight knew he was dead. No one could endure hundreds of nasty spines spearing into him without a twitch or a moan.

He galloped forward, his rifle leveled on Kilgore, who was climbing to his feet. Although Knight's finger twitched, he didn't pull the trigger. "Why'd you kill him?"

"Jessup's got Hellfire," Kilgore said. "They rode toward the Blue-Eyed Bitch, so that must be where they're taking her."

"You knocked me down at the top of the hill. Why'd you do that if you're not in cahoots with Jefferson Avery?"

Kilgore stared at him, his jaw muscles knotting as he ground his teeth together. He stepped forward but did not lift his revolver. "I never saw you. All I had in my head was rescuing Hellfire. She's the boss, after all."

"You're not working for Avery?"

364

In answer Kilgore pointed his pistol at the dead body.

"I was wrong about you," Knight admitted.

"Can we both ride that nag of yours?" Kilgore turned the gun a little toward Knight, hinting that he would shoot him out of the saddle to steal his horse — so he could rescue Hellfire Bonham.

"No need. I see that bushwhacker's horse staked to a mesquite bush over that hill." Knight pointed with the rifle, aware that he was giving Kilgore the chance to shoot him down if that was his pleasure.

"Let me get his rifle and any ammunition on him." Kilgore expertly searched the corpse, making Knight think it wasn't the first dead body the man had plundered.

With a box of cartridges and the dropped rifle in hand, Kilgore made his way up the sandy slope and down to the skittish horse.

"Where were you when the shooting started up at the mine?" Knight wanted to hear Kilgore's response. He still didn't trust him.

"I was patrolling the far side of the property. By the time I worked my way back, most of the shooting was over, but I saw Hellfire getting nabbed. I lit out after her." He paused, eyeing Knight. "You got in the way. I'm sorry if I bowled you over, but I never recognized you. I was too focused on Jessup and his men herding our boss down the side of the mountain."

Knight remained silent as Kilgore stepped up into the saddle. The stirrups were fastened wrong. He rode with his knees bent since the former rider was a much shorter man, but there wasn't time to readjust the tack.

"You ought to be pinning a medal on me for trying to stop the kidnapping," Kilgore grumbled.

"I apologize for thinking you had thrown in with Avery," Knight said. "There'll be a half dozen men down the road in a few minutes."

"Fine, you wait for them." Kilgore turned his horse and put his heels to its flanks. He shot off like he was a Fourth of July rocket.

Knight put his head down and charged after Kilgore. He had gotten the man all wrong. Hellfire must have seen a loyalty in him that Knight, being more suspicious by nature, had not. He caught up with Kilgore, and they raced side by side along the road circling the base of Red Mountain, heading for the road leading to the Blue-Eyed Bitch mine.

"What'll we do when we catch up? Jessup

has four or five men with him."

"One less than before," Kilgore said.

"They still outnumber us two or three to one. Do you think he'll kill Hellfire?"

"He wanted her as a prisoner or he'd have gunned her down."

"Avery might want the pleasure of doing the killing himself," Knight said. "They really hate each other, Hellfire and Avery."

Kilgore looked over at him and started to ask a question. Knight knew what it was, but their headlong race had neared an end. Not a hundred yards ahead rode Jessup's trailing guard. Knight swung the rifle up and got off a shot, intending to spook the man. Instead, he hit him. The man grabbed his right arm, jerked around, and lost his balance as his horse veered suddenly. He went flying out of the saddle.

Knight galloped past. Kilgore slowed and took the time to shoot the fallen man a couple more times. He caught up as Knight drew rein. His horse dug in its heels, skidded along, and kicked up a dust cloud that saved them both. Jessup had left behind another sniper at the bottom of the road to Avery's mine.

Bullets ripped through the dust, not finding a target in either pursuer.

"Damned if we can get past him without

taking a bullet or two." Kilgore hit the ground and made his way to an arroyo. He flopped down in it and began reloading.

Knight started to join him, then realized they'd both be pinned down at the same spot if he did. He angled away and found a place to take cover on the far side of the road, making it impossible to cover both at the same time. The sniper would have to swing from one of them to the other.

Knight took in the situation in a flash. The longer the sniper held them at bay, the closer to the Blue-Eyed Bitch Jessup got — and the sooner Avery would kill Hellfire Bonham. Without conscious thought, he was on his feet and charging the rifleman.

A flash of light off the front sight warned him. He dived and skidded to safety behind a fallen pine trunk as a bullet whipped through the air where he'd been. As if they had worked this out, Knight drew the fire and Kilgore advanced.

When the sniper realized he had another man coming for him from a different direction, he switched back to take a few shots at Kilgore. This gave Knight the chance to continue his attack. Before he was forced to take cover again, he reached a spot within ten yards of his target. He pressed his back against the rock, signaled Kilgore, and waited. The rifleman fired three times, then Knight heard a metallic click as the hammer fell on an empty chamber.

Swarming to the top of the rock, he peered down on the man frantically reloading. Knight knew then how the expression "shooting fish in a barrel" came about. His shot was that easy. With the man looking up at him in horror, Knight steadied his rifle. He was a doctor and had taken a vow to preserve life.

Avery was going to kill Helene.

Knight squeezed the trigger and ended the guard's life.

"Are you going to stand around all day or do we rescue her?" Kilgore's question made Knight swing around.

The hired gunman held out the reins of Knight's horse. Knight jumped, got his leg over the saddle, and landed hard. The horse protested, then bolted, running up the road toward the Blue-Eyed Bitch mine. Knight held on for dear life and finally got his composure back. The rifle he held came up to sight in on the rider ahead.

Jessup's henchman began throwing lead back over his shoulder. Knight ignored how near a couple bullets came and pressed on at a full gallop. When the other man's revolver came up empty, Knight had him.

Almost at point-blank range, he fired.

The round took the rider high in the shoulder and knocked him from the saddle. From the way he moaned and clutched his shoulder, Knight believed he had broken the man's collarbone. Whatever happened next, it wouldn't involve the fallen rider.

Knight pounded up the trail. He heard Kilgore fire several times behind him and wondered if the gunman had killed the downed hombre. If so, he wasn't going to lose any sleep over such blatant murder. Jessup had kidnapped Helene . . . and Jefferson Avery was behind the crime. If either of them came into view, Knight knew he'd have no trouble pulling the trigger. They had started a war. Avery had hired Jessup and his owlhoots, forcing Hellfire to recruit her own small army.

A quick look back told him that Kilgore was keeping up. The man worked to reload his gun. Knight knew he ought to get ready for a real fight, but he wasn't as good a rider and needed both hands on the reins to control his horse.

"Ahead, just ahead. Jessup! He's got Hellfire." Knight wished he could double the speed, but his horse already strained to make its way up the road. Altitude robbed horses of their wind as fast as it did to people.

Jessup twisted around in the saddle and got off a couple shots at Knight. Then Avery's hired gun flew through the air. Hellfire, in spite of her hands being bound behind her back, had risen in her stirrups and thrown herself against him. She slammed down over Jessup's empty saddle and crashed to the ground amid kicking hooves. Curling into a ball, she let the horses step over her and run off.

Knight fired until his rifle came up empty. He missed Jessup every time. He rode up to where Jessup struggled to reload his own pistol, and without thinking about what he was doing, dived from the saddle. He sailed through the air and crashed into the gunman.

Arms wrapped around the kidnapper, he drove Jessup to the ground. They landed in a heap, but Knight was on top. He slammed a hard fist into Jessup's face, opening a cut that bled profusely. Hand smeared with blood, his heart filled with rage, Knight kept pummeling until his arm ached.

"Enough, Sam, enough. Get my hands free." Hellfire Bonham bumped into him to bring him back to the here and now.

He looked down at the unconscious man

and realized he would have beaten Jessup to death if she hadn't stopped him. Rocking back, he looked up at her and heaved a breath. "Let me get my knife out and cut your ropes."

Her jaw was set hard. "Get me free. I need to strangle Jefferson Avery with my bare hands."

Knight drew his horn-handled knife from a sheath at the small of his back. The last time he had used it was to slice away blood-soaked clothing on miners who'd been trapped in the Lucky Draw collapse. Two quick slashes cut the ropes binding Hellfire. She gave him a quick peck on the cheek, then stepped back and picked up Jessup's dropped gun. A quick check showed it was empty.

"Let me reload, and we'll get on up to the mine to take care of Avery once and for all." She reached down to strip off Jessup's gun belt with its cartridge-filled loops and worked at the buckle.

She let out a sudden cry as Jessup grabbed the front of her shirt and dragged her down. He had regained consciousness without either of them noticing.

"Drop the knife," he rasped. "Do it or I'll break her neck." He looped his arm around Hellfire's neck and tightened enough so she turned red and had trouble breathing.

"Here," Knight said, tossing the knife to the ground at Jessup's feet.

The man reacted as Knight had hoped. He loosened his grip on Hellfire's neck and reached for the knife. Knight drew the Colt and fanned off a shot that whistled past Hellfire's ear and caught Jessup in the right eye. The man's head snapped back and he toppled to the ground, as rigid as a plank coming off a sawmill's blade.

Hellfire stared at the body in surprise, then spat. "Took you long enough to catch up with us." She hesitated and then took Knight in a bear hug he thought might break his ribs.

She pushed away when Kilgore came up.

"I took care of two more of them," he said with bleak finality. As he reloaded he asked, "What now, boss? Do we go on up to the mine and flush the rest of the snakes out? We've got a few of your miners on the way."

"Wilcox and maybe three more," Knight said. "It's not much of an army, but we can take Avery by surprise."

"I don't want it to be a surprise," Hellfire said. "I want him to know what's in store for him and to feel the hot breath of hell before I kick him through death's door."

"Three of us can take them," Knight said.

"Avery's expecting Jessup and his boys to ride in. We'll take their place."

"Let's go." Hellfire scooped up Jessup's gun, then took the fallen knife and handed it to Knight. "If you want to cut his ears off for a trophy like those Mexican bullfighters, you can. I won't mind. That was mighty fine shooting."

"You aren't mad that I might have hit you?"

"You could have shot through me if it meant putting an end to him." She spat again on the corpse. "Now quit talking. I want some action."

"There's Jessup's horse. The one you rode ran away." Kilgore led the mount over and handed her the reins.

Hellfire bounced her shoulders once to get ready, then launched herself into the air, landing easily in the saddle. She tucked Jessup's revolver into her waistband and trotted off, expecting Knight and Kilgore to follow.

Knight knew she would ride into the Blue-Eyed Bitch camp whether they accompanied her or stayed where they were. Sparks flew from her eyes, and every word shot out like a bullet. She was fired up and ready to prove her moniker was deserved.

Hellfire Bonham was on the warpath.

CHAPTER 26

"Let us ride in first. That's what you're paying us for," Knight told Hellfire as he tried to keep down his uneasiness. The Blue-Eyed Bitch mine looked deserted. Even if most of the men were in the mine working, someone should have been moving around. Not every worker went on a single shift when it was more efficient to work two twelve-hour shifts every day.

"What? Let you varmints have all the fun?" Hellfire let out a grim laugh. "I was the one who got kidnapped. I'm the one Avery wants, the son of a bitch."

Knight saw the fire burning inside Helene Bonham. He understood how Jefferson Avery had come to name this mine after his ex-wife. Nobody crossed her — and Avery had made a terrible mistake trying.

"Do I have to tie you up so Kilgore and I can root out Avery and whoever else is with him?" Knight looked around, hunting for

375

trouble. Not finding it made him even more cautious.

"I told you that'd be fun, Sam, but later. Not now." She cocked the revolver and tapped her heels against the horse's sides, getting it moving forward.

They had to be riding into a trap, Knight thought. It felt *wrong* in the mining camp.

He and Kilgore did their best to keep up. The horse Hellfire rode smelled its stall and food and wanted nothing more than to be unsaddled, curried, and left the hell alone. They moved up to flank Hellfire. Knight was taken by how similar the Blue-Eyed Bitch looked to the Lucky Draw. Both had bored straight into the mountainside and left black tailings to tumble down the slope like stony vomit. Hellfire had built her office and corral to the right. Avery had staked out the same plan. Where his men bunked down and ate was different, but not that much.

"The yellowbellies all left," Hellfire said. "Avery had better be here."

"There's no reason for any of them to run," Kilgore said. "Jessup's attack was meant to kill us all. Why would they abandon the mine if they thought we weren't a problem any longer?"

The same thought had occurred to

Knight. He rode to the mouth of the mine and listened intently. No sound of men drilling or hammering came from the shaft.

"Something scared them off." He craned his neck to get a better view up the side of the mountain, sure that an ambush would be sprung any instant. All he heard was the drone of insects.

"Let's go to the office. Avery would defend that to his last breath." Hellfire dismounted and let the reins drag. The horse slowly made its way toward the corral where a few other horses milled around, pawing at the dirt and looking as if they would bolt if the gate opened for them.

Knight hit the ground and said to Kilgore, "Watch our back. This feels like a trap."

"Wilcox and the rest will be here in a few minutes, unless they deserted, too." Kilgore made an expansive, all-inclusive sweep of his hand taking in the emptiness.

Knight had to hurry to catch up with Hellfire. He reached the office a few steps ahead of her, put his back to the wall, then kicked open the door. She burst past him, gun leveled and ready to kill whoever was inside.

"Damnation," she said as she stopped short and stared.

He moved to one side and saw Jefferson

377

Avery sprawled on the cabin floor. From the blowflies and other insects feasting on him, he'd been dead for some time. Knight knelt and rolled him over, then looked up. "You're about an hour too late, Helene. Somebody beat you to it. Shot him in the back."

Knight frowned when he saw the wind stirring something stuck on a nail. He pulled it down, identified it as a small brooch attached to a torn piece of cloth, and handed it to her. "Yours?"

"That's mine, all right, but how'd it get here?" Hellfire touched her breast where it would have been pinned. "That cloth isn't even the same color as my shirt."

Knight circled the desk and saw the letters on the floor. He picked them up and only had to leaf through the top few to know what they were. "These are yours." He held them out toward her, as well. "Letters to Avery."

"The son of a bitch kept my love letters?" She looked from the stack to Knight then pushed the letters away using the barrel of her gun. "Take them. Cross out Jeff and put in Sam. It'll save me time and paper."

Knight let that pass. "The safe's open. Do you think he was shot while he was taking something out?" He knelt and tried to

378

reconstruct the scene. "Nothing makes sense unless you're being framed for killing him."

"What do you mean, Sam?"

"You burst in and accidentally tear the brooch off your shirt. He's looking for something in the safe. You shoot him in the back."

"I'd do that," she agreed, "but I would have preferred to see the fear on his face. I wanted him to know who killed him."

"He had the love letters in the safe, grabbed them, and only got halfway across the room before he died. He dropped them under the desk."

"I never did any such thing," Hellfire protested. "Jessup was kidnapping me back at the Lucky Draw at the time you said Avery got shot, remember? Besides, look at the drag marks. Somebody dragged him from outside and dumped him here. He was killed somewhere else, then the scene was set up to frame me."

"So it wasn't you. It wasn't Jessup, either."

"Then who killed him?"

"The mine superintendent might have done the deed," Knight said, thinking hard. "What was his name?"

"Pedro Ramirez. He's a slimy one . . . so low he could crawl under a duck wearing a top hat and never knock it off."

"Do you think he's the one who shot Avery? And made it look like you were the one?"

Hellfire frowned in thought. "He wouldn't have sent Jessup and his cutthroats after me, if that's true. There's not much in the way of law in these parts, but if he wanted to frame me so even the damned fool bluecoats would figure I was responsible, he'd never have sent Jessup when he did."

"Jessup worked for Avery," Knight pointed out. "And Avery didn't suspect his own superintendent was scheming to murder him. But why would Ramirez do that?"

"Let me look in the safe. It's got to be in there somewhere." Hellfire burrowed around in the papers left inside, then rocked back and shook her head. "It's not here. The partnership agreement between me and Avery. We signed it while we were married and never got around to canceling it."

"What agreement?"

"Well, Sam, this goes along with framing me for *his* murder." She glared at the body on the floor. "We are — were — partners in both mines. With him dead, I inherit the Blue-Eyed Bitch. I've got two mighty fine, high-grade-ore silver mines now since he's worm food."

"That would be a motive to kill him."

"I'd have done it for a penny and the satisfaction of seeing him squirm."

"If we don't find who did it, you'll have to be careful about talking like that."

"Like hell I will! Look there." Hellfire bent over and grabbed a pistol that had slid under a chair. "Whoever did this even used my pistol." She sniffed at the muzzle. "It's been fired. They went to a lot of trouble."

"That means the law's on the way. Why else go to such lengths to plant clues, and to use your pistol?" Knight went to the door and looked out, almost expecting to see the bluecoats marching in.

"Who'd be able to steal my brooch and gun? Who knows about the partnership and its clauses?"

"Avery might have boasted enough for somebody like Ramirez to get ideas," Knight said. "He'd have the authority to send the miners on their way, too."

"But he lost control of Jessup and his men. Avery sent them to kill me and if the cavalry found me dead, that would be a disaster for Ramirez."

Knight hardly heard. His mind had leaped forward and passed where Hellfire was at the moment. "If the mines aren't bringing up silver, Ramirez could claim they were worthless and buy them for a song and a dance. He has to know the terms of the partnership agreement."

"And that scurvy-bunch of lawyers in San Francisco who are responsible for running things if me and Avery died would sell their mothers' souls for a buck. Ramirez must know that."

"Any lawyer would. It goes double for lawyers a thousand miles away. They wouldn't want to run what appeared to be played-out mines. They'd put the mines up for sale and Ramirez wins the secret bid." That theory made some sense to Knight. It was the only one that did.

But something else ate at him. "What's happened to Kilgore?"

"He was wandering around outside on guard duty, like you told him." Hellfire leafed through the love letters.

Knight tried to figure out what memories they brought back and failed. Her face had gone utterly motionless.

"I'll find him. If Ramirez is responsible, Kilgore can track him down."

Knight stepped out. Again an eerie feeling worked its way up and down his spine. The Blue-Eyed Bitch being deserted was sinister enough. He had heard stories of miners leaving a mine because of whispering ghost voices, the revenants of those who had been killed in the tunnels. Other tall tales told of Tommy-knockers, those same ghosts warning the living of impending doom. Knight heard nothing. No ghost whispered a warning in his ear, but he felt uneasy anyway.

"Kilgore! Where'd you get off to?" He walked the path back to the mine and stopped dead in his tracks. "Kilgore?"

A boot poked out from under a clump of brush. Knight slipped his Colt from its holster and advanced slowly. As he feared, the boot belonged to Kilgore, and the hired gunman was very dead. A length of rope around his neck showed how he had died. Someone had dropped a noose over his head and then tightened it, silently cutting off both outcry and breath until Kilgore died.

Gunfire from the cabin sent him racing back. He burst through the door and would have been shot if Hellfire hadn't run out of bullets. She pointed her gun — the one that had killed Avery — at him and kept squeezing the trigger. Every time she did the hammer fell on another spent chamber.

"Sam! It was Pedro Ramirez! He tried to shoot me, but I got off the first shot. Then . . ." She stared at her gun as if it had betrayed her. Then she started to think. "It was almost empty because he used it to kill Avery and never reloaded. I only had two shots in it. And I missed him! I missed the conniving rat!"

From the way she ranted and raved, he knew she was all right. If Ramirez had shot her, she would have shown it, waving her arms around and spinning around as if she were a compass needle trying to locate the back shooter.

"Kilgore's dead," Knight told her. "Wilcox and the others will be here eventually. Go to the mine and wait for them."

"How do you know I won't run into Ramirez?"

"I didn't pass him returning to the cabin. If he was in here, the only place he could have run is around the mountainside. If he'd gone up, he would have kicked loose rocks and I'd have seen them. If he went down, that's a mighty steep incline. I won't need to do anything but find his body."

"No, wait, Sam." Hellfire hugged him tightly. "Don't go after him. Wait for the others. Come with me and protect me."

He pried himself loose and smiled at her. "Of all the people I have ever known, you need me protecting you least of all. You take care of yourself pretty damned good."

"I don't want you hurt, Sam."

"Go on. The longer before I get on his trail, the farther Ramirez gets and the longer he has to set up a real ambush."

She gave him a quick kiss, then darted away. He watched her until she rounded a bend in the trail, then sidled around the side of the cabin, wary of an ambush. Ramirez had left distinct footprints in the soft dirt of the trail. As Knight had guessed, the superintendent had lit out like a scalded dog away from the office.

Holding his Colt Navy at his side, Knight kept an eye peeled for a trap as he made his way along the path. Not only might Ramirez be lying in ambush, this was his terrain. The farther Knight went around the mountain, the edgier he got. Never quite sure what warned him, he threw himself to the side of the trail as two shots smacked into the ground in front of him.

Knight scrambled for cover, trying to figure out where his attacker was hidden. When another bullet tore a piece out of his leg, he located the shooter. Ramirez wasn't in front of him. Knight had walked past and the killer had him cut off from retreat to the mine and any possible help he might get if Wilcox and the rest had arrived.

"It won't work, Ramirez," Knight called as he bellied down behind a rock. His wounded leg hurt like blazes, but he forced himself to ignore it. "Your scheme to take over both mines has failed. Hellfire knows what you did. I've removed the bogus clues you planted. And she'll just tuck that pistol of hers into her belt and no bluecoat will ever ask to see it."

"I've got the partnership agreement," Ramirez said. "That'll prove she killed Avery. It'll be my word against hers, and I have evidence."

Ramirez's voice told Knight that the mine super had wedged himself between two large boulders. He couldn't move up- or downhill, but he had a good view of the trail leading away from where Knight lay behind the rock. It was a standoff — as long as Knight had ammunition.

Then it became murder. His.

"Those soldiers are more interested in fighting Indians than they are in a mine owner getting himself killed," Knight argued. "And you know how Hellfire can sweet-talk them. The officer in charge will believe anything she tells him."

"That's why I'll even the score with Jessup. He made a mess of everything. He didn't even kill her when he should have."

"First he tried to kill her, and that destroyed your plan. Avery had to die before

Hellfire, and she couldn't be killed at her own mine. Better to stage the crime and have her arrested."

"Yeah, but now I don't have a problem killing her. She killed my boss." Ramirez laughed harshly. "You and her. You killed my boss. I shoot the two of you and I'm a damned hero!"

Knight took aim and fired into the rocky notch, hoping the bullet would ricochet around and drive Ramirez out. All he succeeded in doing was emptying his gun. He was out of bullets.

He slid his revolver back into the holster and felt something hard and smooth at the small of his back. It was the knife he had used to kill Jessup. He slipped it out. The silver blade caught the sun. He hid it at his side.

Ramirez had to show himself if Knight wanted to make a good throw. Some of the men at the Lucky Draw had practiced throwing their knives at a pine board. Some were pretty good at it. Knight tried to remember how those men had drawn back and then released. Too many just heaved their knives and they bounced harmlessly off the board. He tried to remember why they had failed.

Then he realized, almost too late, that he

had to concentrate on Ramirez. The crunch of a footstep in the gravel gave him scant warning. Ramirez had gotten behind him somehow.

Knight whirled and found himself bowled over as Ramirez charged like a bull. They hit the ground and rolled over and over, arms locked around each other. Knight grunted and heaved, got Ramirez off him, but had his feet kicked out from under him as he tried to stand. Landing heavily, he rolled and avoided a boot crashing down where his head had been an instant before.

He kicked like a mule and caught his attacker in the knee. Ramirez let out a bellow of pain and fell onto him. Again they rolled in the dirt. Rocks jabbed painfully into Knight's back and shoulders. He used his elbow as a battering ram against Ramirez's face. Blood from a broken nose spurted over him.

Through it all Knight had kept the knife in his hand. Ramirez rose above him, a large rock in both hands. He intended to smash Knight's brains out all over the hillside. As he reared back with the rock, Knight lunged. Because of his awkward angle of attack, the tip of the knife didn't penetrate very far, but Ramirez yelped in pain and dropped the rock.

Knight took the opportunity to jerk to a full sitting position and drive the knife in and upward. He knew the instant the blade pierced Ramirez's foul heart. A convulsive shiver passed through the dying man before he toppled forward onto Knight.

For a moment, Knight found himself pinned to the ground, unable to move.

With a heave, he rolled the dead man off him, sat up, then stood, dripping blood. He wiped the gore off the best he could, then sat on a rock and stared. The strain of the fight and the nearness of his own death passed.

He drew in a deep breath and stood up. He started to return to the mining camp when he remembered Hellfire saying the partnership agreement had been missing from the safe. A quick search produced the agreement from Ramirez's blood-soaked coat pocket. He tucked it into his own pocket.

"You were a fool. You'd never have owned both mines, not while Hellfire Bonham is alive."

He made his way back, trying not to stumble too much. The fight had taken the starch out of him. The office was empty. For that he was glad. Hellfire had obeyed him when he told her to go back to the mine and wait for Wilcox and the rest to show up.

Putting one foot in front of the other proved difficult. The leg creased by Ramirez's bullet throbbed. As he neared the mine, Knight found the going got easier. Men were talking, but Helene's voice rang out above all the others. From the sound of the conversation, there were a lot of men there. Good old Wilcox had —

Knight stopped dead in his tracks. Wilcox and three miners had finally arrived from the Lucky Draw, but a dozen horses were tethered near the mine. Blue-coated soldiers roamed around warily, rifles at port arms.

Hellfire was arguing with the obnoxious, wet-behind-the-ears Lieutenant Billings. What he knew and what he would do weren't things Knight wanted to find out, especially when he heard the officer declare in a stentorian voice, "Where's Knight? I've got questions for him."

Hellfire tried to argue with him and divert attention back to how Jefferson Avery had tried to kill her. The lieutenant was having none of it.

"Knight. I want Knight." He fumbled in the front of his jacket and pulled out a paper. He shoved it into Hellfire's face. She glanced at it and brushed it away, continuing her demand that Pedro Ramirez be brought to justice.

If he made his presence known, Knight knew what would happen. He had no idea what that paper was that Billings waved around was, but in his gut he believed it had to be a wanted poster.

No matter how far he ran, everything he had done in Pine Knob caught up with him. Even if the lieutenant wanted to ask him about something else, Knight was covered in blood. Explaining that away would require him to be taken back to Fort Bayard for questioning.

Sooner or later, a wanted poster had to surface. When it did, he would be on the gallows with a noose around his neck before sundown. He backed away, his mind racing with ideas how to escape.

As he turned, he became aware of someone behind him. He tried to fight but a sack dropped over his head and cut off his vision. Then hard blows punched away at his midriff, doubling him over. As he collapsed, a cord tightened around his neck, fastening the burlap sack around his head. Strong hands pulled him out straight and dragged him away, helpless.

CHAPTER 27

Knight let the abductor think he had been subdued, then kicked out when the grip on his arms eased. He struck the unseen kidnapper with a boot but lost his balance and fell. Hard fists pummeled him, and one landing in his belly knocked the wind from him. He thrashed around in the dark, knowing his punches were as weak as a kitten's. Changing his tactics, he tried to strip off the sack over his head.

"Don't," a cold voice said.

Knight winced as a gun barrel smashed into his wrist when he attempted to loosen the sack.

He settled down and waited to recover his strength. His mind ran wild. It finally occurred to him that it wasn't the bluecoats who had nabbed him. They were gathered around Hellfire Bonham, talking about Avery's murder. That realization gave him the answer to the question of who had taken him prisoner.

"Hesseltine!"

The name brought loud laughter. "You're ours, Dr. Knight," said the rotund Pinkerton detective. "We're getting paid for taking this assignment, but if we play our cards right, that fool Donnelly will pay extra. Spurgeon and me might be able to retire from the agency if we can convince him to cough up a big enough reward. I don't think we'll have any trouble at all, either. Donnelly hates you. Oh, yes, he *really* hates you. Men pay for that kind of emotion."

As Hesseltine yanked him upright and shoved, Knight grunted. He staggered a few feet, then tripped on a rock and crashed to the ground. Hesseltine was on him again instantly, dragging him to his feet by his coat collar then steering him along the path. He felt a gun barrel poke into his back to keep him from making a break again.

Knight knew that if the Pinkertons returned him to Pine Knob, he was a goner. They might even decide to kill him for Donnelly, but if they did, they probably wouldn't be given as big a reward. Donnelly might not even pay them anything beyond their salaries because he wanted to torture his adversary and then watch him die.

Slowly. Painfully.

Knight shook his head from side to side, bringing a hole in the sack around enough to give him a glimpse of the trail. They were returning to the mine office where Jefferson Avery had been laid out. He had no choice but to go along and wait for a better chance to escape later.

"Inside." Hesseltine shoved him. Knight crashed into the desk and caught himself to turn and sit on it. The hole in the sack moved so all he saw was Avery's body on the floor.

"You pose quite a problem for us," Hesseltine said. "How do we sneak you past those soldiers? They won't do anything but get in the way."

"That's why you didn't shoot me," Knight said. "If you did, they'd take my body."

"Who knows what they'd do?"

Knight had hit on one of the problems facing Hesseltine. Lieutenant Billings seemed inclined to refer everything back to his superior at Fort Bayard. Not only would the detectives not be given the body, they would lose the right to claim they had captured Knight. If the army found any wanted poster on Knight, they'd keep him — or his body — to make things right with Captain Norwood back in Texas.

"Where's your partner?" Knight wanted

to keep Hesseltine talking, to gain time. What he would do with the extra time was beyond him at the moment. He had to play the cards he was dealt. Stalling gave him a new hand and kept them from spiriting him away.

"Spurgeon got hit pretty bad. You're a terrible shot, but you got lucky and drilled him twice in the arm."

"If the blood is spurting out, an artery got cut. He'll bleed to death without help."

"You? You're offering to patch him up?"

"It's a long way to Sierra Rojo. Doc Murtagh is the next closest doctor."

"Murtagh?" Hesseltine spat. "We came across him and his work. There wasn't anyone in the town with a good word to say for the drunkard." He spat again. "His reputation all the way down to Ralston is the same. He loses more patients than he saves."

"That's not unusual out on the frontier." Knight had caught his breath. He got ready to tackle Hesseltine if the hole in the sack revealed his captor. "During the war we lost a lot more than half."

"That was war. You had men hit with cannonballs and run through with dirty bayonets. Then you operated with filthy hands."

"You've heard of the germ theory?"

"Infection will set in if Spurgeon doesn't bleed to death first. I don't know any of the medical theories. All I know is that he's my partner and —" Hesseltine stopped speaking and stepped away.

And all Knight knew was that his captor's attention had turned to something else. He tore at the sack and ripped open the front. Getting it off his head would take too much effort since it was tied in place. He gasped as he dragged in fresh air and then kicked against the desk, sending himself flying through the air to crash into Hesseltine. They went down in a fighting, thrashing pile.

Knight drove his knee into Hesseltine's thigh and grabbed for the man's left wrist, twisting hard to force the gun from his grip. With all his strength he banged the hand down on the dirt floor. The gun went off, startling them both.

From outside came a shout, "Sarge! Gunfire from the office where they said the body was."

Soldiers!

Neither wanted to be caught by the buffalo soldiers. They rolled over and over and fetched up against the far wall. By the time Knight got back on top, pinning Hesseltine's gun hand down, the burlap had torn enough so he could see. He stared down into the Pinkerton's contorted face. With a heave, Hesseltine threw him to one side.

Rather than returning to the fight, Knight kept rolling, got to his feet, and shot out the door.

"There's one of 'em. Git 'im!"

Two soldiers ran to catch Knight. He put his head down, pumped his legs, and raced down the trail away from the cabin and the mine. As he ran he heard two shots. A quick glance over his shoulder sent a shock through him. Hesseltine had gunned down both of the soldiers, shooting them in the back as they passed the cabin.

If Billings wasn't inclined to chase after him before, he would be now. Losing two of his men, both shot in the back, would infuriate the lieutenant. A court-martial was in the officer's future if he didn't catch somebody to blame for the murders.

Knight put his head down and ran faster. He heard the detective's boots pounding on the ground behind him. He had to turn the tables somehow or he would be on the run forever. Donnelly wasn't giving up, and men like the two Pinkertons showed tenacity because of the huge reward being offered.

Knight reached a tumble of rocks where

the game trail meandered in different directions. He never hesitated. Jumping up, he caught the top of a rock and tried to find purchase. His fingers dragged against the rough surface and left bloody streaks. Kicking hard, he found a toehold that let him scramble up to the top of the rock. He whirled around, fell onto his belly, and waited, intending to jump Hesseltine.

Knight realized his plan had failed when Hesseltine didn't show up. He came to his knees, then heard the click of a revolver cocking behind him. With a hard twist, he spun to the right, fought to stay on the rock, and failed.

He slid down the rough side, losing patches of skin as he went. As much as the abrasions hurt, the bullet that Hesseltine fired at him would have hurt more if it had found its target. Instead, it whined off the rock.

"Give it up, Knight. I won't kill you if you surrender right now!"

Knight tried to get his feet under him and found his foot had wedged between two rocks. He tugged but couldn't get free. Fearing the worst, he looked up to the spot where he had been a moment earlier. Hesseltine stood there, gun pointed at him.

"Don't shoot," Knight said. "You've got me."

"Like dynamiting fish in a barrel." Hesseltine squeezed the trigger. The hammer fell on a spent chamber. "Damn. Don't you go anywhere while I reload." He grinned as he took his time reloading because Knight was too firmly caught to elude him again. When he finished, he took aim, pursed his lips in thought, then put his thumb on the hammer and slowly lowered it. "You stay there, and I'll get you free."

Knight struggled but failed to extricate his foot from between the rocks before Hesseltine came around and stood beside him.

"Don't try anything funny or you'll rot here, unless you want to chew off your leg like a wolf caught in a trap." Hesseltine found a tree limb that looked too spindly for the chore but which proved strong enough to lever up the rock pinning Knight.

He tumbled out, holding his leg. "I think it's broken. I don't have feeling in it."

"Here," Hesseltine said, handing him the limb he'd used as a lever. "Use that as a crutch. And hurry. I'm sure the soldiers won't just let us dance away."

"They're going to track you down."

"Me?" Hesseltine laughed. "It's you they want." He sobered. "And I'm not going to let them have you. Walk!"

Knight hobbled along, using the makeshift crutch although his foot began to ache and then tingle as circulation returned. The leg wasn't broken, and he had known that all along.

Less than a mile around the side of Red Mountain he saw why Hesseltine had spared him. Rance Spurgeon lay propped up against a rock, whiter than bleached muslin. He had tied a tourniquet around his bicep to stanch the blood, but some still squirted out from his forearm in feeble spurts, showing how close to bleeding to death he was.

"You're the doctor. Fix him up."

"Why should I?" Knight considered his chances of using the stick to knock the gun from Hesseltine's hands, but the detective kept far enough away so that wasn't possible.

"If you don't, I'll kill you."

"He might die anyway."

"Try. That's your only chance to see another sunrise." Hesseltine looked at the sun setting over the high mountains to the west. The Mogollon Rim would soon hide the light, making it more difficult to track.

Knight had to stay alive that long. He could lose Hesseltine in the dark. The man was from Chicago. Whatever skills he had as a tracker were rudimentary compared to a boy raised in the Piney Woods of East Texas.

"I *am* a doctor. I took an oath to preserve life." He hobbled to Spurgeon's side, dropped to his knees, and peeled away the blood-soaked cloth. The two bullet holes were deceptively small. All the bleeding came from a severed artery just below the elbow.

He moved the arm around, twisted it, and brought a shriek of pain to Spurgeon's lips. He looked up when he felt a presence. Hesseltine had moved closer and pointed the revolver straight at his head. Even if he knocked the gun out of line, Hesseltine had the advantage of height and position.

"You're blocking my light."

"Work faster." Hesseltine moved a few feet, the gun never wavering.

Knight started to complain about working under such pressure, then let the wound engross him as it always did. A half dozen different ways of approaching the repair and suture came to him. He reached into his pocket, only to feel cold steel barrel pressed into the back of his head.

"Thread. Silver. Metallic. Another miner let me use it on his cut. I need to tie off the artery or he'll be dead in a very few minutes."

Hesseltine didn't reply. Knight took that as agreement to do what had to be done. He pulled out the knife he had used to kill Ramirez. This caused Hesseltine to back up a step, but he still watched silently. Holding the tip between thumb and forefinger, Knight cut into the flesh to expose the severed blood vessels threatening to rob Spurgeon of life. Both bullets had passed through his arm, so all he had to do was tie off the artery.

A tiny loop like a noose dropped over the slippery artery. Drawing the loop closed slowly, he choked off the blood. Somewhere along the way, Spurgeon had passed out, making the operation simpler. Knight knotted the silver wire and began working on the cut he'd made to reach the artery.

"Will he lose his hand? That's his gun hand."

"I can't say. He's lost too much blood to worry about that. Better to be concerned about him surviving the bullet holes and the surgery."

"Either of them kills him, you're the one who did it. You shot him and —"

Knight saw what Hesseltine hadn't. Spurgeon's revolver was inches away. He slid it free, half turned, and moved faster, swinging the stick he'd used as a crutch to smash into Hesseltine's leg. He brought up the stolen gun and fanned off a shot. The bullet missed its target and dug into the dirt beside the Pinkerton detective. When Hesseltine started firing back, almost point-blank, Knight jumped over Spurgeon and slid down the slope. Bullets followed him until he reached a ledge that gave him some cover. If Hesseltine poked his head over the edge of the trail, Knight was ready to blow it off.

He steadied the gun against the rock and waited. Hesseltine had the advantage of height but couldn't circle the way he had before. If he tried, he would end up at the base of Red Mountain before he knew it. Knight cast a glance down. It was a two-hundred-foot drop down the steep slope. As he studied the trail above, he reminded himself that him tumbling down was as likely as having the detective take the fall.

"Did you kill yourself, Knight? Are you setting a trap for me?"

Knight controlled his instinct to shoot when he saw Hesseltine's elbow poking out over the edge. If there was any question that he hadn't plunged on down the hill, he had to use that to his advantage. Hesseltine was trying to lure him into revealing where he waited.

Knight looked around for another way out. He was trapped there as long as the detective just sat back and waited. Even with the threat of the soldiers coming to find what the ruckus was about, Knight was at a disadvantage. The two Pinkerton detectives weren't wanted by the army, not that he knew anyway. Hesseltine just hadn't wanted the soldiers taking Knight into custody and robbing them of the reward Donnelly had offered.

The ledge where he stood was wide enough for him to move around. He could jump to another a few feet back along the trail. Leaning out, he saw crude stair steps up the side of the hill to a point a dozen yards past where he had operated on Spurgeon.

He slipped the stolen revolver into his holster, judged distances, and jumped. His heart was in his throat during the second nothing but two hundred feet of empty air was beneath him.

Knight gripped the rock above the ledge he had jumped to, got ready, and leaped immediately to the next one. He fell into a rhythm, as if taking huge, long steps.

One mistake and he would die.

By the time he reached the next-to-last ledge, he was out of breath. He pressed

404

against the rock, studying his stony ladder upward and gathering his strength. He hadn't thought the foot that had been trapped was seriously injured. Now he wondered. It throbbed like a toothache. Putting weight on it became more difficult.

"A sprain," he whispered to himself. He rubbed the ankle and muscle in his calf to keep circulation going. A misstep meant a long and deadly fall.

With a final leap he got onto the last of the stone steps and clambered up. A few feet from the trail, he stopped and listened hard for any movement. The soldiers would be bad, but he had a chance of talking his way out of being arrested if Hellfire lied for him, bolstered whatever story he told, made life hell for Billings so he wanted only to ride away.

Hesseltine posed the bigger problem. Being taken back to Pine Knob alive was an option that had expired when he made a run for it. With Spurgeon as badly injured as he was, Hesseltine wasn't going to risk transporting a live, fighting prisoner. A corpse would be a lot easier for one man to handle.

Arms and legs moving like a monkey climbing a tree, Knight swarmed up over the edge of the trail, rolled to his feet, and caught his breath. He had come up ten feet from Hesseltine.

The Pinkerton stood with his back to him, examining his partner. "Dr. Knight, you do good work. Rance might just pull through."

"Take him back to Chicago. Send a telegram to Donnelly saying you lost me."

"Why would I do that?"

"See to your partner. Get him back where he can recuperate."

"The money offered for your capture, dead or alive, is considerable. I had plans for that money."

"I'll buy you off. I'll match what Donnelly offered. I can get it from Hellfire Bonham. She owes me, and she owns both mines now."

"Does she? So you two are intimate?" Hesseltine straightened, tugged at his coat, and shifted his shoulders while still facing away.

"I can get the silver."

"You will find this hard to believe, Dr. Knight, but I take my job seriously. Bribing me will not work, not for any amount of silver bullion." Hesseltine moved one foot back a few inches. "I take the job so seriously, as does my partner, that we had no trouble killing Seth Lunsford or the lovely young girl who thought to ransom him from us as we questioned him as to your where-abouts. I shot him to keep him from warning you. Spurgeon killed the girl. Marianne was her name, I think. We are quite serious about taking you in."

Hesseltine spun in a practiced move, his right hand flaring away from his body. But Knight knew the man was left-handed. That hand went for the revolver holstered in the shoulder rig. The Pinkerton had practiced this draw over endless hours. He freed his gun and had it swinging around to fire when Knight went for the gun in his holster.

Never had he moved faster. Never had his aim been more accurate. Hesseltine jerked as the bullet struck him in the heart. His finger tightened on the trigger, sending his round to harmlessly kick up a spurt of dust at Knight's feet.

Knight kept firing as Hesseltine collapsed. "For Seth. For Marianne. For all the others you've killed, calling it your duty, you son of a bitch."

Knight realized he had tried to fire three more times after the gun came up empty. He forced himself to calm down. Henry Hesseltine wasn't going to arrest anyone ever again. And he wasn't going to murder those with information he wanted.

He didn't have the rounds to reload the

detective's gun. He threw it away, then went to Hesseltine and rolled the man over. Death had permanently etched a smirk on his round face. To the very end, he had considered himself superior.

Knight plucked his own Colt Navy from the man's waistband, checked to be sure it was loaded, then edged around the body and went to take care of Spurgeon.

He didn't know if he could kill a man he had just operated on, a man whose life he had just saved. The rage he felt at everything the Pinkertons had done made him think that maybe he could.

But as he made his way around the bend in the trail, he saw it was a moot point. Spurgeon was gone.

"You can't get too far, not in your condition," he called. "Surrender and I'll spare your life."

There was no answer. Knight found where the detectives had tethered their horses. Fresh tracks told him Spurgeon had ridden away on one and let the other trail behind. Catching up with him, injured though he was, presented too difficult a task for Knight with his throbbing ankle.

He shoved his Colt Navy back into his holster. If he wanted to bring Spurgeon to justice, there was only one thing he could do.

Knight limped back along the trail toward the Blue-Eyed Bitch mine, Hellfire Bonham, and the soldiers.

and the soldiers

CHAPTER 28

Knight had to stop and rest by the time he reached the cabin. He glanced inside. Jefferson Avery still sprawled on the floor. And up the hill he found Kilgore's body, but the soldiers' bodies were gone.

As he rested he wondered what had happened. The lieutenant should have sent his men swarming along the trail after him and the Pinkerton detectives when he found two of his men dead. That the other bodies hadn't been touched struck Knight as peculiar, too.

It was almost as if Hellfire had dragged the soldier's bodies off and didn't bother telling Lieutenant Billings about the others. That made little sense since even the callow officer had to write a report detailing what happened at the mine. Knight smiled a little, thinking that Billings would be sent to some far distant post to rot for the rest of his army career after he turned in the report to his captain. Fort Bayard would hum and whisper about the greenhorn lieutenant who had lost two men amid a fight over a mine.

The smile faded when Knight realized it made the lieutenant more dangerous than ever. If he wasn't court-martialed and cashiered he would patrol with a "shoot first, ask questions later" attitude that promised to spark wars between the blue-coats and the Apaches. Knight didn't want to think what it meant for the miners and those in Sierra Rojo and Ralston who depended on the army for enforcing the law.

Hobbling along again, he reached a look-out over the mine entrance, sank behind a greasewood, and tried to figure out what had happened. The deserted area made no sense if the cavalry was still poking around. With no reason for them to lie in ambush, who would they set a trap for? Him? He worried that Billings had a wanted poster from Texas on him, but he had ridden far and fast. Having one catch up with him seemed far-fetched.

"You can come on down, Sam. They rode out a half hour back. By now, there's no telling where they got off to." Hellfire Bonham strode from the mine, looked up at him, and put her balled hands on her flaring hips.

"How'd you know I was up here?" Knight asked. "Never mind." He made his way down the path, trying not to wince as he put weight on his foot.

"Did you get yourself all shot up again? I heard quite an exchange a while back."

"Scratches from falling down the side of the mountain, but no bullet holes except a little gash on my leg."

She came to him and put her hand on his cheek. Her fingers came away bloody, but she checked out the rest of his body to be certain he wasn't lying. Now and then he gasped in pain, but he had been through so much he was surprised he wasn't bleeding from a hundred cuts all over his body.

"You pulled up lame?"

"I'm not a horse. You can't shoot me because I'm gimpy."

That brought a smile to her lips. She had a way about her. She was alive, she had a sense of humor, and she certainly was nobody's fool. That made her about as attractive a woman as he had seen in a month of Sundays, Amelia Parker included.

He turned dour when he thought about Victoria. She was beautiful, but she had stabbed him in the back the first chance she got. It hit him hard to realize their marriage had been a sham, built on lies, and ready to

412

fall apart at the first fuss.

"It's not all that bad. Come on over and set yourself down on this rock." Hellfire dragged him along and shoved him down. She turned, stepped over his leg, and grabbed his boot. Pulling it off nearly made him pass out.

"Not only does it smell to high heaven, but it's all swole up. You did sprain it good and proper." She began massaging it. "If I had some ice, that would work better. Right now, you want to keep it elevated."

Hellfire looked over her shoulder and went on. "I don't have to tell you a thing like that, do I? Not since you're a full-fledged, dyed-in-the-wool sawbones."

"Don't listen to what Dave Wilcox says. He's got an imagination and works hard to spin a story."

"You're a lousy liar, Doc."

He pushed her away. She danced off with his boot and held it out, pretending that it smelled worse than it did. She tossed it back to him.

"All right. I'll just call you Sam." She came closer and said in a low voice, "Maybe I can think of other things you'll like even better. When we're alone. In between the sheets."

Knight realized she thought as highly of

413

him as he did of her, but he was too worried at the moment to continue the banter.

"You want to know what happened, don't you? Me and Wilcox fixed it up with the soldiers. That lieutenant of theirs is one stupid jackass."

"Billings is that," Knight agreed. "But two of his men were killed. How'd you square that with him?"

"He's going to spin a tall tale of claim jumpers and fighting off a whole danged army. To keep things square, I said I'd back him up and say that Avery was behind it all. His soldiers will know it's a lie, but how long it takes for them to get the truth to his captain is the question. I say a week. Wilcox wanted to take odds on it being only a solitary day. We've got a silver dollar riding on it. You want in on the bet?"

He shook his head. Billings's career was over and rightfully so. All he needed to do was make sure the lieutenant didn't resurrect himself using Knight's scalp to do it.

"What went on out there? You stink of gunpowder."

He didn't want to go into the story since there wasn't any reason to burden her with his past. With careful thought, he said, "Two more claim jumpers. I finished off one. The other got away."

"You make that sound like a temporary condition. With that bad foot, you're not going to get very far. Let me take care of it for you."

"I need to do it myself. There's no call getting you mixed up in more killing."

"I can't say I like it, Sam, but I'm not overly bothered by it, either. I didn't get my reputation being a stick in the mud." She patted the gun she carried on her hip. "From all accounts, I'm not as good with this as you are, but I'm better than most men."

He looked past Hellfire to see Wilcox and two of the Lucky Draw miners trudging up the hill. All carried shovels over their shoulders.

Wilcox's expression brightened when he saw Knight. He dropped the shovel and went over. "Damn me, I thought I'd have to dig another grave for you, if we ever found the body." He eyed Knight critically. "You don't look too bad for wear and tear."

"There's more to do." Knight jerked his thumb in the direction of the Blue-Eyed Bitch mining office.

"Take care of all of them except Jefferson Avery," Hellfire said. "I need his body to prove the son of a bitch is dead."

"Kilgore's there and farther along the

415

game trail running around the mountain you'll find a . . . man with a few bullet holes in him." Knight forced himself to keep calm. The memory of how good it had felt to ventilate Henry Hesseltine returned. It was hardly justice enough for the Pinkerton detectives killing Seth and Marianne back in Buffalo Springs, but it went a ways toward sending Hesseltine straight to hell where he belonged.

"I won't ask. Hellfire here's got the army all taken care of." Wilcox waved to the miner to get started on new graves.

"Remember, Avery doesn't get buried," Hellfire said. "I'd let the coyotes eat his carcass, but I don't have anything against the four-legged varmints and poisoning them has to wait for another day."

"Don't go running off, Sam." Wilcox nudged the swollen ankle, grinned at his joke, and joined the miners.

Hellfire waited for Wilcox to get out of sight before she said, "He's working out better than I ever thought. I've been through so many superintendents that I've lost count."

"With two mines to run, do you think he can do double duty?"

"Well, Sam, that's something to discuss at length. The Lucky Draw is more than enough for any man."

"It's good that you're not a man. You can run both of them."

"You noticed I'm not a man? That's a start. What I want to talk to you about is —"

"Let's leave that for later. I've got one more chore before I can think straight."

"There was a second one? The one that took off?" Hellfire looked disgusted. "I can send some of the boys out. Wilcox will walk through a fire barefoot for you. You rest up and stay off that bad ankle." She read his face. "Damnation, you're a pigheaded, stubborn fool."

"If that's what you see, you might as well be looking in a mirror," he said, working his boot around to get it over his swollen ankle. His foot more than filled the boot, but he stood and tested his weight. It hurt, but not as bad as before. For what he had to do, it would be all right. "I need a horse."

"There's a corral full of them. Saddles and anything else you need. Even saddlebags, if you think you need to fill them up for a long trip."

"I patched up Spurgeon. He had lost so much blood that he's not going to be able to get too far." He wrestled with the notion that Spurgeon might die before he found him. Not killing him would satisfy his doctor's oath, but on a personal, deep down human level, he wanted to watch Spurgeon die at the killing end of a gun barrel.

And not just any gun. *His* Colt.

Knight stumbled along a few paces, then realized Hellfire watched every move. He endured the pain of walking more normally as he cut out a horse from the corral and set about saddling it. The whole while she watched him with a gimlet eye. The question of whether she would stop him made him work faster. He wasn't sure how far he wanted to go defying her, and if she ordered Dave Wilcox and the others to physically restrain him, he doubted he would be up to fighting them.

He swung into the saddle and settled himself. If he couldn't keep his friends from stopping him, what shape was he in to fight Spurgeon? That was a question begging for an answer.

"You'll need this," Hellfire said, handing him a leather pouch. "Unless you want to use that bloody knife on his dirty throat."

He bounced the pouch, judged its weight, and heard the sound of metal touching metal. Powder, bullets, wadding.

He touched the brim of his hat and rode past her, not trusting himself to say anything. She was quite a woman. He trotted along the trail. Wilcox already had Kilgore planted and the other two worked on a grave for Henry Hesseltine. The men stopped their work to get out of his way.

"Bring us back a scalp, Sam. It'll look real good nailed to the beam leading into the Blue-Eyed Bitch. We're counting on you," Wilcox called.

As with Hellfire, he didn't trust himself to speak. He waved, then concentrated on the narrow trail. Here and there he saw fresh hoofprints and kept going. As badly injured as Spurgeon was, he wouldn't be hard to find.

Only he was. A trail branched from the one circling Red Mountain and went down steeply. Knight never bothered to dismount and study the tracks. That was the way Spurgeon sought to escape. After a half hour, he still hadn't caught sight of him. It irritated him, but he still had confidence he would overtake the Pinkerton detective before long.

When he reached a good-sized road, he dismounted and knelt to look at the tracks. He pulled himself back to an upright position using the horse as a support. His foot hurt, but his anger boiled over and made it seem insignificant.

"Damn you, Spurgeon. Did you join up with them? Did you?" He stalked around to see more of the tracks and be sure he'd interpreted the signs properly.

He did. Spurgeon was riding with the soldiers. Probably he had found Lieutenant Billings on his way back to Fort Bayard and had spun a tall tale about being jumped by outlaws. His story could change if Billings urged him to tell his commander that it had been claim jumpers, the same ones who had attacked the Blue-Eyed Bitch mine and killed not only the owner but also two of his soldiers.

That tale would bring out the entire Ninth from Fort Bayard and surrounding forts. Knight had no doubt the description of the leader of the claim jumpers would fit him to a T. He had been chased out of Pine Knob and Buffalo Springs. If he didn't do something to stop Spurgeon and Billings, Sierra Rojo wouldn't be safe for him any longer, either.

As he rode, he muttered to himself about killing Spurgeon and the lieutenant, then realized it would never stop. A squad rode behind Billings. Did he kill them, too? What about anybody at Fort Bayard who might send out another company to catch whoever killed them? The house of cards collapsed in a lightning flash. Knight wasn't sure he could stand the thunder, especially if Helene was caught up in the storm.

He didn't owe her anything but felt responsible if he brought down the wrath of the U.S. Army on her for something he did. He rode a little faster, hoping to overtake Spurgeon and learn what tall tale he had already spun.

Knight was forced to pitch camp for the night, never having caught sight of the patrol. He worried that Spurgeon had veered away from the soldiers without him noticing. If he rode back to Sierra Rojo, he stood a chance of finding Spurgeon if the detective intended to telegraph his home office requesting support. From all Knight had heard, Allan Pinkerton did not take kindly to having his operatives killed, especially by those who were supposed to be taken into custody. Knight didn't know how many men the agency could send, but it would be more than enough to find him. After all, two of them had come all the way from Pine Knob and had located him with seeming ease.

All it took was utter ruthlessness and being willing to gun down whoever had information.

Knight said a brief prayer for Seth and

Marianne and hoped no one else in Buffalo Springs had been murdered for information about his whereabouts.

He tossed and turned the entire night, getting almost no sleep and little rest. Lying awake just before dawn, he stared at the stars and wondered if he made a wish on the last one to disappear, would that be the same as wishing on the first star in the evening? Restless, he made a sparse breakfast off what had been put into his saddlebags, then hit the trail.

As he feared, the patrol had gone directly back to Fort Bayard. He reached the post at midday and sat staring into the parade ground for any hint that Spurgeon was there. Knight decided he hoped that the Pinkerton had not even ridden with the cavalry troopers. It was too much to wish for that he had died. The man's body — or a grave — had been high on Knight's list of things to watch for. He hadn't even spotted any buzzards circling above.

He sat straighter when he saw two men carrying a litter from a bunkhouse to the post infirmary. At that distance he couldn't tell who lay on the stretcher covered with a blanket. During the fight at the mine, more than two soldiers might have been shot. He grew antsy, wanting to know and yet not

422

wanting to risk going onto the post. After the stretcher bearers vanished and then returned a few minutes later without their burden, he came to a decision.

He had nothing to lose by seeing if that was Rance Spurgeon, but his safest course required him to wait until sundown, then sneak onto the post. Waiting was nigh on impossible, but he did it.

Slipping over the knee-high mud fence and onto the parade ground proved easy. Letting the darkness cloak him, he stood tall and walked purposefully to the infirmary. He had learned long ago that looking as if he belonged mattered more than anything else. It was a bluff, but what soldier stopped someone who wasn't trying to hide and boldly made his way through the middle of an encampment?

The sentries weren't alert yet, having just chowed down. They watched from towers at opposite corners of the compound. He made certain he came from the west so any light remaining in the sunset dazzled their eyes. By the time the guards' eyes adjusted, he was standing on the steps leading up to the infirmary.

A deep breath, a touch of the revolver at his hip, then he went inside. The low light cast by the coal oil lamp almost blinded him. The trick he had used against the guards worked against him.

His eyes dark-adapted and he squinted from even the pale yellow glow behind the lamp's glass chimney.

"Who're you?" The question came from the far corner of the room.

Knight kept from jumping. If he looked suspicious, he was a goner. "I'm supposed to look at the new patient."

"Who're you? Nobody said anything about anybody lookin' at him." A corporal came over and stood in front of him, blocking Knight's path to the cot against the far wall.

"I'm the doctor from Silver City."

"Didn't know they had one. The only one I know is Doc Murtagh, and I wouldn't let him near even a colicky cow."

"He's in Sierra Rojo. Or Ralston City. It depends on which saloon is closer for him."

"Ain't that the truth." The corporal chuckled, and Knight knew he had said the right thing. He had identified Murtagh as a quack and had shown he knew the territory well enough to be from Silver City.

"I understand your patient's in a bad way. Nobody told me anything more but that he'd lost a lot of blood. Is he one of yours?"

"Nah, he's a civilian. Ain't really sure why the lieutenant brought him back. Wouldn't be the first time he left someone out on the trail to die."

"The patient must know something important," Knight said, offering the obvious answer. There wasn't any need to add that he was the one Billings wanted the shot-up Pinkerton to identify.

"Must be. There's no tellin' what that might be. The lieutenant lost two men. Explainin' that's gonna be hard. Maybe he has the answers." The corporal pointed to the lump on the cot. The blanket rose and fell rhythmically, showing Spurgeon had fallen into a gentle sleep.

For Knight, that boded ill. If Spurgeon wasn't at death's door, that meant he was close to being able to spill his guts.

"I wasn't told anything except that he was in bad shape. What's your opinion on him?"

"You're askin' *me*? Nobody's done that before. Mostly, I watch over 'em until they die, then get a burial detail formed to plant 'em deep in the ground. With the caliche a foot below the surface in these parts, that's usually quite a chore."

"Does the patient have a name?"

"Ain't heard. He was passed out when the lieutenant found him. Or if he wasn't, he was damned close. Looks like he got shot a couple times in the arm. Fancy that. He almost bled to death getting shot in the arm. Somebody patched him up pretty nice. Smooth, even sutures. Them's the stitches that closes a wound." The corporal looked chagrined. "But you bein' a doctor, you knowed that."

"I do. Let me examine him."

"Mind if I watch? I got a hankerin' to be a doctor someday. Hell, if Murtagh can be a doctor, so can I."

Knight cursed his bad luck. He nodded, stepped around the soldier, and went to kneel beside Spurgeon. It took a few seconds to identify him. His face was drawn and he was whiter than the new-blown snow, but this was the man who could put a noose around Knight's neck.

He took Spurgeon's pulse. "Thready. It might be that infection's setting in."

"Ain't gonna contract anything contagious, is he?" The corporal stepped back a pace. "I been through one quarantine here, and it wasn't purty. Eight men died of scarlet fever."

"It's not that kind of infection, unless he starts to cough." Knight played with a couple ways of getting Spurgeon out of the infirmary and back on the trail. Once out of

426

sight of the post, the Pinkerton detective was a dead man.

Knight pushed into the Adam's apple and released pressure twice, producing a dry, hacking cough. He recoiled and stared down. Shaking his head sadly, he said, "Looks like it has become infectious. If you don't want everyone on the post to get sick, I'd better take him back to Silver City where I can look after him. He needs medicine I have there."

"We got plenty of medicine. Well, not plenty. Some. A lot of it's Apache potions. A couple of them scouts we hired were medicine men for the Jicarilla and whupped up potions and powders for curing what ails us. At least they claimed it would. I just stored it in bottles. I wouldn't put it past them red bastards to poison us, if they could."

"Help me get him up. I'll need both of the horses he rode in on and —"

"How'd you know he had two horses? Nobody sending word to you over in Silver City would mention that. And how'd you get here so fast? Even if a courier rode all day, he'd hardly be *there* now. Who are you?"

"I told you. I'm a doctor. I —" Knight lunged for the soldier, hoping to bowl him over. The young man moved faster than any human had a right to. Knight fell past, betrayed as much by his bad ankle as the corporal's speed. He landed on his knees, scrambled to his feet, and chased the soldier outside.

The corporal stood at the base of the steps leading up into the infirmary, shouting his head off. Knight never hesitated. He leaped, his arms circling the man's neck. He bull-dogged him to the ground and shoved his face into the dry dust, stifling his outcry.

"What's the ruckus?" The question came from some distance away. In the darkness whoever asked could not have seen.

Knight tightened the headlock and kept the corporal's face forced down to the ground. The corporal made gagging sounds. To drown that out as much as to alleviate suspicion, Knight called back, "Ain't nuthin' much. Just feelin' my oats."

"If you got some of Georgie's squeezin's you'd for damn sure better share."

"Later. Got plenty to share. Want to get back to the patient."

Knight tightened his hold around the soldier's throat. Gasping sounds told him he had only to twist a little and the youth would be dead. When the corporal went limp, Knight eased up. He had no grudge against him, even if he was a bluecoat. He'd hardly been a tadpole when the war started so hadn't seen any action in the big battles that had sent so many Confederate soldiers into Knight's field hospital.

He jerked around, got to a sitting position, and laid the man's head in his lap while he caught his breath. Knight had to get him inside fast before he stirred and moaned. With his hand clamped over the soldier's mouth, he swung him around and dragged him up the steps and back into the infirmary.

Knight barely smothered his curse. Rance Spurgeon was gone.

CHAPTER 29

"Quit fighting me or I'll do more than tie you up." Knight made loop after loop of bandages around the corporal's wrists to secure him. Then he wrapped his feet together like he was tying up a calf for branding. He checked the gag in the man's mouth and made sure it was secure. "You might get a week of sentry duty or tossed into the stockade, but it's better than getting your throat slit."

The soldier looked at him with wide, frightened eyes.

"I wouldn't have been the one to do it." Knight jerked his head toward the empty cot. "Your patient. He would have killed you as soon as look at you. He's one bad hombre, and I'm doing the army a favor tracking him down so you don't have to."

The bound man kicked and strained against his bonds. Knight let him fight until he was sure he wasn't getting out of the

430

bandages. Being a surgeon and learning how to tie knots that never came loose had its benefits. He hoisted the man onto the cot and then secured him to that.

"So you won't wiggle out the door and draw attention," Knight explained. Satisfied his prisoner wasn't going to get loose or otherwise draw attention, he put on the corporal's blue woolen coat — the coat he hated so much from the war — and left the infirmary without a backwards look.

Spurgeon had broken through a loose board at the back of the infirmary. Knight cursed the fact that it was one of the few wood buildings on the fort. Most were adobe. The Pinkerton would still be scraping at the two foot thick walls if he had been in any of the nearby buildings.

Carefully staying in the shadows, Knight reached the stable area. He didn't know what Hesseltine had ridden any more than he did what Spurgeon's mount looked like. The wounded man could have even taken one of the army horses, though most of them looked malnourished with bony rib cages and gaunt rumps. Horse stealing wasn't anything new for Knight. That was one of the charges Captain Norwood had leveled against him back in Pine Knob.

The difference was that nobody knew he

was on the post and no one had identified him, other than the corporal. He worked his way through the remuda, found a sorrel that didn't shy away from him, saddled up with the McClellan saddle that killed his butt as he settled onto it, then slowly rode away.

As he passed through the opening in the low adobe fence circling the compound, he threw the sentry in the guard tower a snappy salute. It felt strange reverting to ways he had known a lifetime ago when he was a captain in the CSA. Knight heaved a sigh of relief when the sentry came to port arms and didn't draw a bead on him. As he rode away from Fort Bayard he felt prickles up and down his spine. Then he rounded a bend and went down by a stream and disappeared.

Tracking in the dark was too difficult for even experienced frontiersmen. He had heard tales of men using lanterns, but drawing such attention to himself would be dangerous, even if he had a lantern.

But he had a good idea where Spurgeon would flee. The man wouldn't take off across the barren country. Even dazed, he had to know he would die as soon as the sun came up. Instead, he would ride for a town where he could recuperate — and send for reinforcements.

Knight set as quick a pace as he could to overtake the detective. Just before sunrise on the road to Sierra Rojo he spotted his quarry. He allowed himself a moment's satisfaction that he had figured out everything Spurgeon had done, but with the detective in sight, Knight found himself at a loss as to what to do next.

In spite of all the men he had killed, he wasn't a murderer. He had killed in self-defense. Admittedly, some of those deaths he had relished. Hesseltine had deserved his fate. And Spurgeon deserved his. Without any law in these parts other than the inept cavalry, its patrols commanded by greenhorn officers, Knight felt an obligation to take the law into his own hands. Men working for an agency like Pinkertons were not above the law. If anything, they ought to fight to uphold it.

It turned his stomach thinking they had killed two innocents back in Buffalo Springs just to find his trail.

He coaxed the horse into a gallop. The thudding hooves drew Spurgeon's attention and he twisted in the saddle. Knight kept coming, even when he saw Spurgeon pull the carbine from a saddle sheath. The first bullet went high and wide. Then the detective wheeled around and took better aim.

Even weak and injured as he was, he was a decent marksman.

The Spencer's .52-caliber round grazed Knight in the left side, lifted him from the saddle, and threw him to the ground. He lay there, stunned, staring at the pink dawn lighting distant clouds over the mountains. He tried to sit up, but the fall had taken the starch out of him. He shifted his eyes and saw Spurgeon riding slowly toward him. Spurgeon levered in another round and sighted along the barrel, intending to kill his pursuer.

"You don't ever give up," Spurgeon rasped in a weak but hate-filled voice. "That's good for me. You killed Henry, but that just means I don't have to split the bonus Donnelly offered for your scalp. We argued over whether to kill you or take you back alive."

Spurgeon bent low and slid from the saddle to land heavily. Walking proved difficult for him but he came closer, the rifle in his left hand trained on Knight.

"Henry argued we should take you back and let Donnelly have his way with you. I wanted to lug your corpse around." Awkwardly, Spurgeon raised the carbine to his shoulder. "Henry always thought things through and gave us some decent arrests

434

because of that, but this one time he was wrong." In a voice almost too low to hear, he said, "This is for you, Henry."

Knight remained on his back but rolled enough to the left in spite of the pain to pull his Colt Navy. He got off the shot. The bullet rocked Spurgeon back and caused him to fire in the air. The Pinkerton fought to lever in a new round, but the heavy rifle unbalanced him.

Knight's second shot caught him under the chin and drove up through the top of his skull. Spurgeon's head snapped up, and he kept falling. A tiny dust cloud rose around his body where he fell.

"And that's for Seth and Marianne, too," Knight said, climbing slowly to his feet. He stood over Spurgeon.

The detective was dead. As Dave Wilcox had said the night he and Knight met . . . he had never seen deader.

Justice had been served, and yet Knight felt hollow inside. There wasn't any sense of vindication or retribution. Nothing.

He slipped his Colt back into the holster and limped after the spooked horses.

"If you don't stop wiggling, I do declare, I will get Doc Murtagh to fix you up." Hellfire Bonham pushed Knight down and sloshed iodine on the shallow wound on his side caused by Spurgeon's bullet.

"The pain's almost as bad as my foot."

"I can put iodine on that, too, but that's not going to do a danged thing for it. And it's too late to ice it down. We brought in a load of ice while you were gallivanting around, getting your hide all shot up."

"Ice?" Knight fought to keep from falling asleep in spite of the pain. He had ridden for an eternity on the uncomfortable saddle that had turned into a torture device by the time he'd reached the Lucky Draw mine. The ride had pushed him to the limits of his endurance. Now all he wanted was to sleep.

"They freight wagonloads of it from up north of Santa Fe and sell it over in Arizona. Since I'm rolling in the money now, I bought a load for the miners to enjoy."

"It's getting on toward late fall," he said, the bunkhouse beginning to spin around him.

"So? It's still warm enough for ice in your beer to taste good. I bought 'em a couple kegs of beer down in Sierra Rojo to celebrate everything working out so fine. And you were right about Wilcox. He's . . ."

Knight fell asleep — or maybe it was closer to slipping into a coma. For him it seemed like only a second of oblivion before he heard voices again.

"Coming around now."

"Helene?" Knight sat bolt upright in the bed, not knowing where he was.

"None other. You're the only one who calls me that. You're the only one I'll let get away with calling me anything but Hellfire or blue-eyed bitch."

Knight wasn't in the miners' bunkhouse. It took him a few seconds to realize he was stretched out in Helene's bed. Her small cabin was set away from the office and away from the lab where she mixed up her devil's potion of nitroglycerin.

"Why am I here?"

"I figured it smelled prettier than the bunkhouse with all them miners stinking up the place after sweating in the mines all day long. And I put up curtains. Adds a nice, homey touch, don't you think?"

"I shouldn't be here. In your bed."

She shoved him back flat. "Where else would you want to be? Sam, you're one hell of a doctor and even more of a man. That's what I need in my life after living with swine like Avery. I need someone to help run both mines. Wilcox is good, but running both the Lucky Draw and the Blue-Eyed Bitch is too much for him."

"You want me as the foreman on Avery's mine?" His head still spun. Too much crowded in too fast.

"It's not Avery's. It's mine." She giggled like a schoolgirl. "Both are all mine because of that partnership agreement me and Avery never dissolved. I've already contacted the lawyers in San Francisco and worked out the details. Two mines are duly recorded in my name. I'm filthy rich now. And I want you to help me spend some of that mountain of silver."

"How long was I unconscious?"

"Only a few days. I've been spooning in soup broth to keep you alive. It's good now that you're awake. Do you want a steak? I can have the cook whip one up."

"Nothing that heavy. Eggs." Knight sank down in the bed. If he didn't move, his head might stop hurting and let him think better.

"I'll get him onto it. You rest up and before you know it, you'll be up and around." She leaned over him and ran her hand up his leg. "And I do mean up."

With that Hellfire left, whistling a jaunty, bawdy tune.

Knight began mulling over everything the woman had said, and what it meant. What man wouldn't accept such an offer?

He ate the eggs along with some toast,

pleaded weariness, and when it got dark enough, made his way to the corral and picked out a strong gelding. She had offered him a share of the profits from two silver mines, so she couldn't complain about him taking a horse and tack. He stepped up and made his way down the moonlit road going toward Sierra Rojo.

Donnelly would never stop hunting for him. When the two Pinkerton detectives failed to report, he would send others. And the army might be on his trail for horse stealing again. The corporal had gotten a real good look at him and would identify him to save himself from being tossed into the stockade for the rest of his enlistment. Too many people wanted him dead to stay with Hellfire Bonham, no matter how attractive her offer was.

It was time for Dr. Samuel Knight to find another town, somewhere over the horizon, where he could become a gambler or some other profession and try again to leave his past behind once and for all.

Until death came calling for him once more.

ABOUT THE AUTHORS

William W. Johnstone has written nearly three hundred novels of western adventure, military action, chilling suspense, and survival. His bestselling books include *The Family Jensen; The Mountain Man; Flintlock; MacCallister; Savage Texas; Luke Jensen, Bounty Hunter;* and the thrillers *Black Friday, The Doomsday Bunker,* and *Trigger Warning.*

J. A. Johnstone learned to write from the master himself, Uncle William W. Johnstone, with whom J. A. has co-written numerous bestselling series including The Mountain Man; Those Jensen Boys; and Preacher, The First Mountain Man.

The employees of Thorndike Press hope you have enjoyed this Large Print book. All our Thorndike, Wheeler, and Kennebec Large Print titles are designed for easy reading, and all our books are made to last. Other Thorndike Press Large Print books are available at your library, through selected bookstores, or directly from us.

For information about titles, please call:
(800) 223-1244

or visit our website at:
gale.com/thorndike

To share your comments, please write:
Publisher
Thorndike Press
10 Water St., Suite 310
Waterville, ME 04901